MURDER

ON THE

NECHES

A FEN MAGUIRE MYSTERY

MURDER

ON THE

NECHES

A FEN MAGUIRE MYSTERY

BRUCE
HAMMACK

Chapter One

Former sheriff Fen Maguire noticed the hopeful tone of his words as he asked, "Are you calling to tell me there's a murder to solve?"

Candy's chuckle came from the speaker on Fen's phone. "You must be bored after a long winter." Her voice switched from mirth to something more fitting for a legal secretary calling on behalf of her attorney husband. "Chuck needs you to come to the office this morning. Can you make it?"

"Only if you answer one question. Will I need to pack for one week or longer?"

Candy showed her agile mind with her response. "One week but bring laundry detergent."

She cut off the call before he could comment, leaving him with a beehive's worth of questions buzzing in his mind.

Instead of speculating, he looked at his late wife's picture and spoke as if she could answer him. "Looks like I'm going somewhere soon. I appreciate her not telling me where or when until I get to their office, and you can guess why. Thelma would drown me with questions I either wouldn't or couldn't answer."

Fen took a deep breath. "Do you mind if I cut our morning talk and prayer time a little short this morning? It's been a long winter, the wettest early spring on record, and I've come down with a severe case of cabin fever. I feel like the walls are closing in on me." He paused. "Thanks, honey. You were always patient with me." He paused and kissed the glass covering her face before making a slight correction. "I need to change that last statement. You were patient most of the time. I still regret giving you an iron for your birthday."

The smell of sage hit him as soon as he opened the door to his home office. The aroma of fresh-baked biscuits joined the smell of sausage when he entered the kitchen.

Thelma, his cook and housekeeper, sensed his presence and turned from the stove. "You're too early. Why'd you cut short your time with Miss Sally?"

"Candy called."

Thelma let out a huff. "Here we go again. Where are you going this time?"

"Don't know."

"When are you leaving?"

"Don't know."

"Who got killed?" Thelma held up a hand. "Don't waste your breath. You either don't know or you ain't talking this morning."

"Candy wouldn't tell me much. I asked her if I should pack for one week, or longer. She told me one week, but bring laundry detergent."

Thelma huffed. "I'll never understand how you can solve crimes with your mouth clamped shut like a rusty vice."

Fen spoke as he arranged placemats, napkins, and silver-ware on the four-person table with a view of the Brazos River bottom behind his home. "I'll know more after I meet with them. They want to see me as soon as I can get there."

"You'll know everything there is to know and still keep most of it to yourself," said Thelma as she took a baking pan filled with homemade biscuits from the oven.

He filled his mug and returned to the table. Thelma had a reputation to maintain as being the best-informed woman in Newman County and parts of the surrounding Central Texas counties. Her sources weren't always reliable, as she emphasized quantity over quality of gossip, but the accuracy was surprisingly good. The second part of her reputation involved her making sure others stayed informed.

Mechanical chirps from Fen's cell phone caused Thelma to spin and face him. Fen looked at the caller ID and said, "It's Bailey."

"Lord, have mercy. What kind of trouble is that girl in now?"

Fen knew it would aggravate Thelma if he didn't turn on the phone's speaker, but he put the phone to his ear anyway.

"Good morning. How's college?"

Her words came out fast and strong. "I'm wasting my time taking stupid required classes I'll never use."

"I mostly agree, but it's the price you have to pay if you want a college degree. Take a deep breath, let it out, then tell me what's really bothering you."

Frustration colored her next words. "I just did. Most of my professors are clueless about earning a living in the real world. They teach a bunch of garbage I'll never use and make us read books I either don't understand or disagree with. I think they cooked their brains by taking too many drugs when they were in college or reading goofy theories on how things should be."

"What about your art classes?"

"One of them isn't too bad. The other is a complete waste of time and money. The instructor is a grad student with pink hair. He's never sold a painting in his life."

"Are you sure about that?"

Fen realized that was the wrong question to ask when she sprayed out her next answer with extra force. "Of course I'm sure. He's totally into pottery and never mentions painting unless it's something abstract that goes on clay fired in a kiln."

The sound of eggs hitting hot grease brought his attention away for a second or two before refocusing. "What are you going to do?"

"What can I do? I'm paid up for the entire semester. It would be a huge waste of money if I quit in the middle of the term."

"Are you painting?"

"Some, but not like I did when I had a dorm room to myself. Having the studio above the garage spoiled me."

Bailey's problem needed more thought than he had bandwidth to give it. Thelma was lifting fried eggs from a cast-iron skillet, and she didn't appreciate a hot meal growing cold. An inspiration floated by and Fen grabbed it.

"Isn't spring break coming up soon?"

"At the end of the week. My last class is Friday at ten o'clock, so I'll be home Friday afternoon."

"Don't get your hopes up, but I received a phone call this morning from Candy. She wouldn't give me details, but you know what calls out of the blue from her and Chuck mean."

"They don't call unless there's a murder for us to solve."

"I'll call you and let you know what they tell me. You may need to change your plans for spring break."

"What plans? Cory has to work."

Thelma plopped a plate in front of him. "Don't let it get cold."

Bailey whispered. "You're eating breakfast early. I thought I had my call timed better. Do you have the speaker on?"

"Nope."

"Let me talk to Thelma. She'll grill you with questions if I don't tell her why I called."

"I could tell her."

"There's a big difference between could and will. You have an aggravating habit of keeping things to yourself. Give her your phone and let me save you from her wrath. Besides, she'll sulk if you don't eat your eggs before they get cold."

Instead of responding, Fen held out his phone. "It's Bailey. She wants to talk to you."

Thelma took the phone. "Bailey. What's going on that's so important you had to call this time of mornin'?"

Fen dug into his breakfast with his thoughts alternating between a possible murder investigation and how to respond to Bailey's desire to leave college. With any luck, the slow winter months were coming to an abrupt end.

A mental checklist of things to pack appeared in Fen's mind, and he began checking items off. The list was short because he didn't know if he'd go to the sunny beaches of South Padre Island, north to the Panhandle, east to the border of Louisiana, or all the way west to El Paso. Wherever it was, he'd take sketch pads and everything he needed to paint a landscape.

He was buttering a biscuit when Thelma's voice changed. "Pink hair? On a man? What kind of college are you going to? It was bad enough when Millie Shiflet tried to dye her hair red and it came out orange as a pumpkin. Did that teacher do it on purpose?"

Fen kept his head down and swallowed a laugh along with a bite of sausage. Thelma didn't go to town often and colleges might as well be colonies on Mars. Her happy place was on his four-thousand-acre farm and ranch, cooking and cleaning for him and Sam, her husband, who was also Fen's ranch manager. When she ran out of work, she worried about Bailey.

The conversation continued as he ferried dishes to the counter by the sink. This was Thelma's cue to end the conversation.

"I gotta' go. Fen's ready to go to town and I don't want him to leave his phone behind. I never would know where he was." A few seconds passed. "I'll tell him that very thing. Bye, and be careful at that crazy college."

Fen received his phone as Thelma said, "Bailey told me to tell you she expects a call the minute you get out of Chuck's office."

He lifted his chin. "You can't fool me. I'll call her, then she'll call you. That's your plan, isn't it?"

"It wouldn't be if you and Bailey used words more freely. Both of you only tell me what you think I need to know. She may not be blood kin to you, but that gal sure takes after your ways."

A buff Stetson was the last thing Fen grabbed as he went into the garage and started his one-ton diesel truck.

Chapter Two

The metal gate swung shut automatically as Fen turned right onto a gravel road that led him past his former father-in-law's ranch. Their property lines touched, and they extracted liquid wealth from the same rich, underground oil field. Otherwise, they might as well live in separate countries. He wondered for the thousandth time if there was anything else he could say or do to repair their relationship. The only answer that came to him was to let time try to heal them both, especially Sally's father.

Passing over the Brazos River helped clear his mind of past regrets. Sally's memorial service took place over three years ago, and he'd found things to help him move on: continuing to paint landscapes, his ranch, helping Bailey overcome a lousy childhood and adolescence, and solving murders. There was one more, but he'd best not think of Audrey until he knew what his next assignment might be.

The city of Springdale, the county seat of Newman County, appeared fully awake and prospering as cars lined up five and six deep at stop lights. Fen remembered a time when he could count the number of traffic lights on one hand. He regarded this as a sign the years were slipping by at an accelerated pace. Not unusual for someone approaching his late forties.

He drove the usual route to Chuck's law office and pulled around back to a parking lot. Candy must have heard his diesel engine cut off, as she had his favorite mug of coffee waiting for him. Not one to waste time, she said, "Thanks for speeding up your morning routine. I see you had eggs and biscuits this morning."

Fen looked down at his shirt. "I like to keep part of my meals for a snack later on."

She pulled a moistened wipe from her desk drawer and scrubbed a tiny area of his shirt. "Thelma must not have gotten a good look at you before you left. There. Good as new. Chuck likes to wear his food, too. Let's get to his office."

The walk down a long hallway gave Fen time to once again think about the enigma who was Candy Forsythe. She was a blondish woman, attractive but not flashy, brilliant but not pretentious. She rarely turned her head but saw and heard everything. He assumed she was five years either side of his age, but couldn't be certain as Candy never seemed to age. Finally, she was a chameleon who could morph into different roles when required, as evidenced by her participation in the community theater.

Most of the time she was remarkably unremarkable, and Fen thought she'd make the perfect CIA agent. Perhaps she had been at one time, but now she played the part of her husband's secretary. Even though she sat in Chuck's shadow, there was little doubt who ran the office and had the political contacts.

As usual, Chuck sat in a high-backed leather chair, boots on his desk, with a phone to his ear. Fen took his mug of coffee to one end of the couch and settled in while Candy moved to Chuck's desk, closed a file folder, and placed it on the nearest towering stack.

She returned to sit on the other end of the couch as Chuck ended his phone call.

Chuck joined them and settled into a chair near Fen. "I didn't expect you for another ten minutes. You must need something to do."

"I wouldn't mind it."

Candy handed Fen a file folder she'd carried from her desk. "A situation has come up on Lake Palestine. The victim is Dale White, thirty-three, originally from Northern California. A fisherman found him floating in water on the north side of the lake two days ago. His wife reported him missing five days prior to the discovery."

Chuck took his turn. "He was one of those tech guys who got filthy rich, retired three years ago, and has been traveling the world. He and his wife wound up in Florida last November, where Mr. White bought a high-rise condo in Miami. They played in the sand and fished until April."

Candy took over. "Mr. White purchased a Class A motorhome. Their intention was to take several years exploring the USA during the warm months and return to Florida for the winter."

Chuck added, "The motorhome cost upward of a million dollars. That's what I call exploring in style, but he could afford it with plenty left over."

Fen tilted his head. "What's the catch? Other than the guy's wealth, this sounds like something the locals could handle."

The couple traded a knowing glance before Chuck said, "The catch is, too many agencies are involved. Four counties have a portion of their border on Lake Palestine. They discovered the body in the water at the intersection of two county lines, Smith and Henderson."

Fen rubbed his chin. "Are they sure it's a homicide? If he drowns in a lake, the state game warden should lead the investigation."

"The small hole in the back of Mr. White's head led the game warden to conclude the guy didn't drown."

Candy added, "Do you remember what the weather was like ten days ago?"

"Rain, rain, and more rain," said Fen.

"It was worse around Tyler," said Candy. "The Neches River and a series of creeks feed into the lake."

"Ah," said Fen. "With that amount of flooding, someone could have dumped the body near any of those streams and it would have found its way into the lake." He looked at Candy. "Floods have a bad habit of destroying evidence."

Fen stared into his mug of black liquid. "You're holding something back."

A look of mischief spread across Chuck's face. "And what do you think that could be?"

The mug rested on the table as Fen cast his gaze into Chuck's eyes. "The real reason you need me to look into a murder that local sheriff's departments and game wardens should handle."

"It's complicated," said Candy.

Chuck added, "The lead detectives from two of the counties both believe they know who killed Mr. White, and of course, they don't agree on the same suspect."

"So?" said Fen. "The game warden can act as referee."

"It's not that simple," said Candy. "The game warden investigating the case announced his intention to run for sheriff of Smith County. He's the odds-on favorite to win."

Chuck added, "He requested that someone else take over the investigation."

"How, and why did my name come up?"

Candy leaned back. "You underestimate your reputation. Besides, with ten years' experience as a state trooper and ten years as a sheriff, you're the most qualified."

Chuck gave a more cynical response. "My guess is, the future sheriff of Smith County didn't want to run for office with an accusation of favoritism hounding him."

"Why favoritism?"

"Because the lead detective for Smith County also wants to be sheriff. The current sheriff is retiring. In most counties he would be the logical choice as he's familiar with the department. But there are those who don't believe the detective is the best choice this time."

There were times Fen would like to tell whoever initiates these assignments they should butt out and let the locals figure it out. A murder was one thing; a murder wrapped in politics was another. But he said, "Why is there always politics involved?" He took a breath. "Tyler is the county seat of Smith County, and that's the county where the Neches River flows into Lake Palestine."

Candy nodded in agreement. "The other northernmost county is Henderson, and it has more of Lake Palestine's shoreline than any other county. Kickapoo Creek flows into the lake from the northwest and the Neches River flows from the northeast. The game warden believes the original crime scene is somewhere upstream from either the river or the creek."

Fen looked from Candy to Chuck. "Let me summarize. We don't know the original crime scene, the flood is bound to have destroyed physical evidence, there's a squabble over jurisdiction, and important people want to protect a future sheriff from bad press. Couldn't you find a harder case for me to investigate?"

Chuck displayed a top row of nice teeth. "If it was easy, you wouldn't like it."

Candy stood. "I have a file folder on my desk for you. All the police reports are in it. When can you leave?"

"Today. I'll find a place to stay, and Bailey will join me on Friday. She's not enjoying the college experience as much as she hoped. I have my fingers crossed that spring break will do her good."

Chuck asked, "Isn't she good enough already to make a living painting portraits?"

"She has the skill, but not the reputation. It would also help if she looked older than sixteen. Successful people are her sales target because that's where the money is. They want to leave something special for family to remember them by. They take one look at Bailey and assume she's too young to be good enough for what she wants to charge. It doesn't help that patience isn't her greatest asset."

Candy asked, "How's her relationship with that deputy sheriff progressing?"

Fen lifted his shoulders and let them fall. "You may need to ask Thelma about that."

"You can do better than that," said Candy. "Does she still call him every day when she comes home to your ranch?"

Fen considered the question before answering. "She only came home twice this semester. Now that you mention it, she had little to say about Cory. I spoke with her this morning and she sounded like she was mad at him for always working, but she didn't seem very mad."

"Ah," said Candy in a way that told him more than the two-letter word.

Fen stood and took a step toward the door. "I don't know

what 'Ah' means, but a blubbering teen on my hands while I'm trying to solve a murder is something I can live without. If she and Cory break up while we're gone, I'm calling you to come dry her tears."

"No deal," said Candy. "Chuck and I are happy being childless."

Chuck gave his head a firm nod. "Working on divorces is all the drama I can stand. My New Year's resolution was to refuse any more. So far, I've turned down four."

Fen shook Chuck's hand. "Turning down work tells me you have plenty of business."

"Not so much that we'd refuse an invitation to one of Thelma's famous steak dinners after you get home from solving this case."

Candy let out a groan. "Don't pay attention to him, Fen. It's our turn to have you over. I'll expect you the first Saturday after you get back."

The heels of his boots made a clomping sound as he made his way to Candy's desk, where he retrieved the file and received her obligatory hug. She wasn't normally a hugger, but she made an exception for him.

Bright sunshine streamed through a window. He donned his hat and sunglasses before opening the door. The clicking of the handle behind him set his brain in motion. There was much to do before he pointed his truck to the northeast and made his way to Lake Palestine.

Imaginary lists appeared in his mind as he left the parking lot and turned onto Main Street. He started with art supplies to take. As many were already under the camper shell covering the truck's bed, that list proved surprisingly short.

A second mental checklist of clothes to take came to him as he drove north. A traffic light changed from red to green as he approached. He began with socks and added sleep shorts to his list. Before he could get further, a flash of light and a honking horn came from his left. He jerked his head, but not in time to take evasive action. The grill of a bobtail delivery truck struck his driver's door with an explosion of breaking glass and bending metal.

Searing pain shot down his left arm and replaced all thoughts of lists. White spots floated like a thousand fireflies in front of him.

Chapter Three

The first two words Fen remembered hearing after the collision were, "Don't move." The same insistent voice followed with, "You were in an accident. Do you know what day it is?"

The voice sounded like it came from a long way off. Instead of answering, Fen tried to move his right hand to his throbbing left arm. The woman pushed it back down. "No, you don't, Sheriff Maguire."

A bolt of pain brought his gaze toward his left arm that was encased in what looked like an inflatable pillow. The sensations of movement and noise came alive as he spoke through the pain. "Am I in an ambulance?"

"Welcome back to reality," said the woman whose face looked familiar, though he couldn't put a name with it.

"I need to go home and pack."

A sudden jolt took away thoughts of everything but his arm. He groaned in pain.

"Hang on, Sheriff. We're almost at the hospital."

A sharp turn and another jolt brought a new level of pain.

All Fen could do was grit his teeth. He then realized the wailing siren had mercifully ceased its mournful cry.

The back doors of the ambulance parted, and he watched his boots leave the ambulance with the rest of him following. Familiar faces came into view. He matched names with a few, but not all.

Complete sentences made little sense. Phrases floated around him. *Cut the shirt and pants off, X-rays, CT scan, sutures,* and *something for the pain.* Some words seemed directed to him while most were between the scrubs-clad workers hovering around him.

An indeterminate amount of time passed before the brain fog lifted enough for him to recognize Dr. Freestone, the tall, thin-as-a-stalk-of-straw general practitioner.

Fen ran his tongue around what felt like filmy teeth and asked, "What's the damage this time?"

Dr. Freestone looked down at him. "You should live to a ripe old age unless you don't."

"Thanks, Doc, but could you try again and use words I can understand?"

"Glad to. You were in an accident. A delivery truck hit you broadside. The crash knocked you silly."

"My head hurts."

"It should. You have a concussion, and I put eight stitches in your scalp."

"Why does my arm hurt so bad?"

"You separated your shoulder and fractured the radius and ulna. I popped the shoulder back in place while you were napping. The good news is the breaks to those two bones in your lower arm are clean. An orthopedist looked at the X-rays and you don't require surgery. You have a pretty white cast for people to sign."

Fen tried to move and let out a loud moan.

"That's your body telling you not to make any sudden moves."

"When can I go home? I need to pack and drive to Lake Palestine."

"No way. Upstairs in a room is where you'll stay for at least two days. You took a nasty blow to your head that's had you in and out of consciousness for the last six hours. There's a possibility you could still develop a bleeder in the brain. I'm tempted to send you to either Houston or Austin to be near a brain surgeon."

"I'm not riding in another ambulance today."

"It would be in an air ambulance if I sent you."

"Save the life flight for someone who really needs it. I'll be a good boy, do what you say, and not rush getting out of here."

Dr. Freestone chuckled. "You're such a lousy liar. I've patched you up enough times to know you hate hospitals and like to heal on the go." He paused. "I've already spoken to Thelma and Bailey about your injuries and what you should and shouldn't do."

He let out a mournful groan and asked, "Bailey's here? What time is it?"

"About seven thirty in the evening."

"I've been asleep all day?"

"I wouldn't call it sleep. More like resting and talking gibberish. We woke you often enough to check your eyes to make sure your pupils stayed equally dilated and reacted appropriately to light."

Fen took a deep breath and released it through his mouth. "You weren't joking when you said the crash knocked me silly."

Dr. Freestone leaned in and whispered, "By the way, if Audrey is someone you don't want Thelma to know about, you'd better come up with a good cover story."

"Did you tell her I talked about Audrey?"

"Of course not, but I can't vouch for everyone who works here. You babbled mostly about Sally, but Audrey's name came up enough times for me to notice. Thelma's bound to have heard from one of her spies by now."

Fen thought about shaking the doctor's hand, but realized his right hand had an IV in the back of it and the left had a cast covering most of it. Instead, he said a simple, "Thanks for telling me. I'll come up with something that will satisfy her curiosity."

"Make it believable enough so she allows you to rest in peace. She'll sleep in your room's recliner tonight. Bailey will relieve her in the morning. I was going to put you in the ICU, but it's full."

"Bailey?" said Fen. "Her spring break doesn't start until Friday afternoon. She should be in Georgetown."

The doctor shrugged and walked to the door. "I'm not sure you can convince her to leave."

Fen closed his eyes as the door whispered shut. He wouldn't lie to either woman, but he needn't spew out words like a slot machine with a row of three cherries showing.

A man with tattoos on both arms soon arrived. "Hello, Sheriff Maguire. I'm here to take you upstairs to your room."

Fen asked, "Do you realize I'm no longer the sheriff of Newman County?"

"I do, and everyone knows why. You losing your wife and Mr. Newman blaming you for it put you in a tailspin." He continued without slowing down, "Did you have anything to eat today?"

"I missed lunch and supper."

"The nurses have protein drinks at their station they can give you."

"No cheeseburgers?"

The scrubs-clad man grinned. "A decent cheeseburger

wouldn't last five minutes at any of the nurse's stations. Those are the snack-happiest people I've ever seen."

"It doesn't matter," said Fen. "I'm not hungry."

"Then you've come to the right place, and that's a fact."

Fen waited to say anything else until the man had the bed pushed into his room and the bed's electric cord plugged in. "Your face looks familiar. What's your name?"

"Roderick Smith, but everyone calls me Hot Rod."

Revelation came in a flash. "You were in jail when my wife died."

The man seemed pleased that Fen remembered. "Your men arrested me two months before she passed. I stole a car in Bryan and was on my way to Waco when they pulled me over for having only one working headlight. The judge went easy on me because the car was a pile of junk."

"Why'd you steal it?"

"It was shiny red and looked like it would turn a woman's head. Turns out it smoked more than my uncle Sid. I should have known when the owner left the keys in it. I still think they wanted someone to take it."

"Now I remember," said Fen. "I talked to the judge about you and recommended probation."

The man grinned. "And that's just what he did. I haven't been in trouble since. I even found myself a woman who keeps a tight rein on me. Church is twice on Sunday and Wednesday night for good measure."

"I'm glad to hear it," said Fen, and he meant it.

"Time to go," said Hot Rod. "Thelma's been wearing a hole in the waiting room floor all day. I'm getting out of here while the gettin's good."

Two nurses came in, took vitals, and asked if he wanted a protein drink. They also encouraged him to press the call button if he needed anything and showed him how to operate the television. Their last act was to make sure he had a tall plastic glass of ice water.

Fen heard the squeak of shoes on highly polished floors moments before his door swung open. Thelma breezed in without knocking, and Bailey followed in her shadow.

As usual, Thelma was the first to speak. "I've heard fourteen versions of what happened this morning. Three of them said you were minutes away from being with the Lord and Miss Sally. It wasn't until Doc Freestone came out and shot straight with me that I slowed down on praying."

Each took a side of the bed. Bailey looked for a hand to hold but found only a cast. He followed her eyes. "Rest your hands on the cast if you want to. I want you to be the first to sign it."

Thelma handed her a pen. She signed it while tears dripped on his sheet. After producing a tissue, she looked at the wound on his head. "That's a crummy haircut they gave you. You'll need a knit cap to cover the stitches."

"Will a baseball cap do?"

Bailey took the one she was wearing, loosened it, and gingerly placed it on his head. "Let me take a picture of it and you decide."

Fen examined three photos on Bailey's cell phone. "It's high enough that a cap should work fine."

"You won't need it for quite a while," said Thelma with conviction.

He knew Thelma better than anyone, except for her husband, Sam. The tone of her last words meant she intended to keep him under her protective wings until he was out of the proverbial woods from the head injury, and possibly the arm as well. Removing stitches would take a week and the cast would be on for who knows how long. He mentally changed his deadline to arrive at Lake Palestine until Friday so Bailey could drive him, but he'd put his foot down to anything longer.

The door opened and Lou slipped in. Her index finger went to her lips as she said, "Shh." She walked to the bed and whispered, "This is my third attempt at trying to get to see you. The last nurse told me she'd call the cops if I came back."

Thelma challenged the woman. "There's a good reason for them not wanting a reporter asking questions. Fen needs rest, not a bunch of questions."

Lou ignored her and spoke to Fen. "Candy called and told me to find out how badly you're hurt."

Fen tried to gather his strength. "The doctor said a minimum of two more days here. It could be longer. They don't seem too concerned about the arm, but the bump on the head has Doc worried."

"That's what I need to know. There's a big story breaking in Dallas tomorrow that I want to cover. Candy will let me know when it's safe for you to travel."

Lou slipped from the room after giving Bailey a hug.

"Don't you be looking that way," admonished Thelma while looking down at him. "I know Lawyer Chuck and Miss Candy want you to go somewhere and do other people's jobs. When they release you from this hospital, the only place you're going is home."

Instead of responding, Fen took a breath and yawned. He then fluttered his eyelids. "Pain medicine is kicking in." He closed his eyes and pretended to be asleep.

Thelma hovered over him for two long minutes before whispering, "My overnight bag is in the truck. I'll be back in a jiffy."

Bailey whispered back, "I'll stay here and watch him."

Fen waited until Thelma's rubber-soled shoes squeaked out the door. Bailey greeted him with a knowing smile as he opened his eyes.

"You can stop pretending. She's gone."

"You're missing classes. You could have waited until Friday to come home," said Fen.

"Would you have done that if I was in a serious accident?"

"Point taken."

"Thelma called, then your lawyer buddy Chuck called and told me what happened. He said you were in and out of it today and no one could see you."

"How fast did you drive to get here?"

"Not too much over a hundred until after I talked to Chuck. He told me there was no sense in getting in a hurry and to meet him at the towing company's lot. He helped me load everything that was in your truck into mine."

"Everything?"

"He kept a file folder and said he'd bring it to you tomorrow morning."

"Good. We'll need to study it after you relieve Thelma."

Fen didn't want to ask the next question, but he had to know the answer. "How much damage was there to my truck?"

"It bent the frame. It's a total loss. The fire department had to cut off the driver's door to get you out."

Bailey rested her hands on his cast again. "After seeing the damage to the truck and all the blood, I don't know how you survived. Why aren't you in worse shape?"

"I still have one or two of my nine lives left. Besides, we have an assignment."

Bailey looked skeptical. "Don't you mean we had an assignment? There's no way Thelma's going to let you leave the house for weeks."

"I'll be good enough to travel by Friday."

A ray of hope entered Bailey's voice. "Do you think we can shake her so we can work the case?"

"It won't be easy and my mind's like a bowl of oatmeal right now."

"You need brain food."

"Food sounds good."

Bailey unzipped her jacket and dug out something shiny from a large interior pocket. The object was a triangle of aluminum foil. She opened it and announced, "Two slices of meat lover's pizza. You'd better eat fast."

"Bailey's brain food," said Fen with a thin smile. "I'll be thinking much better by morning."

Chapter Four

Sunlight peeked through a gap in the hospital room's curtains. The first person Fen saw was Thelma, hovering over him like she had after every nurse visit during the night. Her questions this morning were the same ones she asked throughout the night. "How are you feeling? Can I get you some water or ice chips?"

"Water, please. I could also use some mouthwash."

"It's no wonder your mouth tastes like the inside of an old shoe. I smelled the pizza Bailey brought last night. You fell asleep before I could get your toothbrush to you."

"Busted again."

"I intend to keep the promise I made to Miss Sally to take care of you. Lord only knows how many guardian angels you've worn out."

Fen didn't want to start his day by listening to Thelma rattle on about the many times she'd nursed him back to health before he had his knee replaced. His gaze shifted to the nightstand. "Thanks for bringing Sally's picture. Could you grab the control and raise the head of this bed?"

The bed creaked and popped as the angle changed. "That's perfect. The cafeteria downstairs should be open by now. Get some breakfast while I have my morning time with Sally."

Thelma gave him a stare. "If it were any other reason, I'd suspect you of doing something foolish, like checking yourself out and heading to who knows where to solve some crime that's none of your business."

With his head tilted to one side, he gave what he hoped would be a look of innocence. It must have worked, because Thelma grabbed her purse and took a step toward the door. "In case you don't know, you no longer have a truck, and Bailey won't be here for another hour. It should be safe for me to leave you alone for about half an hour, even though I doubt they have much worth eating."

She stopped at the door. "If by some miracle they bring your breakfast, leave it until I get back. You have tubes sticking out of one arm and the one in a cast is useless."

The twenty minutes of being alone flew by as he spoke in a muted voice to Sally's photo. He was still talking when Thelma returned early.

What Thelma didn't know was that while talking with his late wife, Fen had come up with a strategy to start the investigation. It wasn't a brilliant plan. In fact, it wasn't even a good one, but it might get his brain working again.

His breakfast tray arrived, and as expected, Dr. Freestone had ordered a soft diet. Fen didn't complain when Thelma made him eat every tasteless bite. Compliance with her demands was the first part of his plan. He'd be the perfect patient, at least for the next two days.

Bailey arrived right on time. Thelma handed her a written list of duties to perform. She then gave Bailey another longer list of what not to do. His sometimes cranky housekeeper even wrote in all caps, NO MORE PIZZA!

Thelma then clarified that she'd be back by noon to feed Fen his lunch. He knew his mother hen well enough to recognize the drill sergeant's attitude masked a caring soul. He also knew that she functioned best with a solid routine and eight uninterrupted hours of sleep every night. Anything less, and she became a porcupine with an ingrown quill.

Thelma left, and Bailey went to the window overlooking the parking lot. Fen asked, "What are you looking at?"

"I'm making sure she's gone. You had all night to think of a way to get us out of town. Let's hear it—after I'm sure she won't double back on us."

A knock sounded at the door and Bailey whispered, "See, I was right."

The door opened but instead of Thelma, Chuck and Candy walked in. Chuck held up a white box. "Extra gooey cinnamon rolls for the wounded warrior and the college student."

"Yummy," said Bailey. "You'd better hide those until I'm sure the food police don't bust us."

Candy placed her purse on a small countertop. "If you mean Thelma, she either knows, or soon will. Belinda at the bakery is one of her phone friends."

Fen cast his gaze to Bailey. "Help yourself to a roll or two. I had breakfast and I don't want to lie to Thelma or even bend the truth for the next couple of days."

Chuck cast him a look that telegraphed suspicion. "Is that devious brain of yours making a strong comeback? If so, Candy and I want to be accomplices."

"It's going to take you two, plus several others."

Chuck rubbed his hands together. "This could be fun."

"You'll enjoy the first thing I have for you to do. I need a new truck."

Candy didn't hesitate. "I took care of that yesterday afternoon."

Chuck interrupted his wife. "The good thing about you giving me power of attorney is that I can spend your money whenever I want."

Candy acted like Chuck hadn't said a word. "It's almost a carbon copy of your last truck, only a year newer. The dealership is putting a new camper shell on it today and they'll deliver it to your home tomorrow morning."

Bailey spoke next. "Mr. Chuck and I retrieved the custom racks for your paintings and supplies."

"Was the camper shell damaged, too?"

Chuck nodded his head. "The fiberglass looked like spider webs in several places, and the glass in the back window shattered. The tow truck driver said the frame bending twisted everything, including the shell."

Fen let out a low whistle. "I knew that truck smacked me good, but not that hard."

Candy looked at her watch. "The only thing left for you and Chuck to talk about concerning your truck is the accident itself."

Fen looked at Chuck. "What about the accident? The guy ran a stoplight."

"And he received a ticket for it," said Chuck as he took a deep breath. "I don't want to alarm you or borrow trouble before it happens, but an accident like the one you had yesterday is fertile ground for litigation. If the guy claims it was you who ran the stoplight, his company may sue for damages to their truck. Corporate attorneys do it all the time to help bargain for a settlement."

"That stinks," interjected Bailey.

Fen agreed, but didn't want to involve Bailey in this part of the conversation. He fixed his gaze on Chuck. "What do you recommend?"

"We have three options. Two of them are preemptive strikes. The first is to file a civil lawsuit seeking monetary and punitive damages, plus legal fees and court costs."

Fen shook his head. "I don't like that one."

"Next," said Chuck, "I could write a letter stating our intention to seek compensation for their driver's negligence, and the company not properly maintaining their truck."

Fen shook his head. "I don't want to sue some guy trying to earn an honest living."

"It's only a statement of intent, not worth much more than the paper and postage, other than it tells the defendant and the attorney you're not a pushover."

"What's the third choice?" asked Fen.

"Do nothing and let the insurance companies fight it out. You probably won't get what you believe your truck was worth, and there could be future complications if your injuries are more severe than originally thought."

Fen had a decision to make, or did he? "I'm somewhere between options two and three. What's coming to mind is to delay and see what the other team does."

"Good choice," said Chuck. "I'll hold off on doing anything for the time being. That way, you can focus on the murder."

Candy took her turn. "Not doing anything is what we need to talk to you and Dr. Freestone about. We're not sending you to investigate if he says you shouldn't go."

Bailey let out a squeak of disappointment.

Fen updated his condition for Candy and Chuck. "The nurses are checking me every hour. So far, they say everything looks normal. As far as my arm, it's going to be useless for quite a while. When I was sheriff, my trick knee often had me walking with a limp or sitting at my desk. If I could solve crimes with one functioning knee, having the use of only one arm won't stop me."

Candy said, "Don't minimize your injuries, Fen."

"I'm not. That's why I won't press Dr. Freestone to release me today or tomorrow. But, by the end of the week, I'm leaving this hospital. Friday morning, Bailey, Thelma, Sam, and I are leaving to find out who killed a rich California man named Dale White."

Bailey let out a gasp. "All four of us?"

"It's the only way. I need Sam to find the original crime scene. I believe it's somewhere on the Neches River, close to where it empties into Lake Palestine."

Candy nodded her head in approval. "If anyone can find evidence in the woods, it's Sam."

Renewed excitement filled Bailey's voice. "Are you still planning on painting?"

"Why not? There's nothing wrong with my right hand and painting helps me think."

The pace of Bailey's words increased. "I'll put the racks in your new truck and pack everything you need."

Fen shook his head. "Sam and Thelma can do that. You're going back to college today."

"No way," said Bailey. "You said we'd go over the case this morning. Besides, I'm sick of school. My time is better spent painting instead of learning a bunch of useless information." She gulped a breath. "And you need someone to drive you."

"Our original deal was for you to leave college on Friday afternoon and join me at the resort we're staying at overlooking Lake Palestine. That's what you'll do."

Bailey's hands rested on her hips. "Thelma and Sam won't know what painting supplies you'll need."

"Sam and I built and installed the rack. He can put it in. As for art supplies, I'll give Thelma a list."

"She doesn't know burnt umber from burnt sienna."

Fen spoke in a calm voice. "All right. You'll gather everything I need in the garage before you leave today. Sam will pack it after they deliver the new truck."

He could tell that Bailey's temper climbed with each answer he gave. She wasn't one to keep her emotions bottled inside. "This isn't fair. You're trying to get rid of me. Why?"

Fen pushed the button that lifted his back and head higher. "Do you want to explain to Thelma that you're playing hooky from college?"

"No, but—"

"Do you want to hear what she has to say when I tell her I'm not staying home past Friday morning?"

Bailey's lips squeezed together in a thin line. "No, but—"

"Isn't that enough to make you go back to college?"

"Not really."

"It's for your own good."

Candy came to Fen's rescue. "Your plan is to lie low for a couple of days and then spring the trip on Thelma. You know she won't let you go alone, so you're taking her with you. Right?"

"Exactly," said Fen. "She cooked for us when we were in Smithville on our last case. It worked out better than anyone thought. She even scared up some gossip that proved useful. This time, I can't lift a skillet or anything else with this arm. I have to swallow my pride and admit I need her help if we're going to solve this case."

Bailey wasn't fully on board yet. "I still don't see why I have to go back to college today."

Candy moved to Bailey's side. "Fen's trying to put Thelma at ease. You know better than anyone how loyal she is. Remember the fire that burned your hand and the skin grafts that followed? Thelma tried to take on your pain, but couldn't, so she did the next best thing. She did everything for you and nursed you back to health. Fen will tell you she wasn't pleasant to be around until your hand healed."

Bailey looked down at the fading scars on her left hand. "She didn't even know me back then, but she treated me better than I deserved."

Candy continued, "When you needed it, Thelma gave you her attention, and Fen had to step back. Now it's Fen's turn to receive her attention, and you'd be wise to step back."

Fen added, "Like I said, it's for your own good to go back to college."

A nod from Bailey followed. "I know she's going to explode when she hears you want to travel to solve the case."

"Exactly," said Fen. "That's why I'm devising a plan to make her think our leaving is her idea."

Chuck interjected, "I hate to throw a wet blanket on this topic, but if Dr. Freestone doesn't give you a clean bill of health, all this planning will be for nothing."

"Chuck's right," said Fen. "That's why I need Candy's help. You know Claire Freestone, don't you?"

"Sure."

"Could you put a bug in her ear about our problem? If Doc Freestone told me there's no travel restrictions, and Thelma happened to overhear him say it, that would ease her mind considerably."

"How will that help?" asked Bailey.

"I'm counting on her insisting she drive me."

"Good luck with that plan, especially the part about driving over two hours from home."

Fen grinned as Candy cast her gaze his way. "You sly devil. You're going for half a loaf, aren't you?"

"Half a loaf of what?" asked Bailey in bewilderment.

Chuck explained. "Fen knows Thelma won't allow him to

drive so soon after a serious accident. She'll insist on being his chauffeur. He's willing not to press her on it. She'll think she's getting her way, and he winds up where he wants to be."

"I get it," said Bailey. "He gets half a loaf, and it's the half he really wanted."

Chuck put the file folder on Fen's bed. "Take this before I forget it. You'll want to put the information in a new folder. Someone's blood made a mess of this one."

Candy added, "I should receive more reports this week. When they arrive, I'll scan them and email them to you."

"Send Bailey a copy of them," said Fen. "I'll need to rely on her more this trip than I ever have."

Chapter Five

Dr. Freestone's arrival marked the end of Candy and Chuck's visit. Fen took a closer look at the man who had advised him for ten years to have a knee replacement. He'd also explained what to expect when Sally's body showed signs of rejecting a transplanted heart. The man of science had shown extraordinary compassion as he mixed hope with stark reality while Sally ever so slowly moved from this world into eternity.

Fen mentally shook himself back into the present. Dr. Freestone possessed keen eyes that seemed to see things other people didn't. He had a lean frame with a retreating hairline that made his head look larger than normal. Not unusual for a man in his early sixties.

"Are you still riding your bicycle to work?" asked Fen.

"You betcha'. Millie wants me to get an E-bike but I'm delaying that until I can no longer outrun Bill Shank's dogs. It's a game we play."

The doctor got down to business. "How's the vision?"

"Good."

"Headaches?"

"Not as bad as yesterday."

"Aches and pains?"

"I feel like the high school football team took turns tackling me."

Dr. Freestone pulled back the covers and pressed on various spots of Fen's abdomen. When Fen didn't scream, the doctor pulled the stethoscope from around his neck and listened to sounds from the neck down.

"Everything sounds good. Let's check your eyes and ears."

Dr. Freestone peppered him with questions about the date, time, place, and details of the accident while shining a bright light in Fen's eyes. "You're healing faster than I expected, but I want to take some more pictures of your brain before I send you home."

"Good," said Fen. "I think it's best if I spend two more nights."

"Now you have me worried. Of all the things you could have said, staying in the hospital isn't one of them. I came here thinking I'd have to order restraints to make you stay even one more night."

Fen explained. "I've been asked to help investigate a murder near Tyler, and I knew you wouldn't want me driving."

"That's not the only restriction I'll order."

"It's complicated, but I came up with what I think is a workable plan. I'll submit to Thelma or Bailey driving me where I need to go. The place we're staying is a cross between a hotel and a luxury apartment with three bedrooms, two bath-rooms, a living room, and a full kitchen. Thelma will do all the cooking and cleaning while she keeps her eye on me. That should satisfy her."

The doctor let out a chuckle. "She'll also make sure you follow my orders."

Fen nodded his agreement. "That's the price I'll have to pay for not dodging that truck in time."

Bailey made her presence known. "You know how Thelma is. She'll worry herself sick if she's not there to take care of Fen and me."

Dr. Freestone took his time responding. "I'll order X-rays and a CT scan today. Depending on how they look, I may repeat the order tomorrow."

Fen interrupted, "If they're clear, can you arrange it where I'll be released early Friday morning?"

"Only if they're clear and you have no dizziness. Have you tried to walk?"

"Not yet."

"Throw back the covers and swing your feet off the bed without help."

Fen did so and sat, awaiting further instruction.

The doctor motioned for Bailey to join him. "Stand on one side and I'll take the other. If he wobbles, we'll put him back on the bed."

Bailey took the side with the arm in a cast while Dr. Freestone gripped Fen's right arm. Fen eased his feet to the floor and the room spun. They both firmed their grip on his arms as he wobbled.

"Just as I suspected," said the doctor after the blanket covered Fen's legs. "You shouldn't have worried about staying two more nights. You're not going anywhere until you can walk to the nurse's station and back without help."

Fen's mind cleared. "Can I practice sitting and walking today?"

"Not until I'm sure you won't fall. The IV stays in, too."

Fen watched the door shut quietly behind the doctor. The unwelcome words came as a bit of a surprise. After a few moments of quiet, he turned his head to Bailey. "This is just a temporary setback. The plan is still the same. You'll go back to college today and I'll lie here and get better. Don't say anything about me getting light-headed to Thelma."

Bailey's chin quivered. "It's all right if we don't get to work this case. There will be others."

"You're giving up before the game starts. Your job for the next few days is to return to school, do well on your tests, and get ready to help me solve what promises to be a very interesting case."

Bailey seemed to pull herself together. "And your job is to rest your brain. Take a nap before they come to run the tests on you."

"That's not a bad idea," said Fen. "Lower the head of the bed some."

When he woke, Bailey was gone. Thelma rose from the chair by his bed when she saw his eyes open. "Do you want a drink of water or some ice chips?"

"Not yet."

"Bailey told me Doc Freestone came by. She said he thinks you're making good progress but wants to take more pictures of your brain and keep you here until he's sure you're all right. I agree, and there's no use trying to talk either of us out of it."

Fen nodded. "Did Bailey tell you she's going back to college this afternoon?"

"Uh-huh, but not until I convinced her you'd be out of here by the time she got home for spring break."

"Thanks for doing that. She can be a little hardheaded."

Hospital aide Roderick Smith's arrival put an end to the brief conversation. "Howdy, Thelma. I'm here to take Sheriff Maguire down to get his picture taken. How are you doing today?"

"Tolerable, Roderick. I hear your truck broke down."

Roderick let loose with a rollicking laugh. "There ain't

nothing that slips past you. We're down to one car, but it's all part of the Lord's plan for helping me get slim and trim. Doc Freestone gave me a perfectly good bicycle and I'm pedaling my way to a healthy body. Started today."

"Are you wearing a helmet?"

"The doc wouldn't let me have the bicycle until I bought one."

Thelma gave a nod of approval. "You watch out for cars and trucks. I'd hate for you to wind up in a hospital bed like someone I know."

"No, ma'am. My helmet even has a mirror sticking out the side so I can see cars sneakin' up on me."

"That's good. A person can't be too careful with all the crazy drivers on the road these days." Thelma took a breath. "What's this I hear about Pooky Jones getting stabbed?"

"Stabbed? He leaned over an iron fence and poked a hole in that big belly of his. All it took was a couple of stitches and he was on his way."

Thelma frowned. "People ought not to spread rumors, especially if they don't have all the facts."

Roderick performed all the things needed to free Fen's bed from electrical devices. "Here we go, Sheriff."

Fen's lunch was barely room temperature when he returned to his room. He ate it as if it were delicious and listened as Thelma ranted about the quality of hospital food and how much better it would be if she brought a thermos of her cure-all chicken noodle soup. He encouraged her to do so and suggested she could ask Sam to give her a break before she pulled another all-night vigil at his bedside. To his surprise, she agreed.

Sam arrived as Fen finished choking down his bland food. Thelma gave her husband strict instructions about what her patient should and shouldn't do. She emphasized his dietary restrictions and confinement to bed. Sam grunted a reply that he understood.

After she left, Sam produced a chocolate-chip cookie and gave it to Fen. He couldn't remember anything tasting so good and washed it down with water.

Sam asked, "Do you want to try to walk?"

"You read my mind."

Fen followed the same routine he'd tried to accomplish with Dr. Freestone and Bailey earlier in the day. He took his time dangling his feet off the side of the bed. Then came the real test as Sam took a firm hold of his right arm. Fen slid off the bed and stood motionless, hoping the room wouldn't move as it had earlier in the day. It didn't, and he took a tentative step forward. The IV tubes restricted the number of steps he could take, but that was all right. Fen knew the day's rest had worked to restore his balance.

"That's good, Sam. I'll get back to bed now. I have some things to tell you."

Sam was the type of man who didn't believe in speaking unless absolutely necessary. He waited silently for Fen to speak.

"I have a special assignment for you."

A nod of his head was Fen's only clue that Sam heard him.

"I need you to look for a crime scene. Someone shot a man in the back of the head about a week ago." Fen took out his phone. "This is a map of Lake Palestine." He enlarged it to display the northernmost part of the lake. "Even though they found the body in Lake Palestine, about here..." he pointed to a spot on the map. "I believe the body came down the Neches River and into the lake."

"Did it rain as hard there as it did here?" asked Sam.

"Harder."

"What about this creek on the other side of the lake?"

"It's possible, but the body was much closer to the east bank."

Sam took the phone from Fen and studied it. As a full-blood Choctaw Indian, his natural habitat was the woods, not indoors. The less time he could spend with a roof over his head, the happier he was.

Sam handed the phone back. "Not much chance of me finding anything."

"I know."

"When will they let you out of here?"

"Friday morning."

"Does Thelma know you're planning to go?"

"My plan is for Thelma to drive me, and we'll meet Bailey there."

Sam grunted an affirmation to the plan. "Thelma drives slow."

"I know."

"Does she know she's driving you?"

"Not yet. When can you leave?"

"Tomorrow, around lunchtime."

"Can you have my truck packed with my art supplies by then?"

"Bailey stacked everything in the garage. It won't take long."

When Thelma returned, she and Sam traded places. They parted without speaking to each other, which wasn't unusual, at least not for them. Fen wondered if they communicated by telepathy more than words. It was the strangest relationship he'd ever seen, but it worked for them.

After another bland meal, followed by a cup of Thelma's chicken noodle soup, Fen thought about his plan while she watched a game show on TV. It continued to come together, but there was still one hurdle to overcome. Thelma needed to believe Fen was well enough to travel and participate in a murder investigation.

The nurse came in with his evening dose of pain medication. Any refinements to the plan would have to wait until the next day.

Chapter Six

It was difficult to catch Thelma sleeping, but that's what Dr. Freestone did Thursday morning. Not only was she sleeping, but a puddle of drool formed a damp circle on the pillow her head rested on in the hospital's recliner.

The doctor gave a quick smile and turned his attention to Fen. "Are you ready to walk this morning?"

Thelma bolted upright, wiped her mouth, and jerked a blanket off. Still groggy from getting precious little sleep for two nights straight, she rose slowly from the chair.

Fen answered Dr. Freestone's question. "I'm ready, willing, and hopefully able."

"Let me check you over first." He began by shining a bright light in Fen's eyes and spoke as he searched for anything amiss. "Yesterday's tests all came back clear. How did you sleep last night?"

"I don't remember."

"Attempting humor this early in the morning is another good sign. How are the headaches?"

"They lost the battle with the pain pills."

More poking and prodding. "You're not screaming like a little girl when I mash on all the important things under the hood, so that's another good sign."

Dr. Freestone turned to Thelma. "Come to the other side of the bed and be ready to ease him down if he can't sit, stand, or walk."

Thelma scurried to obey.

Fen looked at Thelma. "I tried this yesterday with the Doc on one side and Bailey on the other. It didn't turn out very good."

"Don't be in such a hurry," said Thelma. "Slide your legs over the side and get used to sitting up."

"That's what I was going to say," said the physician. About fifteen seconds passed. "Any dizziness?"

"Not a bit."

"Good. Stand when you're ready."

Fen knew from yesterday's trial run with Sam that he'd have no trouble. After taking a slow couple of laps to the door and back, the doctor okayed him to walk down the hall to the nurse's station with Thelma pushing his IV stand.

Once Fen was back in bed, Doc Freestone made his pronouncement. "I walked in here with my mind made up to order another round of pictures of your brain, but I don't believe those are necessary. I still want to keep you here one more day and night without an IV, just to be sure."

He turned to Thelma. "Make sure he drinks plenty of water and go with him on a walk every other hour until bedtime. If he becomes dizzy, sit him in a chair if you can. If not, ease him down to the floor and get help. I'll be by early tomorrow morning and release him to go home. You'll receive written instructions on what he can and can't do."

Fen asked, "Can I drive?"

"Drive? No. You'll be on pain medicine for your arm. You can travel as a passenger and hopefully you won't get in another accident."

"I'll see to that," said Thelma.

The doctor left, and the morning passed with Fen taking walks every two hours and frequent trips to the bathroom. It came as a pleasant surprise when he received a regular meal for lunch. His plan to travel to Lake Palestine was working out, but one major hurdle remained. He had to convince Thelma to drive him there.

It turned out he'd wasted his time worrying. Sam stopped by at the same time a worker removed Fen's empty lunch tray and closed the door behind her.

"I'm leaving the county," said Sam in a flat tone.

Thelma didn't budge from her chair or seem surprised.

Sam directed his next words to Thelma. "Go home and sleep tonight."

"But..." That's all she said before clamping her lips together.

Sam shifted his gaze to Fen. "Everything's packed."

Fen nodded as Sam turned and left.

Thelma waited for the door to close before she stood and glared at him. "You have some explaining to do."

Fen took a deep breath to propel his words. "After they deliver my supper, you're going home to get a full night's sleep. Tomorrow, after I'm released, you'll pick me up and drive us to Lake Palestine. Me, you, and Bailey are staying at a resort for at least a week. We'll each have our own bedroom and there's a full kitchen in the apartment. We need to investigate a murder, and I've already wasted three days."

Instead of arguing, Thelma simply asked, "Is that where Sam's going?"

"He's going to look for the original crime scene."

Instead of arguing or asking for more details, Thelma simply asked, "Are you ready to take another stroll down the hall?"

The afternoon passed much the same as the morning, with short naps for both of them between walks. When his supper tray was delivered, Thelma looked at him and said, "Send me a text when you know what time you want me to pick you up. I'll have everything packed and have a bed made for you in the back seat of that new truck."

He bid his trusty watch-dog good night, amazed once again at how three short sentences from Sam had changed Thelma from a cantankerous taskmaster into a compliant and trusted friend. She was a paradox, a sometimes pain in the neck, but no one questioned her loyalty.

For the first time since firefighters extracted him from his truck, Fen was alone. He unplugged his cell phone from its charging cord and punched in a number. He both dreaded and looked forward to hearing the voice of the woman who answered.

"What a pleasant surprise," said Audrey.

Fen could see her face and smell her scent as she continued. "You're breaking the agreement. We're supposed to limit our calls to every other week. Is everything all right?"

"Yes and no," said Fen. "I was in a little fender bender earlier this week."

He should have known Audrey wasn't one he could fool so easily.

"Where are you calling from?"

"Our local hospital."

"How long have you been there?"

"Since Tuesday morning."

She let out a gasp. "Your delay in calling tells me this wasn't a simple fender bender. Start at the beginning and give me the full story. I'm especially interested in knowing the extent of your injuries and why you haven't called before tonight."

Fen began with the trip to Chuck and Candy's office Tuesday morning and recounted details of each day's events, giving special emphasis to Thelma's almost constant presence in his room. He ended by telling her of his impending trip to solve another murder.

Audrey, a plain-spoken and very attractive attorney, responded by saying, "My first inclination is to drive to Newman County and take a baseball bat to the other side of your head for not calling me sooner."

"I wouldn't blame you if you did."

She then asked, "Did you treat Sally this way?"

"Only once. We had a very brief talk after I came home with stitches in my arm from a drunk with a knife. I didn't call her from the hospital either."

"Then I'll follow her example. We agreed to wait five years before making a final commitment, but that won't happen if you pull a stunt like this again."

"You drive a hard bargain, counselor, but I'll agree to your terms as long as they apply to you, too."

Audrey chuckled, which told him she was well on the way to forgiving him. "I guess you're partially justified for not calling sooner due to Thelma's constant presence with you this week. I understand your desire to ease her into the idea of another woman coming into your life."

"Don't forget my brain being scrambled for a couple of days."

She came back with, "Don't plan on using that excuse in the future. If you're well enough to solve a difficult murder case, there's nothing wrong with the gray matter."

A yawn slipped out before he could stifle it.

"Get a good night's sleep," said Audrey. "Something tells me you're going to need it."

"Good night, Counselor."

"Good night, Sheriff."

Fen replayed the conversation with Audrey as he lay waiting for the pain medicine to take effect. After losing his wife Sally when she refused a second heart transplant, he never dreamed he might meet someone else. He certainly wasn't looking when he met Audrey a few months ago while he was in Smithville on a case. He didn't regret their decision to keep their relationship long distance for now. She had a son she wanted to see settled in his career before embarking on a relationship, and he wanted to give Bailey the best shot he could at her career.

As he pulled the sheet up to his chest, it occurred to him that Thelma wasn't the only paradox. He'd spent the first portion of his day speaking to the photo of his late wife, divulging his innermost thoughts. Tonight, he'd spoken with a woman who was very much alive and well on the way to repairing and capturing a heart he thought would never heal. He fell asleep remembering the light floral scent that had stayed with him for months.

***

BRIGHT SPRING SUNSHINE streamed through his window when Thelma blew into his room at ten fifteen. "Did Doc Freestone release you?"

Sitting up in bed, he ignored her question and said, "I hope you brought me a change of clothes. They went scissor-happy and cut off everything but my boots and belt."

"I figure they knew better than to ruin custom-made boots and that fancy belt you got for Christmas."

Fen spoke as he examined the contents of a plastic grocery bag and clothes on hangers. "Turn your head and I'll shuck this gown and get dressed as best I can."

The sound of a zipper was Thelma's cue to turn toward him. He then answered her original question. "I'm officially discharged, but I have to wait for someone to take me down in a wheelchair." He sat on the bed and held out his socks toward her. "Help me on with these, would you?"

He continued his thought as they both wrestled his socks and boots onto his feet. "We can't check into the resort before four o'clock, so we're not in a rush."

"That's good, because I'm not driving fast. That new truck needs to break in slow and this will be the only chance it will have before you try to push your big foot through the firewall. It's a good thing I'll be driving you if you need to go somewhere."

"That's the deal—either you or Bailey," said Fen.

"If you get tired of my driving, then you two can go in her truck. That gal drives like she stole it."

Fen thought to himself that in her prior life, she'd done just that. Hotwiring cars and taking them for a joyride on the streets of Houston was how Bailey learned to drive as a young teen. Thankfully, she had amended most of her ways. Her rough edges had smoothed considerably since she'd come to live with him. Her driving, on the other hand, could use a little refining.

A knock on the door sounded and Thelma went to swing it open. A wheelchair appeared with Hot Rod Smith pushing it.

"Good morning, Miss Thelma. Howdy, Sheriff."

Both wished Hot Rod a good morning in return.

Hot Rod positioned the chair in front of Fen and locked the wheels. "Isn't it an irony, Sheriff? They won't let you go until you can walk on your own, and then they make you ride out in a wheelchair."

"It's one of the great mysteries of life."

Thelma issued a word of caution. "You go slow and easy taking Mr. Fen downstairs. I hear that you're driving way too fast and running stop signs on that bicycle Doc Freestone gave you."

"That's what I like about this town." Hot Rod chuckled. "There's always someone looking out for me. It's like wearing a shock collar that reminds me to tighten up the way I'm actin'."

Fen didn't know whether to believe him, but it seemed to pacify Thelma, which made the trip to the ground floor much more enjoyable.

Once outside, Fen inhaled a full breath of spring as Thelma retrieved his new truck. She pulled to the curb as Hot Rod locked the wheels on the wheelchair and he took his first step of freedom.

"Put him in the back," shouted Thelma.

Fen mumbled, "So much for freedom."

"What was that?" asked Thelma over the clatter of the diesel engine.

"I said we need to stop at the pharmacy and pick up a prescription for pain medicine."

A wide smile drew Hot Rod's lips upward. "You two are something else, Sheriff. Be careful and try not to come back unless you're bringing cookies."

Fen shook the hand of the man who, like Thelma, had once been locked in the jail he supervised.

"One more thing," said Fen to Hot Rod. "Would you mind pulling off my boots? Thelma went to the trouble of making me this nice bed and I don't want to get the sheet dirty."

"My pleasure, Sheriff. You can rest easy with Thelma driving."

After Thelma stopped at the pharmacy, then Ray-Ray's Drive-In for cheeseburgers, he chased down his noon painkiller with root beer and stretched out on the makeshift bed. He slept all the way to Chandler, a small town on the north bank of Lake Palestine.

Chapter Seven

It took a few seconds for Fen to realize where he was and why his legs wouldn't lie flat. They were bent at the knees like a flap on a cardboard box. He lay with his eyes closed listening to the truck engine drone, a soothing sound that only a diesel engine makes. After pushing up with his good arm, he saw pine trees pass by. "Where are we?"

Thelma didn't move her head. "We're about five miles from Chandler on Highway 31. You've been asleep for hours."

"It must have been the combination of medicine and the cheeseburger."

He looked over her shoulder and noticed she had the cruise control set at fifty-five miles an hour. He stated the obvious. "It smells new and runs good."

"It should. Before Sam took the window sticker off, I took a peek. Do you have any idea what new one-ton diesel trucks cost these days?"

"I was afraid to ask."

"You'd better get well quick and sell some more paintings."

Fen took his phone out of his shirt pocket and activated the maps application. "We should pass over a portion of Lake Palestine in a few minutes. After that, we'll cross the Neches River. There's a park I'd like you to stop at. I think we can walk down to the river from there."

"You sit back and let me do the driving. Sam sent me a text and told me he parked by the bridge. He followed the Neches downstream to the lake, and now he's working his way upstream. Nothing yet."

Fen did as she instructed until Thelma announced, "We're coming up on a bridge."

He righted himself but kept a pillow under his cast. Before him stood a long bridge, spanning what appeared to be the back portion of the lake. They crossed the bridge, and a sign came into view. "We're about to cross Kickapoo Creek. Sam may need to search here if he can't find anything on the Neches."

"If there's anything to find, he'll let us know. If not, then it ain't there."

"That's what I'm afraid of."

The town of Chandler came into view. It looked like a laid-back little town with the normal smattering of fast food and locally owned restaurants. A new Starbuck's coffee shop on the main road gave evidence of the town joining the twenty-first century. Thelma turned on her blinker, slowed, and pulled off Highway 31.

Fen noticed two small road signs. The first gave notice of a public boat ramp on the right side of the bridge. The second pointed to a park on the opposite side of the road and what looked like an enormous parking lot.

He sat up straighter with his feet flat on the floorboard. "The bridge crosses the Neches River and is the dividing line between Henderson and Smith County. Let's check out the boat ramp first."

It was awkward putting on boots without the use of both

hands, but, with Thelma's help, he accomplished the task. They walked until the road turned into a boat ramp, sloping downward into the river.

"This ain't much of a river," said Thelma. "The Brazos back home beats this one by a long shot."

Fen responded with only a grunt as his thoughts fixed on Sam's search for the original crime scene. He spoke out loud. "There's a sidewalk leading under the bridge to that big parking lot across the highway. If I were Sam, I'd park here or, more likely, on the other side of the road."

"Why there?"

"Did you see how many cars and trucks are parked there? At least ten or fifteen. Everyone's been cooped up all winter and they're ready to get outside and take long walks in the woods and by the river."

Thelma cast her gaze to the concrete sidewalk leading under the bridge. "Do you want to walk or drive to look for Sam's truck?"

"Let's walk."

Traffic passed overhead as they made their way north. The parking lot was part of a small park and the trailhead for several walking paths. The search for Sam's truck didn't take long. Thelma spotted it first and moved an open hand in a sweeping motion. "He's out there, but only the Lord knows where."

A dull pain settled into Fen's left arm that was supported by a sling. "Let's get to the resort. I'm expecting a phone call and a visitor this evening."

Thelma turned and walked beside him. "I hope whoever it is doesn't stay long. It will be time for your next pain pill soon and another at bedtime. The way the last one knocked you out, you may not remember what they have to say."

It was on the tip of Fen's tongue to tell her he'd delay the next round of painkillers if necessary. Instead, he considered his options and told Thelma what she wanted to hear. "You're right. I'll ask him to come by after supper and tell him nine-thirty is my bedtime."

She nodded her approval, then turned a squint-eyed gaze toward him. "You gave up too easily. If you're thinking about doing something foolish like going somewhere with whoever it is, you can forget it. He can come after supper, but you'll be in bed by nine o'clock."

Fen sensed the need to negotiate. "Our meeting will take place at the dining room table. I need space for papers."

Thelma responded with, "You can lie on the couch. I looked at the photos of this fancy resort. There's a nice coffee table you can reach from where you'll be laying. Whoever is coming can sit in a chair looking at you."

It wasn't a bad compromise, so Fen walked on without countering her last bid.

"Who are you meeting?" asked Thelma as they approached his truck.

"I was wondering how long it would take for curiosity to get the best of you. His name is Tim Gladly. He's the game warden who was coordinating the investigation."

"You said *was*. Why ain't he still in charge?"

"It's complicated because there's politics involved. Tim announced his intention to retire from state service and run for sheriff of Smith County."

Thelma held up both hands. "Don't say another word. You lost me when you mentioned politics. One of the best days of my life was when you didn't get re-elected sheriff of Newman County." She cut him a glare and announced. "The next best day will be when that lawyer buddy of yours stops sending you all over the state fixing other people's problems."

"That won't be anytime soon. You're not the only one who made a promise to Sally."

Frustration clouded Thelma's face and seasoned her words. "I know all about that promise, and there has to be some sort of escape clause or statute of limitations."

"There is. Didn't I tell you?"

A huff escaped her as they both climbed into the front seat. Once inside, she stared at him. "If I had a dollar for everything you don't tell me, I'd be a rich woman."

"Not rich, but better off." He made his smile disappear and put on an expression reserved for serious conversations. "Sally told me I could stop solving crimes when I put an engagement ring on another woman's finger, or when eight years have passed since she died, whichever comes first."

Her gasp seemed to take the air out of the cab of the truck. Thelma put her hand over her heart. "That's only five years from now." She shook her head and said, "Too soon. Way too soon."

Her countenance changed to one that communicated impending betrayal. "It's going to take me every bit of five years to get used to the *idea* of you and another woman, let alone taking the plunge again. I'm not sure I could stand it even if it's ten years. Sam and I might have to leave."

"You're borrowing trouble again," said Fen as he pointed toward Highway 31. "There's less than ten miles to the resort. I won't be any help carrying in the luggage, but Bailey should be here soon."

"I'll take care of the luggage. Put your seatbelt on and rest easy."

They arrived at the resort's entrance and followed the signs directing them to a building marked Guest Registration. Fen reached for his door handle once the truck shut off. "You stay here," said Thelma. "I'll get us checked in."

Fen liked the idea of not having to get out, but the reservations were in his name, and he didn't want to chance Thelma causing a scene when asked for ID and a credit card. She guarded her own identity as if it were a nuclear secret. She grudgingly agreed to him coming inside but insisted on going with him.

All went well with check-in until the desk clerk passed them off to a salesman who tried to sell him a timeshare. Fen told him no thanks, but the man persisted. That was his biggest mistake of the day, and possibly his career.

Once back in the truck, Fen asked, "Did you enjoy telling that man what he could do with his timeshare?"

"He deserved every word. Did you see the look on his face when I asked him if he owned what he was trying to sell? I knew he didn't. I could see it in his beady eyes."

Fen countered with, "He's just trying to make a living."

Thelma shook her head. "The Bible says to let your *yes* mean yes and your *no*, no. Anything more is sin, and that man was trying to make you a sinner."

The pain in his arm had intensified to a steady throb, so Fen stopped talking. Thelma took the hint and pulled Fen's bottle of pills from the truck's cupholder. She unscrewed the top and handed him a capsule. "The sooner you take this, the better. Hang on and I'll follow the map to where that cute gal told us to go."

An asphalt road made a serpentine path up and down hills dotted with pine and hardwood trees. Condo complexes were scattered throughout the property, each with three stories. The truck rested in a parking spot as Fen's phone rang. He dug it out of his shirt pocket and activated the speaker.

Bailey's voice sounded after Fen issued a greeting. "I'm almost at the resort. Where do I go?"

"Follow the signs to the registration building. Tell them you're staying with me and get a map of the resort. They'll circle where we're staying."

Thelma spoke over him. "Don't let them try to sell you anything."

Fen sighed and said, "The guy wouldn't dare after what he experienced a few minutes ago."

Bailey's chuckle traveled over the line. "Did Thelma set him straight?"

"I certainly did, and I'll come back and tell him again if he gives you any trouble."

Concern seasoned Bailey's words. "You sound stressed, Thelma."

"Don't worry about me. I want to hear how you're getting along with your classes and that handsome deputy."

"Let's just say I'm glad to be here with something different to think about."

"You'll get your chance," said Fen. "We have an appointment with a game warden after supper tonight."

"What about Sam? Any luck in finding the original crime scene?"

"We found his truck, but he won't let us know anything until he has something to report."

"I'm pulling up to the registration building, so I'll see you in a few minutes. I'll call if I need help."

Fen knew Bailey's last remark was as hollow as a box of air. Bailey's misspent early years made her street-smart well beyond her years. If she encountered any problems, she'd solve them herself.

Chapter Eight

F en grimaced with each jarring step to the third floor as
Thelma acted as his shadow, fully prepared to catch him
if he stumbled or fell backward. After entering the condo, she
made a quick review of the three bedrooms and pronounced.
"You're in the last bedroom. It's the biggest with a king-size
bed. I know how you like to spread your papers out when
you're thinking. You have your own bathroom."

Fen scanned the condo, which didn't disappoint. A hickory
dining room table and chairs gave the first hint of the advertised
upscale, rustic vibe. The bedrooms carried on the motif with
more hickory furniture. A stylish kitchen came fully stocked
with dishes, silverware, pots and pans, and newer appliances. A
back patio overlooked thick woods but gave a peek at the
resort's indoor water park, another outdoor pool, and a putt-
putt golf course complete with a waterfall. The marina, swimming beach, and dockside restaurant were somewhere out of
view.

Fen concluded this would be a perfect summer get-away

for a family. It would also do nicely as a base of operations for a murder investigation.

Thelma picked up his bag and carried it to his bedroom. When she came out, she said, "There's a jetted tub and a separate shower."

"I'll take showers. It worked all right in the hospital," said Fen.

"I'll need to tape a garbage bag over your cast before you do. Don't be trying to do it yourself."

Fen walked to the bedroom, sat on the side of the bed, and eased himself down. Thelma nodded her approval as she pulled off his boots. "That's the first smart thing you've done all week. Bailey and I will unload everything and put it away. I'll make out a shopping list and send her to the store."

Bailey's voice sounded from the living room. "That won't work, Thelma. I stopped at a big grocery store only a couple of miles south of here. The brands differ from our store back home. You'll gripe like a centipede with sore feet if I make a substitution you don't approve of."

Fen spoke from his horizontal position. "Bailey's right. You two unload my truck. Thelma, you do the shopping. Bailey can unload her truck and get settled into her room while you're gone."

Thelma huffed, but it was more out of habit and fatigue than genuine disagreement with the plan.

Bailey asked, "Do you want your easel and painting supplies upstairs?"

"No, he doesn't," said Thelma.

Fen found a compromise. "Only my sketchbook and pencils."

It took three trips for the two women to ferry everything Thelma brought upstairs. Fen knew without looking that one of the heavier items was a large, cast-iron skillet.

The spring-loaded front door closed with a firm thud, and Bailey soon appeared in his doorway. "She's gone."

"Good thinking about sending her away."

Bailey sat on the edge of the bed. "I call it self-preservation."

Fen felt the effects of the medication. "Has college improved any since the last time we talked?"

"Not a bit."

"What about your love life?"

"Almost non-existent. What about yours?"

"No change. I'm still a lonely widower."

"There's a city attorney in Smithville who wouldn't mind doing something about that."

Fen had to be careful. Bailey had a woman's intuition, along with the rare ability to detect evasion and deception. He'd tell her the truth, but one bite at a time.

"I'm in the doghouse with Audrey. I didn't call her for several days after the accident. Let's just say it had a chilling effect."

Bailey let out a soft whistle. "That sounds like something stupid I'd do."

"The good news is," said Fen in a more upbeat tone, "you and I can devote all our time to solving a murder." He picked up his phone. "And speaking of a murder, I need to make a phone call."

"Do you want me to leave?"

He shook his head. "I'll put it on speaker but leave the talking to me."

It wasn't long before Fen had Tim Gladly on the line. "We're here. My assistant Bailey is with me and my combination cook, housekeeper, and nurse went to the grocery store for a week's worth of groceries."

Tim asked, "Do you want me to bring you up to date over the phone?"

"I'd rather hear it in person. Can you come here later this evening?"

"I'm busy until about seven thirty. Is that too late?"

"Not at all." Fen gave him the number of the condo and saved the rest of his words for later.

Bailey rose from her seat on the bed. "That wasn't hardly worth listening to."

"Set up an easel in the living room. I want you to paint when I'm not sending you on errands. It will help you think."

"Are you going to paint?"

"Not tonight, but tomorrow we may look for something to sketch."

<hr>

Texas Game Warden Tim Gladly arrived at fifteen minutes before eight. He was stockier than Fen pictured and shook hands like he meant to get to know you better. "That's a nice cast you have on that arm."

Fen took off his baseball cap and lowered his head for inspection. "This is what my doctor worried about more than the arm."

Introductions of Bailey and Thelma came next. Fen motioned for the gathering to move to the living room, where he stretched out on the couch. With the dishes done, Thelma covered a yawn. "If y'all will excuse me, I'm way behind on my television watching." She looked at Fen. "I'll bring your last pill of the night to you at nine o'clock when Mr. Gladly leaves."

Her door shut and Bailey whispered, "You'll have to excuse Thelma. She's subtle as someone driving a thumbtack with a sledgehammer."

"I like her," said Tim. "I bet she can cook up a mean chicken-fried steak and gravy."

Fen confirmed it with, "She brought her cast-iron skillet from home." He paused. "But we didn't come this far to talk about food. What can you tell us about the victim that isn't in the report?"

"You already have the demographic data. From what I've been able to gather, Dale White was brilliant and a royal pain in the backside. He not only was the smartest man in the room, but he made sure everyone knew it. 'Chronically obnoxious' is the way one of his former employees described him."

Bailey asked, "Was he really that smart?"

"Smart enough to retire at thirty with millions coming in every year to fund whatever hobby he wanted to take up. He was an adrenaline junkie who looked for the next challenge or physical thrill."

"What was he doing living at Lake Palestine? This seems like a nice, quiet lake in a sleepy part of East Texas."

"Someone bet him he couldn't win a national fishing competition. Lake Palestine was one of his stops across the USA to prove them wrong." Tim relaxed into the chair. "I know it seems far-fetched to you and me, but the guy had already mastered surfing, rock climbing, endurance running, white-water rafting, and sailing. His wife told me that after he won a small bass fishing tournament, he would take up motocross racing."

"Tell us about his wife," said Fen.

"Her name is Talia Goldberg. She's a free spirit, like Dale. They got together in college, where she was into long-distance running." He took a breath. "Before you ask, she has an alibi, and it's air-tight. She was back in California attending a cross-training competition when he went missing."

"Who sounded the alarm that Dale White was missing?"

"A fishing guide named Hunter Mason. Hunter was supposed to pick Dale up at the marina for a morning session of fishing. He didn't show, and Hunter mentioned it to me. I told a Smith County deputy, and he did a wellness check. Mr. White's mansion-on-wheels and his motorcycle were where they should be, at the RV park on the north end of the lake, but Dale was nowhere to be found, and his wife was in California. Five days later, after heavy rains, another fishing guide found Dale's body floating close to the RV park."

"Who found him?" asked Fen.

"A fishing guide named Tran Wilks." Tim cast his gaze at Bailey. "How old are you?"

"Nineteen. Why do you ask?"

"Tran Wilks is only a year older, but he knows this lake better than guides twice his age. He's a quiet young man with a boyish face and a clean record." Tim cleared his throat as if buying time to find the right words.

Fen and Bailey glanced at each other. The quick look didn't go unnoticed by Tim, who leaned forward. "The reason Tran Wilks doesn't have a rap sheet is because no one's been able to catch him." He paused. "At least that's what some claim. I'm not so sure."

"What do they say he's doing?" asked Bailey.

"Nothing serious. It's a more general disregard for rules and laws, especially those related to hunting and fishing."

Fen tilted his head. "Men like that are a dime a dozen. What aren't you telling us?"

The question earned a chuckle and an explanation. "They told me you were sharp. All right, here's the story regarding Tran Wilks. He's one of the smoothest talkers I've ever met. A real redneck Romeo. A female dispatcher from Henderson County resigned because of him."

Bailey asked, "What did she do?"

Tim rubbed his chin. "Fell in love with him, even though she knew he had other women in four counties waiting in line. The story is she lost her job because she'd call him from work and tell him where game wardens and deputies were working. Again, that's more rumor than fact. Officially, the dispatcher left to attend college."

Fen wanted to follow this trail as far as it took him. "When did she quit?"

"Her last day was December thirty-first. She quit before things went public. The last I heard, her father gave her an offer she couldn't refuse. She's gone back to college in Nacogdoches and doesn't come home on weekends."

Bailey tilted her head. "You seem to know a lot about her and her family."

"I recognized her voice over the radio when I was working in Henderson County, but I know her father even better. He's Detective Clay Matson."

Fen was still feeling the effects of the painkiller, but this revelation was like being hit in the face with a pail of ice water. "Clay Matson? He's the lead detective from Henderson County. That means he's been investigating Tran Wilks."

Bailey released a low whistle. "The Redneck Romeo picked the wrong dispatcher to court."

"Now my being here is making sense," said Fen. "What kind of man is Clay Matson?"

"He's a solid family man but can be a little impetuous when making arrests. He likes quick solutions to crimes."

Fen spoke out loud, mainly to himself. "It sounds like Tran Wilks's luck ran out when he discovered the body in the lake."

"Not necessarily," said Tim. "Tran took the body to the Smith County side of the lake. Clay claims the body was floating on the Henderson County side of the lake and it should be his case to solve. Smith County has the body, and their detective believes that's enough to make it his case since the exact location of the body in relation to the underwater middle of the Neches is in dispute."

Bailey gave her opinion. "I bet Detective Matson wants it to be in Henderson County so he can get back at Tran for costing his daughter her job, breaking her heart, and banishing her from home."

"That thought crossed my mind," said Tim.

Fen recognized another thread to pull. "The detective from Smith County is Bobby Sealy. You did the initial investigation. What can you tell us about him that isn't in the file?"

"He's the chief detective in the Smith County Sheriff's Department and my primary competition in the next election for sheriff. You can draw your own conclusions about why he wants to solve the case."

"Is he honest?" asked Fen.

"I'd call Bobby Sealy ambitious, but I'm biased towards the other candidate."

Fen took a full breath and let it out slowly. "This is shaping up to be a three-way tug of war to see who solves the murder first."

Tim held up two fingers. "Not three, only two. Someone high in the food chain called you in to make sure the investigation doesn't get ugly. I'm washing my hands of it. If I can't win the election on my record and reputation, I'll retire and go fishing."

"That's similar to what I did, but instead of fishing, I paint landscapes." Fen thought for a minute and said, "Don't kid yourself about being able to stop chasing bad guys cold turkey, though. Once it's in your blood, it's hard to give it up."

Tim ignored the remark and rose. "You can call me if you need me, but I don't think you will."

Bailey saw the game warden to the door and came back to the same chair she'd vacated. "What now?"

"You're going fishing and I'm having company visit me tomorrow."

Chapter Nine

Fen sat on the couch with a sketchbook in hand, artist's pencils at the ready, and a blank page staring at him. It was one thirty in the afternoon and he'd done nothing but move from his bed to the couch, still wearing his pajamas. His lethargy broke when the lock on the front door clicked and Bailey rushed in.

Thelma headed her off. "Don't take another step, young lady. Where have you been all day? Your lunch is in the microwave, probably cold as a polar bear's toenails."

Bailey's voice trilled with excitement. "I've been at the activities center earning money."

Her words had Fen's attention, but Thelma spoke before he could. "You'd better explain why you didn't call."

"I was busy. Besides that, going to college got me out of practice for checking in with anyone." She spoke at a pace that didn't allow anyone, even Thelma, to shoehorn in. "This resort is really cool; it's jam-packed with families here on spring break. There's a coffee and smoothie bar, a regular bar for adults, Blue Bell ice cream by the scoop, a special section in the same building for kids to watch movies, an exercise room, and swimming pools all over the place. I stayed in the activities center after I took a walk and checked everything out. That's where I got the job."

Bailey had to take a breath, so Fen squeezed in a question. "Can you elaborate on the job?"

Closing the door to the fridge, with a bottle of water in her hand, Bailey traversed the open plan from the kitchen through the dining room to the living room. She plopped into a chair, took a swallow of water, and gave details. "After breakfast I loaded my backpack with two medium-sized sketch pads and pencils and took a walk."

"You should have told me where you were going," said Thelma.

"You were taking a shower."

"Next time, leave me a note."

Bailey had a story to tell, so she didn't respond to Thelma's demand. "Anyway, I wound up in the activities center, bought a cup of coffee, and started drawing sketches of some of the little ones who were watching movies. Before long, some older kids came out of the arcade."

Her eyes sparkled with excitement. "Did I tell you about the arcade? It has cool games for older kids to play, but they're not free. I think it's a bit of a rip-off, but I guess that's between the kids and their parents."

Fen interrupted. "We're waiting for the part where you earn money."

"Oh, yeah. It was so cool. I was sketching portraits and caricatures when this woman came to see what I was doing. It turns out she's the manager of the whole resort. We talked while I worked and before long, we negotiated a deal for me to work as many hours as I could, not too early in the morning or late at night. I made sure she understood my need for flexibility. The money to pay me is coming out of her advertising budget and, unlike many of the activities here, the sketches go to the guests at no cost. I did the math based on how many sketches I can complete in an hour. She's paying me what I normally charge. I should go back to college with two grand in my pocket."

"Are you sure you'll be available to take me places I need to go?"

Thelma spoke up. "You'll be safer if I take you, and you'll be safest if you stay on the couch and let your arm and head heal."

"Speaking of," said Fen as he looked at Bailey. "I won't need you today. I arranged for Detective Sealy from Smith County to come here at four this afternoon. Detective Matson from Henderson County will be here at seven o'clock."

Bailey rubbed her hands together. "That means I can work the rest of the day and into the night. I'll need to cut off about nine tonight. I'm meeting Tran Wilks tomorrow morning at the marina. He finally got back with me after his morning session of fishing."

Thelma walked out of the kitchen. "What did he sound like over the phone?"

Bailey turned her head so only Fen could see her wink. She turned back to Thelma. "His voice was soft and silky. It reminded me of some of the slow Elvis songs you like."

"Nobody sounds as good as The King."

"This guy does."

"Then you ain't going without a chaperone."

"Yes, she is," said Fen firmly. "I want to know more about this young man, and Bailey's the right person for the job." He turned his gaze back to Bailey. "You'll fish for forty-five minutes, grow tired of it, and spend the rest of the morning drawing the most realistic portrait of him you can."

Bailey's smile contained a scoop of mischief. "If he looks

half as good as he sounds, I'll do an oil painting of him. It's bound to sell."

Fen brought reality into the discussion of Tran Wilks with words of caution. "Don't get too lost in Tran's eyes and silky-smooth words. There's a detective who thinks he's a viable suspect in a murder case. Find out if Tran took Dale White fishing. I suspect he did. In fact, it wouldn't surprise me if Mr. White hired multiple local guides to speed his learning curve to become a competitive angler."

"What do you want me to do after tomorrow morning?"

"If Tran gives you other names, schedule more fishing trips."

Bailey huffed. "It's going to be hard for me to pretend I like to fish. The only way I like them is on a plate, battered in corn-meal and deep fried."

"Don't forget the hush puppies," said Thelma. "It's not a fish dinner without hush puppies, French fries, and coleslaw."

Bailey stood. "Now you've made me hungry, and I need to get back to work."

"Not before you eat."

Bailey had one more question. "Any word from Sam?"

"Not yet," said Fen.

Absolute certainty marked Thelma's words. "Focus on something other than Sam. He's more at home in the woods than I am in the kitchen. We'll hear from him when there's something to report."

DETECTIVE BOBBY SEALY arrived at precisely three-thirty that afternoon. Thelma answered the knock and showed him into the living room before retreating to her bedroom.

The earlier discussion with Bailey had stimulated Fen

enough to take an awkward shower, shave, and dress. His sketch pad remained blank.

The first thing Fen noticed about the detective was his smile. Plastic was the word that came to mind. Despite this, Fen extended a hand for the man to shake. "Make yourself comfortable and pardon my not getting up. I had a run in with a delivery truck. That's why I'm several days late taking over for Tim Gladly."

"I appreciate you coming, Sheriff Maguire, but you wasted your time."

"Oh? Are you close to solving the case?"

Fen's initial impression of the man who sat in front of him with shiny cowboy boots was lukewarm. Sealy's posture was too stiff and his handshake overly firm. Fen imagined the caricature he'd draw of Sealy wearing an oversized cowboy hat, a badge the size of a dinner plate, silver spurs that jingle-jangled, and a steely-eyed look meant to strike fear in the heart of any desperado who crossed his path.

"I'll make the arrest in another day or two," said Sealy, with unwavering confidence. "It's a matter of making sure I've done a thorough background check."

"You must be talking about Derrick McDonald, the ex-marine. What makes you so sure he killed Dale White?"

"If you know his name and service record, then you have copies of my interviews with Mr. McDonald."

"You were very thorough when you interviewed McDonald and the other residents of the RV campground. It seems McDonald wasn't the only person who didn't get along with Mr. White. How did you single him out?"

"McDonald is the only one who not only threatened him but had a physical confrontation."

Fen didn't want to press too hard on their first meeting, so he backed off. "I'm not saying you're wrong. In fact, I think you're on the right track by suspecting McDonald. He may be seventy-two years old, but he's a former Marine with thirty years of service before he retired. You made it clear in your report that he didn't approve of Mr. White, his lifestyle, or his politics."

When Detective Sealy didn't respond, Fen moved on. "Your reports weren't the only ones I received. It seems Detective Matson from Henderson County has his own suspect. Have you looked into Tran Wilks?"

"Of course I did. The Wilks boy brought the body to shore in Smith County. That gives me jurisdiction."

"Isn't that in dispute?"

"Not to my way of thinking. Tran Wilks wasn't sure exactly where he found the body. That put the case in Tim Gladly's lap, and now it's in yours. Still, the body wound up in Smith County and there's nothing to prove he died elsewhere. The flood washed away all evidence of another crime scene."

Fen changed the direction of the conversation. "Why do you think they called me in to help with the investigation?"

He shrugged. "You tell me."

"No. I want to hear what you have to say."

Detective Sealy pursed his lips. "All I know about you is what I read online and picked up from our current sheriff and some of the older highway patrol officers. Your reputation is spotless, and you're a famous artist. You own a large ranch with cattle, crops, and oil wells. You also have a knack for solving hard cases. I suspect you have friends in high places that call on you when small-town cops or sheriffs get stuck. This case isn't one of them. Like I said, there's going to be an arrest in another day or two and it's going to stick."

"By the way," said Fen. "Why is the sheriff retiring?"

"He's old and sick. We'll all miss him, but life goes on and there's no shortage of criminals who need to be in prison. Derrick McDonald is one of them."

Fen issued a forced smile. "Thanks for coming to see me. I want you to know we're on the same team. The person, or persons, responsible for killing Dale White needs to be locked behind bars. If you're absolutely sure it's Derrick McDonald, and you have the proof that will hold up under tough scrutiny, then do your duty. If there's any doubt, I'm here to help."

Detective Sealy stood. "It's clear to me you're not convinced McDonald did it, but I am."

Fen considered saying that he'd seen careers shipwrecked because detectives rushed to make an arrest. A feeling, a hunch, came alive that told him there was much more to the murder of Dale White than Detective Sealy suspected. On the other hand, Detective Sealy could be right.

Thelma came from her room after the front door shut. Fen asked, "Did you hear it all?"

"It wasn't easy, but I heard enough to know he's too sure of himself."

Fen didn't respond but retrieved his sketch pad and drew the caricature of Sealy he'd pictured earlier. As he sketched, Fen hoped the interview with Detective Matson that evening would either confirm or deny his hunch.

Chapter Ten

The gnawing need for movement hit Fen as he waited for Detective Clay Matson to arrive. Thelma had served another meal of excellent quality and huge portions, but it had followed an afternoon snack of coffee with two varieties of cookies. The bloated feeling should be easy to fix with a long walk, but convincing Thelma he was up to it might be difficult. He'd attack that problem after the interview.

The knock on the door came five minutes early, which suited Fen fine. Thelma insisted he remain on the couch while she retrieved the visitor.

Clay Matson's flat-top haircut came into view as soon as he removed his felt cowboy hat. A square jaw gave his head the appearance of a box made up of equal dimensions. Broad shoulders and a western-cut sports coat continued the geometric impression of right angles. The round mound above his belt broke up the hard edges. Fen occasionally fought the battle of the bulge, but Matson had lost it.

"Come in," said Fen. "Have a seat."

As was her custom with most guests, Thelma offered something to drink. Matson accepted coffee and settled on a club chair across from Fen. When she arrived with a platter of cookies, Matson nodded his appreciation and didn't need an invitation to dig in.

Thelma excused herself after saying she appreciated cooking for people who liked to eat. Matson responded with a grunt. It was all he could do with his mouth full.

Fen waited until his guest washed down the cookie and returned his mug to the trivet on the hickory coffee table. The detective pointed to the cast and took the lead. "Tim Gladly told me about the wreck and that it would delay you getting here."

Fen ignored the opportunity to elaborate on his circumstances and asked instead, "What do you think of Tim?"

Matson didn't hesitate. "He's one of the finest men I know and a darn good lawman most of the time."

"Only most of the time?"

Matson looked down, then back up. "You'll have to cut me some slack if I seem out of sorts. This murder case is personal to me." He stood. "I don't know who you are, who sent you, or why my sheriff told me Tim was off the case and that I'd be answering to you. Then you take your sweet time getting here, and that jerk detective from Smith County won't cooperate with me in sharing information. He's already blown the perfect opportunity to solve the case."

Fen stood also. "I don't know about you, but I'm in no mood to sit in this fancy condo. Let's take a walk."

Thelma stormed out of her room but didn't get far. Fen gave her a narrow-eyed stare reserved for special occasions. "Detective Matson and I are going for a much-needed walk. We may be gone quite a while. Don't wait up."

His tone and expression had the desired effect. Thelma made a tactical retreat without comment.

Once outside, Fen led the way down the staircase and into the parking lot, all without saying a word. Once they were on a blacktop street heading downhill, he said, "I met with Detective Sealy this afternoon. He told me he knows who killed Dale White and why."

"He's wrong."

"He told me he has all the proof he needs."

"Did he tell you what it is?"

"No."

"That's because he doesn't have any."

"What do you mean?"

Matson came to a stop. "A fishing guide named Tran Wilks claims to have found the body in the lake. He tied a rope on it and pulled the victim to shore on the Smith County side of the lake."

"I already know that," said Fen.

"Did you know Detective Sealy had his men keep me away from Wilks's boat? He claimed total jurisdiction until Tim Gladly arrived and straightened him out. By that time, Sealy had finished his interview with that low-life Wilks and released him without checking his boat or impounding it. I had luminol with me but couldn't get within a hundred yards of them."

Fen's opinion of Detective Sealy dropped another notch. He also knew what happened to Matson's daughter because of her involvement with Tran Wilks was clouding a father's judgment.

"Let's say there was blood or other evidence in Wilks's boat. How did the murder go down?"

Matson searched Fen's face. "Now I know why they sent you. You listen and ask intelligent questions." His shoulders relaxed as he continued, "Here's what I believe happened. Dale White couldn't help but make people mad at him. It came naturally to him. The list of people who hated him stretches as far as the eye can see then keeps going. Tran Wilks is a cocky kid who believes he's God's gift to humanity. He uses people for what he can get from them and tricks customers into giving big tips."

"How does he do that?" asked Fen.

"From what I hear, he has the slickest, low-key script in the business." Matson's words came faster. "I've had several people tell me they believe Wilks does research on the next day's customers to find out their interests, family history, and anything else he can find out about them. Little by little, in three or four hours, he'll get to know them inside and out. Then, he tells them some wild story and hits them up for a donation of some sort. It's usually to pay off a large vet bill for a dog or cat he doesn't own. Sometimes it's a make-believe medical bill for a relative. Anything that pulls at heartstrings."

Matson summarized. "He's very convincing and manipulative."

"I get the picture. How does that fit in with the murder?"

"Dale White wasn't the type of man who gave a rip about anyone but himself. He also could read people. Once he made a deal, there wasn't any renegotiating. Tran Wilks believes he can talk anyone into anything. To him, an agreement to go fishing for a certain price is only the beginning."

Fen took over. "I can see how sparks might fly if two people like that got together. Let's assume they did. What's your theory about what happened?"

Matson threw out his chest. "I believe Dale White made a handshake agreement with Tran Wilks to take him fishing and teach him what he knows. I wouldn't doubt that agreement included ways to cheat in tournaments."

Fen ignored the last comment, as it was pure speculation.

The detective continued, "Somewhere along the north shore of the lake, the two had a disagreement that turned ugly.

Tran Wilks uses his trolling motor to pull into the channel of the Neches and follows it upstream into thick woods. White's in the front seat casting his rod. Wilks pulls out his pistol and shoots White in the back of the head."

"I get the idea. What does Tran Wilks do then?"

"He dumps the body overboard. The vegetation in that part of the Neches is thick. The body sinks and gets hung up on something underwater. Wilks leaves the area and goes about his business. Days later, the rains come, the body fills with gases, and it floats. The current intensifies and sends what's left of Dale White into the lake."

Fen countered with, "But Tran Wilks is long gone."

"That shows he's afraid of the flood washing the body into the lake. He finally comes back but has no intention of going as far up the river. He's looking for the body in the lake and finds it. He takes it to shore so no one would suspect him."

Standing under the glow of a streetlight, Detective Matson appeared sure of himself. He added a postscript. "The worst thing about my story is Detective Sealy is going to arrest the wrong man, and Tran Wilks will get off."

Fen extended his hand for Detective Matson to shake. "You've given me a lot to think about. I'm going to keep walking. You're welcome to come, but it's going to be quiet."

"No, thanks. My daughter's home from college for the first time this semester, and I need to spend time with her."

The road wound its way past more condo complexes, past a swimming pool, and tennis courts. Fen kept walking and stood in front of a sign with an arrow pointing to a building with a familiar name. He took the sidewalk to a central plaza that was abuzz with people. The sign above the double doors read, ACTIVITIES BUILDING.

Three girls he judged to be about twelve years old swung the door open in front of him then swerved to miss him. Their high-pitched giggles acted as horns to warn others to clear a path. Each carried a page torn from a familiar-looking sketch pad.

Fen made it inside before the door closed. Most of the room's activity was taking place against a far wall. Bailey spotted him and motioned with a frantic wave. He navigated his way through the sea of youthful faces and examined the sketch on her pad. She'd captured both the innocence and mischievousness of a pre-teen boy's expression, as well as his exaggerated ears and legions of freckles.

"I'm so glad you're here," said Bailey. "It was busy this afternoon, but nothing like it is now. Can you spell me?"

"Have you eaten supper?"

She shook her head and kept sketching. "I'd kill for a slice of pizza, an ice cream cone, and a bathroom. Not necessarily in that order."

"Finish that one, then take a break. I could stand to wash my ears out with cheerful sounds."

"Hey," said a teenage girl with braces. "I want you to do my picture. He's old."

Bailey gave the girl a withering glare while Fen took a seat beside his protégé and dug in her backpack for another sketch pad and pencils.

"He's not old," said Bailey. "This man is the best artist you'll ever meet. He taught me everything I know."

The girl wasn't convinced. "I still want you to do mine."

Fen took over. "If you don't like the one I do, Bailey will do another for you at half price."

"Oh? That sounds like a good deal."

The girl standing beside the reluctant patron slugged her in the arm. "Ginger, you're a complete dweeb. If there's no charge for a sketch, half the cost of two sketches is still nothing."

"I don't get it."

Bailey focused on finishing the sketch and mumbled, "It will all become clear when you work and pay bills."

It had been a while since Fen did caricatures, but he soon fell into the rhythm and time lost its meaning. After several pre-teens walked away with their prize sketch, it surprised him when he looked at his next customer. She was a woman in every sense of the word. The spandex shorts and top proved it. He couldn't decide if her light blue eyes belonged to a fallen angel or the real thing.

"Where's your daughter?" asked the woman. "I watched her before I went to work out. She's very good. How is she with portraits?"

"Even better than with caricatures, and she's not my daughter. More like a protégé."

The woman flashed a smile that glowed as if her teeth were infused with neon. "You don't hear that word thrown around very often. If she's learning from you, that means you're the true professional artist."

Fen considered pulling a business card from his wallet but thought this might be a lead for Bailey to pursue. "I specialize in Texas landscapes. Bailey's the artist you want if you're in the market for a portrait."

"I might be, but I'll settle for a sketch tonight."

"She'll be back before long if you'd like to wait."

"I'd rather see a sample of your work, but not a silly sketch."

"It will be rough. When we're working a crowd of this size, it's five minutes max to finish, then move on to the next customer."

"That's fine. A simple sketch will do."

Fen spoke to himself and the woman at the same time. "I'm looking for quick inspiration. Your clothes and physique lead me to believe you love to stay active. What's your favorite sport?"

"Rock climbing."

"And your name?"

"Destiny Roe. What's yours?"

"Fen Maguire, and the name of the other artist is—"

"Bailey Madison," said Destiny. "I picked up her business card earlier today."

Fen went to work with confident pencil strokes. Long ago, he learned to carry on a conversation while he worked. It made the time pass for the customer and it kept him in practice with extracting information. The latter was essential in his other occupation of solving crimes.

His eyes focused on the drawing as his words worked independently. "You have two very interesting names, Destiny and Roe. Do you believe names are more than random letters put together and given to us by our parents?"

"I've never given my name much thought."

"Destiny means an inevitable outcome."

"Kind of like fate?"

"Uh-huh."

"Are you saying that no matter what choices I make, I'll end up at the place destiny predetermined?"

Fen smiled as he kept sketching. "All I'm saying is that's what your name means. You choose if you believe it or not. I go back and forth on the predetermined theory until I give up and think about something else."

Destiny shook her head. "There's no confusion with me. I chart my course and make my own breaks." She paused. "What about my last name?"

He stopped drawing, but only long enough to flash a glance at her. "That word is even more interesting. A roe is a gazelle, a small, graceful animal with speed and agility. The word is used in the Bible to describe a beautiful woman."

She leaned forward. "That's very flattering, except the part about being fast. A woman could take that the wrong way."

Fen kept drawing without missing a beat. "Let's put the words together and see what we get. Your destiny was, and is, to be a beautiful woman."

Destiny leaned forward. "Are you coming on to me?"

A guffaw sounded from over Fen's shoulder. "If you knew him, you'd know the answer to that question. He's the most one-woman man you'll ever meet."

The ripping of the top page from the pad put a quick end to the discussion. "All through," said Fen. "Here's your five-minute sketch."

The woman sat motionless for several seconds. "This is fabulous. How did you get so much detail in such a short time? The rock formation looks like many I've climbed in the past, and the strain on the muscles in my arms comes across so clear."

Fen said, "It takes the study of anatomy and geology to get those right. You'll notice I spent little time on your hands or the details of your ears. Those take me a long time and I'm seldom satisfied with the results. Bailey nails them every time."

Fen stood. "Thanks for coming by, Destiny. I need to get back to the condo, but I'm leaving you with an outstanding artist."

He shifted his gaze to Bailey. "Come talk to me when you get home. There's something important we need to discuss."

Chapter Eleven

F en sat with his good arm's elbow resting on the dining room table. He'd already heard more than he wanted from Thelma about him staying too long at the Activity Center the previous night. With his back to the kitchen, he watched steam rise from the day's first cup of coffee and thought about Bailey spending the morning in a bass boat with Tran Wilks.

The door to Bailey's bedroom creaked, and she entered the living room with her mouth yawning wide, her eyes barely open. Loose, navy pants covered her from the waist down, while a hooded college sweatshirt covered the top of her head and torso. She shuffled into the dining area wearing tattered house shoes.

Thelma glanced at her. "I'm glad to see you're not going fishing half-dressed. It's bound to be cold on the lake this early."

Fen said, "It's supposed to get up to ninety today."

Bailey winked at Fen. He knew what was coming and smiled.

"I'm prepared for cool weather or the heat. There's a bikini underneath the circus tent. The bottom is a thong and there's not much to the top either. I'll shuck the top layer once the temperature reaches eighty."

Thelma shook her head. "I don't understand why you two insist on shortening my life by saying things to get me riled. I checked the clothes you brought and the skimpiest thing I found was cut-offs that show off too much of those pretty legs."

Bailey stood and pulled down her pants. "Do you mean these?"

Thelma groaned, but Fen put a note of seriousness in his voice. "Don't forget what we talked about last night. Tran Wilks has a reputation, and it's not good. He breaks rules and hearts. Detective Matson came up with a theory about Tran being the one who killed Dale White."

Thelma delivered a second cup of coffee to the table. Steam rose in front of her as Bailey said, "From what you told me last night, Detective Matson *wants* the killer to be Tran Wilks. Perhaps he wants it so much that he made up a story and tried it out on you. If you think it's true, so will a jury."

"I never said I believe that's what happened, only that it's plausible. If we take only the basics of the story, any other fishing guide could have done the same thing." He took a breath. "That reminds me, did you make a reservation with any other fishing guides?"

"Two more. All other appointments for next week are fully booked. The guides' names are Shane Wesley and Melody Brine. Shane has a three-star rating while Melody's is four point two."

"What rating does Tran Wilks have?" asked Thelma.

"Four point nine. The highest of all the guides."

Fen issued a final warning. "Remember that this is only the second day of our investigation. Don't think you have to return with the case solved. From what we know of Tran, he's smart, careful, and calculating. Don't scare him off by asking too many questions."

"How many is too many?"

"One, if it's the wrong one. You lived on the streets long enough to know that." Another related idea came to him. "Use today as a time to study how he'll try to play you. His reputation leads me to believe there are two things that will interest him about you. One is how much money he can get from you."

Thelma spoke from the other side of a bar. "If either of you say what I think the other is, I'm going home and taking her with me."

Bailey went to the kitchen and gave Thelma a hug. "You worry too much about me, and I love you for it."

Fen glanced past the embrace to the kitchen window. "First light. You'd better trade in those house shoes for tennis shoes and get going."

"You don't need to worry, either. I've been around guys long enough to know they expect a girl my age to be at least ten minutes late."

"You're probably right, but if his schedule is as full as all the other guides, today will be your only chance to speak to Tran."

Bailey delivered her second quick hug of the day. This time, Fen was the recipient. "I know my assignment. I'll get him to talk, and he'll never suspect a thing."

After the door to Bailey's bedroom closed, Thelma moved to the table and whispered, "When that girl tells both of us not to worry, that's when I get an itch between my shoulder blades."

"Are you itching?"

"Like I rubbed up against a patch of poison ivy."

"Me, too."

Itching or not, Fen knew he had to let Bailey spend time

with the young man despite his dubious character. If he hadn't broken his arm, he'd be bouncing across Lake Palestine with Tran at the helm. As things were, relying on Bailey was his only option.

"See ya' later," were Bailey's only words as she hustled out of the condo. The self-closing front door did its job with a resounding thud.

"I'm going to worry myself sick until she's back here for lunch," said Thelma.

Fen ran his finger around the rim of his coffee cup. "Staying here worrying would be a complete waste of time. I need you to be my driver this morning."

"Where are we going?"

"To talk to an ex-marine before he goes to jail."

"When are we leaving?"

Fen shrugged.

Thelma wagged her head. "That bump on your noggin is still affecting you."

"What makes you say that?"

"You used to be a lot sharper. You'd tell me about the man without me having to ask."

Fen knew she was right and set out to give her some information. "He retired about twenty years ago and lives at a lakeside RV park."

Thelma tapped her temple with an index finger. "Use your brain. He wouldn't be living beside a lake in an RV if he wasn't an avid fisherman. He's a former Marine. Those people take pride in being early risers. I bet he's stepping onto his boat right now with a thermos of coffee. He'll fish a couple of hours if they're not biting and three if they are. Then, he'll go home for breakfast. If we get there any earlier than nine-thirty, we'll be sitting in his driveway wishing we were here."

Stunned speechless, Fen considered how to respond.

Thelma's logic was sound and convinced him to postpone traveling the miles to the RV campground until later that morning. This left him with the option of congratulating her or countering her recommendation to wait. By praising her, he'd admit she was right and he was wrong. If he mounted an argument against her recommendation to delay, that would be petty and violate what he knew to be prudent. He needed to find middle ground, and fast. A more tacit response came to mind.

"I'm going for an early morning walk. I'll eat when I get back."

Thelma grinned. "You just don't want to admit I outsmarted you this morning."

The door made the same thudding sound as it closed behind him. His thoughts turned from Thelma's self-congratulations to what he'd ask the former marine. It occurred to him that Derrick McDonald might not be there to ask, but not because he was on the lake fishing. Detective Sealy may have made a pre-dawn visit that included an arrest warrant and chrome-plated handcuffs.

It didn't take long for Fen to realize that only a few souls were out and about as the morning sun peeked through the pine trees. Footfalls sounded from behind him, and he moved closer to the ditch on the side of the road. The sound of a runner approached from behind.

"You're up early," said a familiar voice.

He turned and beheld more spandex and the same glowing teeth he'd seen last night. "Destiny. I didn't have you pegged as an early riser."

She ran in place as he walked. "Cardio in the morning and strength training at night. We're marking time until it warms up enough in the places with challenging rocks to climb."

Fen noted that she used the pronoun *we* but didn't

comment on it. Instead, he said, "You could always go some-place south of the equator during our cold seasons."

"That's the plan this fall. Some climbers like to scale frozen waterfalls. Not me. Give me a warm cliff and I'm a happy girl."

Destiny slowed to a walk. "I did some research on you and Bailey last night. You're a true renaissance man and she has a brilliant future ahead of her as an artist. Have you ever thought of combining your talents?"

"That's what we were doing last night. She took a break, and I took her place until she returned."

"That's not what I'm talking about. You specialize in land-scapes while Bailey's portraits are stunning. Would you consider painting that rock formation you did last night while Bailey painted me straining to achieve the final difficult hold?"

This caught Fen completely off guard, but he had a quick response. "I like the idea but need to run it by her. She's always looking for work." He paused. "If she's agreeable, I'll let you and Bailey work out the details. I'll honor whatever financial agreement you come to."

"Thank you. I can't wait to see the finished work."

"Only if it's your destiny, Destiny."

"That's clever, James Fenimore Maguire."

Destiny Roe lived up to her surname of a gazelle as she resumed her run at a blistering pace. Fen thought about how excited Bailey would be if she landed the job painting a rock climber dangling from a cliff. He'd need to minimize the cliff for Bailey to capture a close-up of Destiny straining.

He walked on, giving more thought to the work. He'd never done such a project. Perhaps Bailey would have a better idea of how to capture both the landscape and Destiny with details enough to satisfy their client.

Fen continued his slow-paced journey until he passed the back side of the indoor water park. This left him with a mostly uphill journey back to the condo. His mind shifted from the alluring woman he guessed to be twenty years younger than himself to a man fifteen years older. Such was the life of solving murders. You never knew who you'd meet, who'd become a suspect, and who would have nothing to do with the crime.

Chapter Twelve

The morning sun had done its job of taking the chill out of the air. Even light jackets were discarded by the time Fen and Thelma arrived at the RV Park. The lakeside location on a gentle hillside overlooking the northeast corner of Lake Palestine made it a perfect location for anglers. It boasted a long dock and a ramp to launch boats. The place where the Neches River escaped heavy woods was within sight. On the downside, the road that snaked in front of long lines of travel trailers looked in need of fresh asphalt ten years ago. Some campsites had rusting tin covers for the travel trailers, while others were open to the elements. The fast-growing spring grass needed a haircut.

Fen told Thelma to ignore the sign on a tin building at the camp's entrance that read ALL VISITORS MUST STOP AND REGISTER.

"Are you sure we shouldn't stop?" asked Thelma.

He pointed. "No one's there, only a clipboard. Old campgrounds like this become lax on security. The clipboard is so they can advertise exclusive access. We're looking for site number twenty-seven."

They followed the road nearest the lake. The lot numbers started at one and progressed to number nineteen. The road made a gentle turn uphill and curved to run in the direction they'd come. Thelma pulled into a driveway with sprigs of spring grass shooting up through the gravel. "This is it," announced Fen. "Do you mind waiting here?"

"Not a bit. Take your time."

Gravel crunched under Fen's boots as he approached a three-quarter-ton pickup with its hood up. He wondered if it was yawning from old age or overwork.

A man stood on the front bumper with the back side of dirty jeans wiggling as his gruff voice filled the air with a volley of profanity.

"Are you Derrick McDonald?" asked Fen.

"Who's asking?" asked the man who didn't extract himself from whatever he was doing to the engine.

"My name is Fen Maguire."

"What do you want?"

"To ask if you killed Dale White."

That was enough for the man to put his feet on the ground and stand upright. He squared his shoulders. "If you're another cop, go ask your buddies. I've already told them all I know."

Fen took inventory of the man who stood ramrod-straight in front of him wearing a T-shirt that might have been white at one time in its life. His face had more crags and creases than the cliff Fen sketched the previous night.

"Which buddy?" asked Fen. "There's Game Warden Tim Gladly or Detective Bobby Sealy. The second one thinks you killed Mr. White, and the other wants me to find out the truth."

The man's eyes narrowed in suspicion. "Are you some sort of special cop?"

"Something like that. I was once a highway patrolman and a sheriff. I get called on from time to time. Sometimes it's making sure cops don't screw up and other times it's giving a fresh perspective on investigations."

"Which one applies to Dale White's killing?"

"Both. I have copies of all the officers' notes, witness statements from both men, and other documents that might help me."

"What about Detective Matson, from Henderson County? Do you have his reports?"

"Yes, and I spoke to him yesterday. He doesn't think you did it."

"He's right. I thought about killing that California dreamer, and I'd probably sleep well if I'd done it. But that sorry slick of slime wasn't worth the cost of a bullet."

Fen wanted to further gain the man's trust, so he pointed to the fifth-wheel camper. "How do you like living here?"

"It was better in years past," the man spat the words in anger.

"What made it better?"

McDonald pointed down the hill. "Do you see that motorhome through the trees?"

"I couldn't help but notice it."

"It's parked in the spot Lisa and I came to every year after I retired. We had a standing reservation, an agreement with the park owner that we'd rent that spot every year, from February until mid-May." Some of the man's anger seemed to dissipate as he looked toward the lake. "When Lisa got sick and died, I was delayed coming. It seems Dale White took a liking to our camp-site. It's amazing what thirty thousand dollars did to the park owner's memory of our agreement."

The man's story hit a nerve of sympathy within Fen. Derrick had lost his life partner and wanted to come back to their special place to grieve. But that didn't change the fact Derrick freely admitted to hating Dale White. From a legal standpoint, it was circumstantial evidence against the plain-spoken former marine.

Fen wanted to concentrate on the facts of the case and not get entangled in emotion. "Did you go fishing the days before the big rains?"

"I fish every morning at first light," said Derrick. "I sleep very little at night, so I fish every morning and take a nap in the afternoon."

"What about when it was raining hard, like the days before they found Mr. White's body?"

"I figured if fish don't mind getting wet, I don't either."

"Did other people in the campground have a hard time getting along with Mr. White?"

Derrick dragged a dirty hand across a whisker-stubbled chin, leaving a trail of grease. "He reminded me of a second lieutenant fresh out of college I had to serve under." His head wagged as he gave an opinion, accompanied by an icy stare. "What a pompous jerk. Not a lick of common sense. It didn't take long before he had a rash of unfortunate accidents."

Fen looked toward the lake. "I understand what you're saying."

Derrick kept talking. "If I didn't know better, I'd say they were brothers."

"Were you investigated for any of the lieutenant's unfortunate accidents?"

"Not formally, and there's nothing in my record that says otherwise."

The true meaning of Derrick's words shone through the response that smelled of evasion. It seemed likely the grizzled man told a story to young Marine non-coms about how 'others' handled similar situations and escaped punishment. It was pure speculation on Fen's part, but he could picture it happening.

"Let's focus on Dale White," said Fen. "I understand you two had an argument that turned physical. Is that true?"

"Not the way I count physical. He stuck a bony finger in my chest and the next thing he knew, it pointed back at him. It was a simple dislocation that I popped back into place while he was on the ground crying and threatening me with arrest."

Fen took a step to the left to catch the shade of a pine tree. "I'm surprised he didn't file charges."

"He wanted to, but his wife talked him out of it. She filmed the whole thing, and it showed he poked me first. In fact, she told him not to be such a baby and to get tougher."

"I wouldn't have expected that reaction from his wife."

Derrick's smile was the first of the conversation. "Physically, she's one heck of a woman. I hear she's into cross-training competitions and ultra-marathons, but that's just trailer talk. All I know is she runs past here about the same time I throw back the covers. A lot of people here own dogs and they make a racket when she runs with that headlamp throwing light all over the place."

Fen turned and looked down the hill. "Isn't her name Talia Goldberg?"

"That's what I hear. She's one of those modern women who didn't take her husband's name. Can't say I blame her."

"And that's their motorhome, on the first row?"

"Hard to miss, isn't it?" Derrick looked at the extravagant motorhome. "I guess it's hers now. Dale White has no need of it. You could say he's downsized his permanent residence."

He shifted his gaze back to Fen. "Aren't you going to ask me where I was when Dale White went missing?"

"Not unless you want to say something different from what you told Detective Sealy or the game warden. Besides, it wouldn't do me any good. The coroner couldn't be sure of the exact day, let alone the time."

"I'm surprised you're telling me that."

Fen shrugged like the revelation made no difference. It was all part of the game of gaining trust. He knew from experience that leaking small, non-consequential bits of information some-times kept suspects talking and made future conversations more productive.

"Thanks for giving me a chunk of your time," said Fen. "I didn't notice a car to go with Dale White's palace on wheels. Is that normal?"

"Talia usually leaves after her run. She drives a new Land Rover. If it's not in the driveway, she's gone. I don't know where she goes, but I'm willing to bet that someone here in the park does. If my Lisa was still alive, she could tell you."

Fen thought of Thelma and her ability to glean informa-tion. She'd need a plausible cover story to infiltrate the camp-ground, but that shouldn't be a problem. If anyone could make up a convincing tale, she could.

After thanking Derrick again for his time, Fen returned to his truck where Thelma waited.

"That's a rough-looking man," said Thelma. "Did he do the killing?"

"He says he didn't." Fen pointed to the road. "Turn around and let's go back the way we came. Stop at the fancy motorhome."

Thelma did as instructed. Parked beside the driveway was a trailer used to haul a vehicle and a bass boat that looked almost showroom new. "She's not here," said Fen, mainly to himself.

"Who ain't here?"

"Talia Goldberg, the victim's widow."

"Do you know where she is?"

"I was hoping you'd find out for me."

"That's no problem. All you have to do is knock on a few doors and ask."

Fen shook his head. "I'd prefer she not know I'm asking."

"Why not?"

"It's more of a gut feeling than a reason. She goes somewhere nearly every morning after a run. I'd like to know where and if she's meeting someone. It may be perfectly innocent, but then again, it could lead to something."

Thelma's eyes flashed with mischief. "Leave it to me. Finding out what people are doing is my specialty. I'll even give you a two-day delivery of information, guaranteed. It would be one day, but I need to take care of you."

"Forget about me. Bailey will be back for lunch, and she'll be at the activities center if I need her."

"Do you promise to stay on the couch?"

"No. I may want to go to bed."

"You'd better be flat on your back when I get back this afternoon. You've jostled that arm too much today."

Fen countered with, "You take care of getting me information on Talia Goldberg, and I'll be careful with my arm." He then asked, "What's your plan?"

"I'm going fishing."

The answer was more than he expected, even though it made no sense.

It was almost time for Fen's next pain pill when they climbed the steps to the condo. The mending bones in his arm had felt every bump in the road on the trip home. As much as he wanted to make more progress on the case, he had to admit that lying on the couch with a pillow supporting his cast brought relief. So did the pain medicine, but it dulled his mind.

He wanted to quiz Bailey on her fishing expedition with Tran Wilks, but that would have to wait until the afternoon.

The pain pill was kicking in and Thelma had draped a fleece throw over him before she left to gather information and gossip. It wouldn't be long before a nap put thoughts of everything to flight.

Fen's eyes were fluttering like butterfly wings when his phone rang. He retrieved it from the coffee table. Sam's name came up on the caller ID. He fought the sleep that threatened to overtake him again and tossed back the fleece throw that felt surprisingly heavy.

"Sam," he slurred through lips that felt swollen. "Did you find something?"

"Yeah, but it's not much."

"Did you take photos?"

"Yeah. I'll send them."

"Do you have the GPS coordinates?"

"Yeah."

"Are you going home?"

"Too many people here, and I don't like cops."

"Does Thelma know you're leaving?"

"Uh-huh. She's snooping at the RV park."

"She told you not to call me, didn't she?"

"Yeah."

"Thanks, Sam. Be safe driving home."

The line went dead. Fen wondered what he'd do without Sam, but he didn't wonder for long, as the medicine had pinned him to the couch. He needed to find out which side of the Neches Sam had located evidence on to know which detective to call, but he'd worry about that after his nap.

Chapter Thirteen

F en didn't know how long he slept, but something like a guilty conscience told him it was too long. Sam had sent him information that might be crucial in solving the case and he was wasting valuable time sleeping.

He retrieved his phone and went to the message from Sam. As promised, he'd included photos and two GPS coordinates. He stabbed the first photo with his finger and enlarged it. At that moment, the front door opened, and Bailey walked in.

"Thelma told me not to wake you. I'm surprised you're not sound asleep."

"I was. Come here and look. Sam sent me photos and GPS coordinates."

Bailey dropped her backpack on the dining room table and joined him. "I can't see anything."

Fen took his index finger and thumb and enlarged the photo.

"What is it, and where did Sam find it?" asked Bailey.

"It's the corner of a wallet buried in the bank of the Neches, on the Henderson County side."

Bailey sat back. "I could walk past that a hundred times and never see it."

"It's Dale White's wallet. Sam checked for a driver's license then put it back exactly where he found it."

"Isn't that tampering with evidence?"

Fen shrugged. "Not if we go there before dark and discover it."

Bailey giggled. "I like the way you think. It reminds me of how I used to justify things I did."

Fen scrolled to the next photo. "Uh-oh. Things just got more complicated."

Bailey squinted as Fen enlarged the photo. "Is that a pistol?"

"Only the end of the barrel, sticking out of the mud. It's on the opposite bank."

"That means there's a crime scene on each bank. Who has jurisdiction?"

"Both detectives will want it. If ballistics show this is the gun that killed Dale White and it belongs to Derrick McDonald, Detective Sealy will insist on taking over the case."

"What if the pistol belongs to someone else?"

Fen puffed out his cheeks. "That will complicate things even more. Detective Matson from Henderson County could claim Tran Wilks killed Mr. White and threw the gun across the river. That's assuming he could tie the gun to Tran."

"I'm back to my original question," said Bailey. "What if the pistol belongs to someone other than Tran or Derrick McDonald?"

"Let's worry about that later. For now, you and I need to get to the coordinates Sam sent me."

"We could go to the parking lot at the Highway 31 bridge and each walk one bank."

Fen shook his head. "I may have a better idea. Let's check

the coordinates first." Fen pulled up an app on his phone and punched in the precise location.

Bailey leaned into the map. "That's about halfway between the Highway 31 bridge and where the river flows into the lake."

Fen asked, "Have you ever paddled a kayak?"

"No. I borrowed a canoe once and had to swim to shore."

"That's not very comforting, but I'll have to risk it. There's a place to rent kayaks near the bridge. We'll find the wallet and the pistol, then I'll make a phone call."

"Who will you call?"

"Tim Gladly."

"The game warden? I thought he was out of the picture."

Fen slipped his foot into his right boot. "Whether he likes it or not, he'll get credit for finding the original crime scene."

They arrived at the Highway 31 bridge in the middle of the afternoon and rented a two-person kayak fifteen minutes after parking Bailey's truck. Pushing off from the bank proved a wobbly, harrowing experience, but they remained upright. Under Fen's guidance, Bailey allowed the gentle current to take them downstream with her making occasional strokes with the paddle. She soon caught on to the flow of the river and gave course corrections as needed.

Fen kept track of their progress and instructed her to move out of the main current as they approached the coordinates. Sure enough, the corner of a mud-caked wallet stuck out of the debris-strewn bank. He looked across the river to the other bank. If he didn't know better, he'd swear a harmless stick protruded from the mud. He slipped his phone out of his shirt pocket and tapped the picture of Tim's face.

"Hello, Fen. Do you have the case solved already?"

"No, but I need your help. Where are you?"

"Pulling up to a boat on Kickapoo Creek."

"Leave it. That's close to where Bailey and I are. We found

something on the banks of the Neches about halfway between the bridge and the lake. It's much more interesting than a life jacket violation."

"What is it?"

"A wallet and what looks like a pistol sticking out of the mud. One on each side of the river."

"I'm on my way."

As they waited, Fen wished they'd brought bottles of water and mosquito repellent, not necessarily in that order. He gave Bailey a questioning glance. "Why aren't the little bloodsuckers eating you alive?"

"It didn't take too long this morning before I had to take off my sweats. My cutoffs and tube top left plenty for the mosquitoes to dine on. Tran came prepared with high-powered bug spray. I guess it hasn't worn off yet."

Fen slapped his neck. "Speaking of Tran, did you glean much information from him?"

"He's everything he's advertised to be. A smooth talker with black hair and dimples any girl would love to kiss."

"Don't let Thelma hear you say that."

"No worries with that. It was nothing but business as far as I was concerned."

"Did you catch any fish?"

"He knew right where to go. I caught four in the first thirty minutes. We still hadn't said hardly a word to each other when I put my rod down and took out my sketch pad. He looked confused but didn't say anything for the longest time. He finally asked me if I was going to fish."

Mimicking an east Texas drawl, she recounted the rest of their conversation. "Naw, I'm an art student in college and I'd rather sketch you."

"Is that why you keep looking at me?"

"Uh-huh. You have a sexy face. I bet you have girlfriends

lined up for each day of the month."

Dropping the fake drawl, Bailey continued, "He told me he has one serious girlfriend, but she went off to college and broke off the relationship before Christmas."

"He's smart," said Fen. "He mixed truth with a lie, making it less likely you'd confront him. Also, he played the sympathy card by pretending to be the faithful one left behind."

"I asked if I reminded him of her. He said I didn't. He described an athletic girl who's tall and has dark hair. You know the type: made good grades, was homecoming queen, and sang in the church choir."

"Something tells me that didn't stop Tran from coming on to you."

Bailey dipped her head and brought it back to meet Fen's gaze. "He said he didn't believe I was in college until I told him details about the school and my classes. Even after he knew I wasn't jailbait, he still wasn't interested in me."

"That's not what I was expecting," mused Fen.

Bailey shrugged. "He seemed like a nice guy who was stuck on only one girl."

"Anything else?" asked Fen.

"I reeled my line in and told him I needed to work on an art project. I was sketching portraits of fishing guides while on spring break. I hoped to sketch at least three, but I'd only found two guides so far."

"How did he react to that news?"

"He became real concerned when I told him I had a fishing trip planned with Shane Wesley." Bailey tilted her head. "He became protective. Told me Wesley was nothing but bad news and an outlaw. It surprised me how serious he became."

"Perhaps we should give Mr. Wesley a surprise."

"What did you have in mind?" asked Bailey.

"Send Thelma in your place."

Bailey let out a hoot and a holler. "I'm all for it. To tell you the truth, it unnerved me the way Tran looked at me when he was talking about Wesley. I'm good at reading what's on men's minds, and I'm sure Tran was warning me."

"I was kidding about Thelma taking your place, but I'm not anymore," said Fen. "You'll stay at the resort, earn money, and perhaps start on a portrait."

She raised her eyebrows in question.

"Did I tell you I may have scored a painting gig for both of us?"

With a shake of her head, Bailey said, "I think I'd remember if you had. When did that happen?"

"While I was out taking a walk. Destiny Roe was running when—"

Bailey interrupted. "The smokin' hot woman you did the sketch of last night?"

"Yeah. Her idea is for me to do a distant painting of a mountain with a serious cliff overhang, and you'd do a close-up portrait of her suspended in air, searching for the next finger and toe holds."

"That sounds awesome and very challenging," said Bailey. "When can we start?"

"As soon as you make the arrangements. You decide the price and I'll agree to it."

Doubt clouded Bailey's face. "Does she know how much your landscapes bring?"

"She didn't ask, and I didn't tell her, but she'd done research on both of us. Money didn't seem like it mattered to her."

The sound of an outboard motor puttering up the river put an end to the discussion. The sight of Tim Gladly weaving his way upstream was a welcome relief to Fen. He swatted his neck and came away with blood on the palm of his hand.

"Where's the gun?" asked Tim as he approached.

"On the far bank," said Fen as he pointed to a spot on the Smith County side of the bank. "Unless I'm mistaken, that's a wallet sticking out of the mud on this side."

Bailey paddled backward to get the kayak out of the way.

Tim took photos of the scene, put on gloves, and retrieved the wallet. He extracted a driver's license and made the announcement. "It's Dale White's Florida driver's license." He glanced inside. "There's several hundred-dollar bills and credit cards. It doesn't look like his death was motivated by a robbery."

After placing the wallet in a plastic evidence bag, Tim used a paddle to dislodge his boat from the shore. In no time, he crossed the river to the Smith County side. "Where is it?" he asked.

"Upstream about six yards," said Fen.

"Your eyes are better than mine. Wait. There it is. You're right." Tim followed the same procedure of establishing the chain of custody by taking photos, then placing the gun into a plastic bag.

Fen steadied the kayak by holding on to a low-hanging branch until Tim pulled alongside them. "We searched every inch of these banks and found nothing. How did a one-armed man and a young artist do it?"

Bailey answered before Fen could. "Artists are used to paying attention to details."

Fen didn't contradict her, even as skepticism crossed Tim's countenance.

Tim's gaze bore into Fen's. "I suppose it had nothing to do with a Choctaw Indian?"

"What Indian?" asked Fen. "You'll find no trace of footprints along either riverbank."

Tim looked away. "I'll forget I ran the plates on a truck

parked for several nights near the river." He cleared his throat. "This puts me in an interesting position. I'm not sure which detective to call."

"Call them both and tell them what you found."

"*I* found nothing."

"Sure you did," said Fen. "Like I said, you won't find any footprints on either bank, except for what the crime scene technicians discover. I guarantee they won't match mine or Bailey's."

"I guess you know this puts me back in the middle of a tricky investigation."

Fen fixed his mouth so he didn't smile. "I have a feeling in my gut that the middle is going to be the safest place for you." He swatted another mosquito. "And I'm absolutely sure that if I don't get out of this mosquito factory, I'm going to itch all night."

Bailey took the hint and dug her paddle into the water. She'd become proficient enough to navigate and paddle upstream. They were pulling out of the parking lot when two sheriff's department SUVs pulled in. One was from Henderson County and the other from Smith County.

Fen looked straight ahead. "Things are getting more interesting by the minute."

Chapter Fourteen

Thelma stood with hands on hips and met Fen and Bailey at the condo's door. "Where have you two been?"

Fen spoke as Bailey walked past the unsmiling woman. "We've been boating." He, too, walked past her as if he hadn't noticed the angry tone in her voice. "Not really boating; kayaking. We went down the Neches and then back to the bridge. It was a productive afternoon, and don't pretend you don't know where we went. Sam told you what he found."

Thelma's hands dropped from her ample hips. "He shouldn't have said anything about what he told me."

"That's between you and him," said Fen. "What did you learn about Talia Goldberg?"

Thelma shook her head. "First, you tell me exactly what you and Bailey did."

"I just did," said Fen.

Bailey circled back from her room. "It was fun, except for Fen getting chewed by mosquitoes. We rented a kayak and drifted downstream until we found the places Sam told us to look. We found the victim's wallet on one bank and a pistol on the other. Fen called Tim Gladly, the game warden, and he bagged and tagged the evidence. I paddled us back upstream; we made it out of the river without making a mess or getting wet. We returned the kayak and now we're here."

Thelma looked at Fen. "If you had a regular brain, you'd take it out and play with it. How were you planning on swimming with a cast on that broken arm?"

"I wasn't planning on swimming. Besides, we wore life jackets."

Thelma let out a huff to show the inadequacy of his response. She directed her gaze toward Bailey. "I know Fen will scratch himself raw tonight. What about you?"

"I took a shower in bug spray this morning. It lasted all afternoon."

Thelma narrowed her gaze. "If you used bug spray, that means you peeled off your britches and sweatshirt. Did you let that man spray you down?"

Bailey grinned. "He got all the hard-to-reach places."

"Girl, you'll be the death of me," growled Thelma.

Fen came back with, "No, she won't, because you'll take her place on the next fishing trip. She learned from Tran Wilks that the next fishing guide, Shane Wesley, has a reputation that makes Tran look like a choirboy."

Bailey added, "There was something about Tran's eyes and the serious tone of his voice that told me I'd best not be alone with that man named Wesley."

She continued before Thelma could speak. "Before you ask, Tran didn't say or do a thing that made me suspect him of being anything but a nice-looking guy making an honest living."

Thelma lifted her chin. "That part about me taking your place is the first sensible thing either of you has said all day."

Fen had heard enough. "What's wrong with you, Thelma? Are your hot flashes coming back?"

She looked down. "It ain't nothing like that. Me and Sam had a fight. He tramped through the swamps for days, eating who knows what, sleeping who knows where, and having no luck finding clues or evidence. I suggested we get a room somewhere and sleep before he drove home. He wouldn't hear of it. Said dodging people kept him from doing his job of looking for evidence. Besides that, there's a mama cow at the ranch that's springin' heavy."

Fen placed a hand on Thelma's shoulder. "Cows have calves all the time and not all of them make it. That doesn't bother Sam. What else is wrong?"

Thelma's chin quivered. "I told him I wanted us to have some alone time at a hotel. It hurt my feelings something awful when he chose cattle over me." Her eyes clouded over. "You getting hurt again and Bailey putting herself in danger with strange men has me worried sick. All I can think about is something bad happening to you two or Sam."

Of all the things that Thelma could have said, those admissions weren't what Fen expected. Sam and Thelma's relationship was almost beyond comprehension. Yet, every so often, they displayed remarkable vulnerability. When they did, Fen clamped his mouth shut and allowed time to heal them, especially Thelma. As for him and Bailey, she had a point. Investigating and solving murders involved its share of risks. Whatever he said wouldn't be adequate.

He looked at Bailey and motioned with his head toward her room. Obviously uncomfortable, she took off. He thought of Sally and how she would have known how to comfort the hurting woman. As it was, he knew whatever he said would be inadequate. He retrieved a tissue and handed it to Thelma, who took it without a word. Leaving her alone to recover the best way she knew, by cooking, Fen retreated to his room.

Except for the kitchen, all was quiet in the condo until

Thelma served a supper of tossed salad, meatloaf, mashed potatoes, green beans with chunks of bacon, and apple pie for dessert. Both he and Bailey knew the best way to help Thelma get back on an even keel was to ask for seconds.

Bailey was pushing the second helping around her plate when Thelma lifted her head and looked at Fen. "I appreciate both of you putting up with me. It isn't often I get my feelings stomped on or turn into a worrywart." She shifted her gaze to Bailey. "You don't have to eat any more. I'm all right."

"Good," said Fen. "Did you find out how Talia Goldberg spends her days?"

The question put the gleam back in Thelma's eyes. "I'll give you the short version."

Fen knew Thelma's idea of a short version differed from his, but he said nothing and let her proceed at her own pace.

"I told you I was going fishing, and that's what I did. I figured standing on the dock drowning worms would attract the type of person I was looking for. It took almost two hours, but a woman named Florence came with her pole and parked beside me. She thought I was a new camper and I'd sneaked my trailer past her."

Fen grinned. "You went fishing, but it was for information."

"Right," said Thelma. "Until you get to know someone, it's best to let them come to you and do the talking. It isn't always possible, but most retired people are curious about strangers. I told her enough to satisfy her, so when I started asking her questions, she'd feel obligated to tell me."

"You're a genius," said Bailey.

"It's common sense if you take the time to study people. Most folks like to talk about themselves while others enjoy talking about others. Florence likes both."

Bailey pushed her plate toward the middle of the table and leaned forward. "What did she say about Talia?"

"First," said Thelma, "I need to tell you how I got her to talking. I told her I was the cook and housekeeper for a rich artist who was in a recent accident and wanted to take time off from painting to let his arm heal. That's all I needed to tell her, and it was truthful enough for her to ask me a slew of questions."

Thelma took a sip of water. "I showed her photos of Fen's landscapes on my phone and gave her one of his business cards. That made her trust me all the more."

"Is that when you started asking her questions?"

"Not exactly, but it's when I took the conversation off me and put it on the victim. I told her I'd read something about a man named Dale White being murdered at the campground."

A wide smile of satisfaction parted Thelma's lips. "Instead of saying what I knew happened, I said something close to the truth but left enough hanging so Florence would correct me. She told me real quick that Mr. White didn't die at the campground, but that it surprised her it hadn't happened there."

"Did she name possible suspects?"

"The main one is Derrick McDonald, but there are others who had reason to dislike Mr. White. Florence said he was the easiest man to hate she'd ever met."

Fen asked, "Did she say why?"

Thelma gave her head a firm nod. "She said it all boiled down to too much money. It made him like a spoiled brat living in a man's body. He had crazy opinions about anything and everything. He'd pick a subject: politics, religion, food, education, decreasing the world's population, you name it and he called you a fool if you didn't agree with him. He even believed that people with an IQ below one thirty shouldn't vote."

"He sounds bored," said Bailey.

"I agree," said Fen. "He was roaming the world for something that would satisfy him."

"Speaking of that," said Thelma. "I'm not sure he didn't have more than one fish on the line."

"What does that mean?" asked Bailey.

Fen took over. "Great wealth has a way of attracting attention. Sometimes that attention comes in very attractive human packages."

"Oh. I see what you mean." Bailey shifted her gaze back to Thelma. "Did Mr. White have a shapely fishing partner?"

"Florence thinks he did," said Thelma, "but if so, she didn't know who she was, other than to say she'd eliminated all the women from the campground."

Fen brought the conversation back around to his original point. "We know Dale White went somewhere in his boat every day. Where did his wife go?"

Thelma released a huff. "If you'd had a little more patience, I'd have told you. She runs every morning and leaves later to work out at a gym in Tyler. Florence says it's one of those cross-training places where people do crazy exercises. Every other day she goes with another woman who drives a white sports car."

"What make and model?" asked Bailey.

"The only thing Florence knows about cars is they don't run without gasoline."

"Hasn't she heard of electric cars?" asked Bailey.

"She's heard of them but thinks they're a flash in the pan and won't be around long."

The conversation gave Fen one new idea and confirmed the need for Thelma to take Bailey's place fishing with Shane Wesley.

Bailey must have read his mind, because she asked, "Wouldn't it help if I found out who the woman is that's going to the gym with Talia Goldberg?"

Fen couldn't help but smile at her quick mind. "It shouldn't be hard." He turned to Thelma. "What time does the mystery woman pick up Talia?"

"About nine-thirty."

Fen returned his gaze to Bailey. "Park at the boat launch outside the RV park, look for a sports car and wait for two women to leave in it. If Talia leaves by herself, go back the next day."

"What will you do tomorrow?" asked Bailey.

"Rest," Thelma interjected. "He's going to stay on the couch. No more boating, or any other foolishness."

Fen partially agreed. "A day of thinking is a good idea, and my brain works best when I'm drawing or painting." He tapped the table while looking at Bailey. "I like the idea of you and me doing a two-panel painting of a cliff and a close-up of the climber. Whether Destiny hires us or not, let's do it."

"Hopefully I'll see her tonight and get a commitment from her." Bailey rose. "I'm going to take a quick shower and get to the activities building. I need to catch up on caricatures. The two-panel painting will be sweet, but I'll keep tracking the number of sketches I complete."

"That's an excellent decision," said Fen. "Things don't always turn out the way we think they will."

Chapter Fifteen

I t came as a surprise when Fen heard Bailey and Thelma talking in the pre-dawn hours. Bailey, like most college students, had an aversion to starting her day before the sun appeared in the east. Thelma was a different story. Her days began and ended early.

Instead of struggling with buttons and zippers, Fen tugged on gray sweatpants with elastic at the waist. A fleece throw sufficed as a covering over the loose-fitting T-shirt he'd slept in. Leather house shoes completed the early-morning ensemble.

His only early morning greeting as he entered the living room was, "Bailey? What are you doing up so early?"

Her eyes twinkled. "Too excited to sleep. We got the job. Destiny came by last night and we negotiated a deal on the paintings."

"You were both satisfied with the price?"

She responded with a firm nod. "She wants two rectangular paintings, each slightly taller than wide, but when put together with a gap in the middle, wider than tall. I charged her full price for what we both charge for paintings the size of the canvases we'll use."

"That's perfect," said Fen. "Did you take photos of her?"

"Some, but she's coming here this evening and will bring her climbing gear. I'm not familiar with everything rock climbers wear, and I don't want to ruin my painting by making a silly mistake."

Fen had to admit that he too felt the tingle of excitement that comes at the start of a new project. "I'll spend the day doing sketches of various rock formations and searching for photos."

Bailey was several steps ahead of him. "Destiny sent me photos of various places she's climbed. I'll send them to you after breakfast."

That was Thelma's clue to enter the conversation. "I know how both of you are when a new project comes along. Now you're involved in two things at the same time." Her gaze focused on Bailey. "You'll go back to college needing to catch up on your sleep then you'll miss classes."

It was Fen's turn to receive a word of warning. "As for you, the couch and bed are where you're going to be today."

Fen ignored the second part of what Thelma said. She was right about Bailey being involved in too many projects. "There's a change of plan for today. Bailey stays here and works on sketches until it's time to go to the Activity Center. Thelma and I will do surveillance."

Thelma nodded in agreement and said, "It's about time you used me more. But there's no need for you to come. All I'm going to do is sit in that new truck and wait for Talia Goldberg to drive by."

Fen responded with a two-word reply. "I'm going."

As she started to open her mouth again, he interrupted, "Did you plan on carrying binoculars with you?"

"Why should I?"

"Can you read a license plate from forty yards away?"

"Oh. In that case, I'll park closer to the road."

Fen shook his head. "We're to see, not be seen."

Thelma threw up her hands. "The only thing I see now is that you're making up excuses to come with me when you don't need to. Why?"

Fen shrugged. "Let's call it an itch I need to scratch."

"Horsefeathers," mumbled Thelma. "If there's an itch, it's from mosquitoes."

Changing the subject, Fen asked, "Is there a reason I don't have a cup of coffee in front of me?"

"If you're well enough to climb downstairs, get into a truck, and bounce five miles to a boat ramp by a lake, you're in good enough shape to pour your own cup of coffee."

Fen stood, but in an obvious show of remorse, Thelma held out a hand to stop him. "Don't you dare. Go back to bed and I'll bring it to you. You haven't had your time with Sally, and it ruins your day if you don't."

With coffee on the nightstand, Fen held the framed photo of his late wife. As the door closed, he whispered, "Thelma's back to her usual self. I don't know what I'd do without her."

———

TIME PASSED QUICKLY as Fen spent the early morning sketching. He became so engrossed in drawing a craggy mountain that it surprised him when Thelma asked if he planned on wearing what he had on.

"I guess so. I don't plan on doing anything but sit in the truck."

Bailey brought him a baseball cap while Thelma helped him tie his tennis shoes. Otherwise, he looked as he had since dawn. He went down the stairs ahead of Thelma, still clinging to the throw like a shawl.

"How's the arm?" asked Thelma after he climbed into the passenger seat of his new truck.

"It feels better than I thought it would. If it's not hurting any more than it did this morning, I'm switching to Tylenol this afternoon. Those pain pills are way too strong for me to think clearly."

"You're a stubborn man, so I won't say anything until tonight. You'll need something stronger unless you want to stay awake talking to the hoot owls."

Fen thought the compromise sounded reasonable. "You're probably right. The pain is one thing, but the itching under the cast is getting worse. I'll save the hard stuff for nights and use over-the-counter meds during the day."

Thelma didn't complain, so he counted the agreement signed and sealed. She allowed the truck's engine to warm before pulling away from the condos. The posted speed limit on the resort's narrow streets was fifteen miles an hour. Thelma never got over ten until they reached the main road, where she bumped the speed up to fifty. A line of cars stacked up behind them until she turned onto the road leading to the campground. Only two of the drivers honked as they passed.

The lake came into view, and it was a sight to behold. A small armada of boats in all shapes, sizes, makes, and colors dotted the waters. Houseboats, pontoon boats, cabin cruisers, bass boats, and sailboats all skimmed across the water.

Fen spoke, but he didn't direct the words to Thelma as much as to himself. "I remember the time Sally and I rented a tiny sailboat. I tried to tack into the wind. The sail came around and the boom struck me above the left ear. I went into the lake and she came in after me. It scared her so much she made me promise we'd never sail again."

"Did you?" asked Thelma.

"Five stitches in my head and a scared fiancée were enough to convince me that boats should have motors."

Thelma's voice softened to a lament. "She never told me that story."

"Some stories don't deserve retelling. Some are good, some bad."

"Amen to that. I've got a suitcase full of them."

The mood had turned somber, but not for long. A string of three Smith County Sheriff's Department SUVs followed an unmarked car down the road leading to the fishing pier. They turned left, passed the unmanned tin building, and entered the campground.

Fen groaned.

"Do you know why all those cops are here?" asked Thelma.

"I have a good idea, but I hope I'm wrong." He pointed. "Follow them."

"We're not looking for a mystery woman?"

"Not today. This is more important."

Fen's phone rang before Thelma could start the truck. He looked at the caller ID and activated the device. "I'm glad you called, Tim. I'm at the campground where Derrick McDonald is staying. A convoy of Smith County deputies along with Detective Sealy just entered the park. There's only one reason for that much manpower. Derrick McDonald will leave here in handcuffs."

Tim groaned even louder than Fen. "That puts the cherry on the top of my day, and it's not even noon yet. Detective Matson arrested Tran Wilks about an hour ago. Finding Dale White's wallet in Henderson County was enough to get arrest and search warrants. It's going to be hard to explain why two men are in jail for killing the same man."

Fen asked, "What about the pistol? I doubt they could run ballistics on it yet."

"It's a ghost gun. No serial number, so there's no tracing it back to either suspect." Tim paused. "What are you going to do about Detective Sealy?"

Fen had mixed emotions about how to proceed. "I'll try to warn Sealy, but I'm pretty sure he won't listen. If he doesn't, and the killer turns out to be someone else, his career may come to a grinding halt."

"Are you saying you think Tran Wilks killed Dale White?"

"I don't believe there's enough evidence to convict Tran Wilks or Derrick McDonald. What we have is one detective who's emotionally in over his head and another who's trying to make a name for himself with voters."

"That second one is why I can't be involved in this case. I hate to do this to you, but you're going to have to work this without me." He paused. "By the way, why are you at the campground today? Did you get a tip that Sealy was going to arrest Derrick McDonald?"

"I was following up on another lead. I'm not convinced Derrick or Tran either one had anything to do with Dale White's murder."

"Do you have another suspect?"

"Not yet, but the grieving widow interests me."

"According to Detective Sealy, she has an alibi."

A bell went off in Fen's brain. Detective Sealy's reports didn't include details on Talia Goldberg's alibi, only that she had one. But he remembered now that Tim Gladly said she was out of state when her husband died.

The call ended after a quick salutation. Fen motioned for Thelma to proceed. "Follow the road, but don't park close to any of the cops' vehicles."

Thelma spoke as she put the truck in gear. "Did you notice

the white Land Rover leave the park while you were talking business?"

Fen shook his head in disgust. "I missed it."

"A woman was driving but didn't have anyone with her."

"Thanks for noticing. I'll need to come back and talk to her."

"We'll need to come back."

"Right," said Fen. "We'll come back, but for now, I need to talk to a detective who's about to step in a big, stinky cow patty."

"That's one way to learn to watch where you step."

Fen gave her a knowing glance. "I have a feeling it's a warning he won't heed. I believe Sealy prefers to learn his lessons the hard way."

The truck came to a stop and Fen climbed down. He walked toward Derrick McDonald's travel trailer as deputies and Detective Sealy exited the trailer with their suspect in custody. Fen waited at the only unmarked vehicle for Sealy to arrive.

"I don't have time to talk, Sheriff Maguire. There's a trailer to search, and I want to make sure we collect every scrap of evidence."

"Being thorough is the hallmark of a good investigation. I'm sure Detective Matson is doing the same thing after his arrest early this morning."

"What are you talking about?"

"Matson arrested Tran Wilks a little after dawn for the murder of Dale White. His suspect was in jail hours ago."

"He arrested the wrong man."

"Reporters could say the same thing about you."

"I have arrest and search warrants signed by a judge."

"So does Matson. Do you realize what that means?"

"Yeah. He's wrong."

"Perhaps," said Fen. "It also means it won't be long before the press finds out that two detectives from neighboring counties arrested different men for committing the same murder. You're both claiming it happened in different counties."

An accusatory stare came from Sealy. "You're trying to give the credit to Matson."

"You can't back up that claim any more than you can prove Derrick McDonald killed Dale White." Fen kept his voice in an even tone. "And for your information, Detective Matson can't prove Tran Wilks killed Mr. White, either. Tran and Derrick will get lawyers. Lawyers will make sure the press knows, and that's when things will really get interesting."

Sealy's eyes darted back and forth as he considered what to do.

Fen considered spelling out to the man more of what would happen and how it could lead to public ridicule and legal action that might cost the county a ton of money.

Sealy straightened his shoulders and turned a resolute gaze to Fen. "I have evidence to collect."

Fen turned and walked away.

Thelma waited until his door closed before asking, "Is that cow poop I'm smelling?"

"Uh-huh. Let's go back to the condo where I can think about how we're going to solve this case before something else goes wrong."

Fen took out his phone and punched in a number. Lou Cooper answered on the second ring. "Are you finished with the story in Dallas?"

"I sold it last night."

"Are you ready for another?"

"Always."

"Come to the resort. I'll get you a single room if they have a vacancy."

Chapter Sixteen

Fen used the ride back to the resort to do some soul searching. He concluded that multiple reports from biased sources plagued his investigation. An overly protective father and a man hungry for advancement were the primary culprits, but he had done a lousy job of verifying much of the information in the police reports. That needed to change, and the perfect person to help him was on her way.

Once in the condo, he sat on the couch and pulled out his phone. Lou answered with the sound of road noise in the background.

"Where are you?" asked Fen.

"Trying to fight my way out of Dallas traffic."

"What route are you taking?"

"Interstate 20."

"That's perfect. Did you receive a folder of police reports from Candy?"

"Yeah, but I only glanced at them. Some seemed light on facts and heavy on opinion."

A smile crossed Fen's face. "I should have talked to you

before they released me from the hospital. I need you to verify much of what's in the reports, and I want you to start in Athens, the county seat of Henderson County. Focus on the reports from Detective Clay Matson. Stop for lunch and reread them. Look for anything concerning his daughter quitting her job in lieu of getting fired. I couldn't find anything, but that may have had more to do with brain fog from the pain medicine."

"Isn't her name April Matson?"

"Correct. Her father shipped her off to college to get her away from Tran Wilks. I understand she's home for spring break this week."

"I'll try to contact her and ask for a meeting this afternoon."

"You read my mind," said Fen.

For gathering information, few matched Lou's ability to uncover hard-to-find documents and talk people into sitting down for interviews. Her straightforward approach with politicians sometimes cost her steady employment, but her fact-based stories claimed their fair share of scalps.

"Anything special you want me to find out?" asked Lou.

"Three things. First, did she really resign under pressure? Next, is she still in contact with Tran Wilks? Finally, why does her father hate Tran so much?"

"This sounds like an East Texas version of Romeo and Juliet."

"It could be. Some people call Tran the Redneck Romeo."

Lou released a guffaw. "I'd like to review that stage play."

Fen offered a word of caution. "Don't forget how the two lead characters wound up. One murder is all we're here to solve."

Silence settled in for a few seconds until Lou asked, "What are you doing about solving the case this afternoon besides taking a nap?"

Fen ignored the dig. "I'm calling the sheriff of Henderson County. None of the documents in the file have his name on them."

"Is that unusual?"

"Not for a small county where they try to handle things informally."

"Is that all?" asked Lou.

"One more thing," said Fen, hoping trepidation didn't leak into his next words. "There were two arrests made this morning. I may want you to sit on that story for a while."

Fen knew how much Lou hated it when he put conditions on her breaking a story, but it was an agreement they'd made a long time ago. She collected stories of him solving crimes. The books she'd write later were to supplement her retirement income after they both retired. Sometimes, when it helped the case, he'd allow her to sell a portion of the story. This worked out for them both... most of the time. This time, he wasn't sure and needed to blunt her attack.

"Before you cuss me out," said Fen., "remember our deal."

"How can I forget it when you tease me by telling me two people are already in jail? Don't you realize it's only a matter of time before that's reported?" A tinge of anger filled her voice. "Why can't I write and sell the story of the arrests? It's already public information."

"Perhaps not. My instructions from Chuck and Candy are to settle a jurisdictional dispute, solve a murder, and keep two detectives from ruining their careers." He added, "At least that's how I'm interpreting my assignment. If I don't do something fast, I'll fail the last one."

"You're talking in circles," said Lou. "Use small words so I can understand you."

"Very well. Two suspects are in two separate jails for the same crime. Two detectives from separate counties put them there this morning. Neither has enough evidence for a conviction. Both have ulterior motives for arresting the people they did. One or both are wrong. I think both could be."

"Could be, or are, wrong?" asked Lou.

"Either way, I fail."

Lou let out a huff of resignation. "One more question. How do you plan to rectify this?"

Fen was between the proverbial rock and a hard place and didn't like it. He realized in that moment that the investigation needed a good jolt of reality. It was up to him to shake things up and worry about the consequences later.

"Are you going to answer me?" asked Lou.

Fen's voice hardened. "I'm calling both sheriffs and telling them what will happen if I allow you to release the story you're going to write as soon as you stop. After that, I'll pray that my bluffs work."

This brought a gasp from Lou. He could see her collect herself and say, "You know I haven't written the story yet. Aren't you afraid at least one will call your bluff?"

"I'm not bluffing. Five o'clock is the deadline for both men to be released. It's also your deadline to finish a dynamite story. If detectives can arrest in the morning, sheriffs can un-arrest in the afternoon."

"I wish I could record your conversations. They'd make tremendous additions to the future book."

Fen wondered if he'd already bitten off more than he could chew. "Don't get greedy. I'll tell you how they react to the arm-twisting. In the meantime, write the story, interview April, and find answers to the three questions I gave you."

"I'm pulling off the interstate now."

Fen had been looking out the patio door during the entire conversation and didn't realize a small audience had listened in. Bailey spoke first. "That conversation gave me goose bumps. Are you really going to threaten two sheriffs?"

"Of course not. I'll simply insist they choose the most practical option. If they choose not to, it will be their loss."

Thelma placed a platter of lunch meats and cheeses on the table. "Come and eat while you can. Fen's back in fighting form. That means everyone's about to get busy."

Fen walked toward his room.

Bailey asked, "Aren't you going to eat?"

Thelma answered for him. "He will after he calls those two sheriffs. Once he hits his stride, there's no stopping or slowing him down."

Fen closed the door to his room and pulled out his phone. Doubts buzzed around his head like a swarm of bees. He punched in a series of numbers. While waiting for someone to answer, he asked himself, "What's the worst thing that could happen?"

He didn't like the answers that came back, but something had to get the case moving.

A female's voice answered. "Smith County Sheriff's office."

"This is Sheriff Fen Maguire. I'd like to speak with Sheriff Blankenship."

"One moment, please."

It took more than a moment, but a voice that sounded like it had swallowed crushed gravel came on. "Hello, Fen. It's been a while."

"Too long. I guess you know I'm up in your neck of the woods."

"Yep. You spoke with Detective Sealy this morning. He said you tried to keep him from arresting Derrick McDonald."

"He misspoke. I simply questioned the haste of the arrest when all he has is circumstantial evidence. Did he tell you about the arrest in Henderson County for the same crime?"

"It must have slipped his mind."

"Their detective arrested Tran Wilks for the same murder."

"Is their evidence better than ours?"

"About the same in quality and quantity."

Fen prepared for the worst. "Expect a story to break either tomorrow morning or tonight that won't be flattering for either detective."

Sheriff Blankenship stayed silent for several seconds. "There's a pack of attorneys in Dallas that love to file lawsuits for false arrest and imprisonment. If you were me, what would you do?"

"Get McDonald out of jail as soon as possible. You can always re-arrest him if your man can build a better case."

"That's a huge risk. McDonald may be old, but he spent plenty of time in the Marines learning to kill people."

"I spoke with him, and he didn't deny he had a powerful motive. In fact, it was too strong for him to use a gun. He's the type that would use his hands."

"I'm getting the idea your money is on Tran Wilks."

"Not at all," said Fen. "It seems both detectives made up their minds early that they had the killer and stopped looking."

"Keep talking," said Sheriff Blankenship.

"We both know that after you rule out alcohol, drugs, or spur-of-the-moment arguments for homicides, you look for a money angle. After that, see if there's a love triangle."

"Is that what you're doing now?"

"Yes; a fender bender kept me sidelined for several days but I'm working on it day and night now."

He waited for the sheriff to comment, but the silence stretched for several seconds. He hoped the lawman was seriously considering his suggestion. Fen had run out of things to say that might persuade the sheriff to release Derrick McDonald.

Blankenship cleared his throat. "I appreciate the information and the heads up on the press taking a swipe at me and my department. It isn't the first time, and it may not be the last. I'll talk it over with the district attorney tomorrow and see what he recommends."

Fen rolled his eyes. "Tomorrow will be too late."

"There's a simple solution to this," said the sheriff of Smith County. "Quickly find the person or persons who killed Dale White, and both arrests go away."

"That's easier said than done," said Fen.

"If it was easy, they wouldn't have sent you. Happy hunting."

The call ended, leaving Fen to stare at his phone. Had he misread Sheriff Blankenship, or did the wily old sheriff have some other reason for leaving Derrick McDonald in jail?

The next phone call finished with what Fen believed to be better results. Henderson County's sheriff wanted no part of litigation that could come from a premature arrest based on flimsy evidence.

Fen called Lou to inform her of the results of his two conversations. She answered her phone with a question. "Did your bluff work?"

"One did and one didn't," said Fen. "Henderson County is processing Tran Wilks out of jail as we speak. My powers of persuasion didn't work in Smith County. Sheriff Blankenship will meet with the district attorney tomorrow morning."

"Either you're slipping, or that sheriff needs to retire. This story asks a lot of questions he won't want to answer."

Fen wanted to scratch his head, but his cast prohibited the use of his left hand, and the right held his phone. He refocused on Lou's last statement. "There's an outside chance they'll release Derrick McDonald tomorrow or sometime soon. If they do, they'll likely avoid any long-term repercussions."

"How much time?"

"That will depend on how loud Mr. McDonald and his attorney holler."

He imagined Lou shaking her head. "But why risk keeping him locked up when they could pick him up again if they find more evidence?"

"Sometimes sheriffs and district attorneys dig their heels in. No offense but reminding the press who the people elected to make tough decisions can pay off in the long run." Fen smiled. "There's a rumor going around that some reporters believe they're entitled to all information, all the time."

Lou huffed. "If you're trying to get a rise out of me, it won't work. I'm way too busy." She paused. "Do I still need to wait until five o'clock to sell the story?"

"No. Run it as soon as it's ready. The only condition is you go easy on Henderson County. They listened to reason."

"I don't like it, but I'll tone that part down. By the way, I'm meeting April Matson at four thirty in a coffee shop."

"That means you don't need to waste time talking to me."

"Do I have a room to come to?"

Fen crossed his fingers. "Of course, but first come to our condo. I'll text you the room numbers."

Chapter Seventeen

L ou arrived at the condo looking road-weary but smiling all the same.

Thelma opened the door for her and said, "I was about to give up on you coming. Come in and have a seat. I'll get you a glass of iced tea."

Lou thanked her and joined Fen in the living room. "Any trouble finding our condo?" he asked.

She pushed a wayward lock of shortish, mousy brown hair away from her face. Lou frequently had a tired look about her. Fen believed the primary cause to be three failed marriages to fellow reporters who drank too much coffee and hard liquor, not to mention their predilection for philandering. She now drank in moderation, but the addiction to caffeine stuck to her like a coat of glue.

Lou drained half the glass of iced tea before answering. "No. The desk clerk gave me a map for my condo. I went there first and unloaded the car. It's a step up from the rooms I usually stay in. I'm looking forward to a steamy bath in that jetted tub."

She took inventory of his cast and the stitches in his scalp. "You look better than I thought you would. It shouldn't take long for the hair to grow back."

"The stitches and my arm under the cast are competing for the prize of which can bother me the most."

"Ex-husband number two was responsible for me wearing a cast on my arm that was very similar to yours. It cost him his car and all the attorney's fees for our divorce. At first, I thought it was a good trade for not filing charges on him. Then, the engine blew up on my way home from the courthouse. He didn't know how to maintain a car or a relationship."

Thelma asked, "Is that a true story?"

"True enough to go in the memoir I'll write someday," said Lou. "He'll be dead and gone from a worn-out liver before I publish it."

Fen didn't want to spend the night talking about lovers, livers, or anything else that didn't bring him closer to solving the murder. Some invisible switch had clicked inside him, and he desired to follow even a faint scent if it led to whoever killed Dale White.

"Did you sell your story?" he asked.

Lou didn't smile when she said, "The next time you have a scoop for me, make it with more meat on the bone and in a bigger market. I sold it, but only to the newspaper in Tyler. Even a dinky local TV station didn't want it."

"They must be strapped for cash," said Fen. "You may need to start a YouTube channel."

Lou grasped the hair on each side of her head. "Look at this mop. It's not made for viewing on a screen of any size or description."

Fen got back on track. "What about your time with April Matson?"

Lou's eyes came alive. "This is an interesting twist. First, let me describe April to you. Picture the perfect girl-next-door face with alabaster skin and soft, dark curls cascading down her back."

Thelma drew near. "I can see her. She looks like a 1940s Hollywood actress. What about her figure?"

"Hourglass with the perfect amount of sand up top and on the bottom."

"And a tiny waist?" asked Thelma.

"Miniscule, and long, lean legs. You know, dancer's legs."

"I can see her, and I bet she's sweet and innocent as a two-week-old lamb."

"We both get the picture," interrupted Fen. "What did she have to say?"

"Plenty. The last thing you wanted to know was why April's father hated Tran so much. The answer lies in the way I described her. She's an exceptional young lady in every way. That girl almost drips beauty, brains, and grace. I wouldn't blame any father for keeping a close eye on a daughter like that."

Thelma added, "That don't mix with the Redneck Romeo." She looked at Fen. "If she was your daughter, you'd run him off, too."

Fen moved on. "What about her quitting so she wouldn't get fired?"

"According to April, that was a rumor that got out of hand. Of course, she knew the locations of deputies, state troopers, and game wardens. During slow times at the dispatch office late at night, she'd call Tran to stay awake. Very early in the morning, she'd call to wake him up."

Thelma jumped in. "Being a fishing guide, he had to get up way before sunrise."

Lou took over again. "She says Tran was always home in bed if she called him before midnight and they never talked between midnight and an hour and a half before dawn. She wasn't calling him so he could do something illegal. Most of the calls were to wake him up. It's what young people in love do. She didn't quit to avoid discipline. The reason there's no paperwork is that the only thing they did wrong was fall in love, and only her father thinks that was wrong."

Fen rubbed his chin. "That may be, but Tran has quite a reputation as a poacher and a ladies' man."

Lou took another drink of iced tea. "April says he earned the reputation as a flirt and knows he's sowed his fair share of wild oats. As for the poaching, she says he may have done some of that when he was a teen, but not any more than half the boys in the county. She thinks most of the talk is because it's so easy to believe he could be the handsome bad boy your mother always warned you about."

"What do you believe?" asked Fen.

"I think April believed every word she said."

"That wasn't my question."

Lou finished her iced tea before answering. "She told me Tran's saving his money so he can join her in college next fall."

The front door opened, and three heads swiveled to watch Bailey come in. Thelma poured a tall glass of iced tea for the young artist without asking if she wanted any. Lou rose to receive a hug while Fen waited his turn to receive a greeting.

"How's the arm and head?" asked Bailey.

"Getting better every minute. How were sales?"

"Steady but dropping from where they were. I think the novelty is wearing off."

Fen motioned for Bailey to sit. He turned to Lou. "Catch Bailey up on who you spoke to today and your impressions of her."

Lou gave an abridged version of her coffee shop meeting with April Matson.

Bailey turned to Fen when Lou had finished. "I'm missing something. You went to your room to call the two sheriffs and gave them an offer they couldn't refuse. Are you telling me they refused?"

"Uh-huh. One sheriff listened to reason and released Tran Wilks. The sheriff from Smith County was a different story. Derrick McDonald is still in jail and Lou sold the story."

"Holy smoke," said Bailey. "April's father will want to skin you alive."

Fen acknowledged her words and added, "I doubt I'll get a Christmas card from Detectives Matson or Sealy. They're both smart enough to discover the story came from Lou, and she's part of my team."

Bailey puffed out her cheeks. "I don't know about the rest of you, but I'm driving five miles an hour under the posted limit in both counties."

Thelma chimed in. "You should do that all the time. It saves gasoline, cuts down on wear and tear, and—"

Fen interrupted with a direct question for Bailey before Thelma launched into one of her long-winded lectures on proper driving habits. "Didn't Tran talk about April when you went fishing with him?"

Lou's hand went up like a cop stopping traffic. "Hold on. Back the truck up and tell me about Bailey going fishing with one of the two suspects."

Thelma didn't hesitate to speak her mind. "I want it on record that it wasn't my idea and if I had my way, I wouldn't have let her do it."

"Duly noted," said Fen with exasperation seeping into his words. "It was my idea, and I take responsibility for it. I trust Bailey to sense danger and do whatever is necessary to avoid it."

Lou moved on quickly. "Now that we've established Bailey

went fishing with Tran, I'd like to hear from her if he talked about April."

"He never used her name, but I could tell he wasn't interested in me, no matter how much bait I dangled in front of him. I shaved my legs, wore my shortest cut-offs, and might have forgotten to wear a bra. No reaction."

Thelma gasped. "Child, if you do that again, I'll cut a switch from the peach tree and teach you a lesson you won't forget."

Lou chuckled, and Fen had to cover his mouth to keep his grin from busting out. He cleared his throat and asked, "Did you two talk about anything other than what you already told us?"

"He was interested in college. I told him about the art and business classes I'm taking. He wanted to hear more about a degree in business."

Lou nodded. "That fits with what April told me. She's studying to become a nurse, and he wants to own or manage a marina."

Fen summarized. "We've stirred the pot enough for one day. Let's talk about tomorrow's assignment." He looked at Thelma. "I want you to go back to the boat ramp where we parked yesterday and look for Talia Goldberg leaving. The binoculars are still in the truck. I'm particularly interested in knowing if someone leaves with her."

"I can't be two places at the same time. I'm supposed to go fishing with that guide named Shane Wesley."

He looked at Lou. "I have something else for Bailey to do. That leaves you to find out what you can about Tran Wilks from a man with a sketchy reputation." Another thought came to him. "See what this Wesley character thinks about Detective Matson—or anyone else in law enforcement."

"What time?"

"Be at the marina at first light."

"There are only three things wrong with this assignment. I hate fishing, I'm allergic to early mornings, and I'm extra surly to men early in the morning. There could be another homicide if he's chatty before my first three cups of coffee."

"There's a thermos you can take."

Thelma chimed in. "I'll make the coffee extra strong and have something for you to nibble on."

"I rarely eat before noon."

"That's because you don't get up early enough. You spend a few hours fishing and talking and you'll be ready to eat. I guarantee it."

Lou directed her attention to Fen. "What else? There's a couple of hours you haven't filled yet."

"Verify the information in the file, especially the reports from Detectives Sealy and Matson. Also, do deeper research into Talia Goldberg and the money she'll inherit."

Lou shook her head. "I don't need much sleep when I'm doing research, but looking for money is a deep rabbit hole. I'll do it, but it won't be tonight or tomorrow. I'm exhausted from the work I did in Dallas."

Fen hadn't considered the amount of work Lou had done prior to being thrown into a murder investigation. "Forget about Talia Goldberg. I'll focus on her and the money angle."

Bailey asked, "What about me?"

"You need to eat, then get back to the activities building and keep sketching."

"That's not much of an assignment."

"I need a driver to take me wherever I need to go at a moment's notice."

"That suits me," said Thelma. "I feel better knowing you two will keep each other from doing something crazy."

Fen closed out the assignments. "You and I will also meet

with Destiny Roe tomorrow, show her our sketches, and sign the contract for the paintings."

Bailey's eyes widened. "I forgot all about meeting with Destiny tonight. I'll text her to see if I can stop by her condo on my way to the activities center."

"Be sure to find out what time we're meeting tomorrow. If she can't meet until afternoon or evening, you'll have tomorrow morning open."

Bailey sighed. "I think it may be a late night for me."

Thelma pulled dinner plates from the cabinet. "I told you things were going to get busy. One day you'll listen to me."

Chapter Eighteen

Fen's day began with Bailey sequestered in her room, drawing sketches of Destiny Roe defying gravity on the face of a cliff. Thelma puttered in the kitchen, mumbling something about the deficiencies of the electric stove. He took it in stride and counted it a blessing that she directed the complaint to an appliance and not him.

His phone chirped and vibrated on the tabletop while showing the name of the caller. He put down his first cup of coffee and picked up the device. "Good morning, Chuck. I was wondering how long it would take you to call. How's Candy and everything in Newman County?"

Chuck didn't acknowledge the cheerful sound of his voice and got right to the point. "I thought you understood your assignment. Can't you put Lou on a leash?"

"The leash works fine, but she keeps slipping out of her collar."

"I'm failing to find the humor in this. Did you know she was selling the story?"

"I made sure she did."

"Do you realize this is red meat for attorneys?"

"You worry too much. I considered the pros and cons before I gave her the green light. I still think it's an acceptable risk."

"Your idea of an acceptable risk and mine are miles apart. There were two solid suspects and now only one is in jail."

Fen stilled his emotions. "They're not solid suspects. We've uncovered discrepancies between the reports and what's really going on here. I believe we'll have much more information by the end of the day. We might even have a new suspect to throw on the pile."

Chuck released a long sigh of frustration. "I still don't like that you tried to bully two sheriffs into releasing the suspects after judges signed arrest and search warrants. You're to work *with* the good guys, not against them."

"I've had all night to think about that. The sheriff from Smith County is an old fox who knows how to play this game better than both of us put together. He had his reasons for not releasing his suspect yesterday. I'll go out on a limb and predict the second suspect will be back in his travel trailer by noon."

"From where I sit, that limb doesn't look strong enough to hold you and your predictions. Get this case solved as soon as you can and get home."

"Is something else brewing that I need to know about?"

"It's not boiling yet, but it may be by the time your cast comes off."

The call ended, and Fen put the phone back on the coffee table. Thelma appeared at his side. "Don't you worry about what Chuck says. He's just a messenger." She took his coffee cup to refill it. "Candy's the real brains. If she calls, you'd better sit up and take notice. Until then, keep doing what you know is right."

"Right now, I think it's right for me to eat a full breakfast."

"I'll mix up the pancake batter and start the bacon to frying."

It wasn't long before Bailey followed her nose into the dining room. "Is that bacon?"

"Uh-huh," said Thelma. "Bacon, pancakes, a maple syrup and strawberry topping, and a dollop of whipped cream on top. Not the stuff that squirts out of a metal can, but real whipped cream."

"Brain food," said Bailey.

Fen moved from the couch to the dining table. "Why do you call your favorite dishes brain food?"

"They make me happy, and I think better when I'm happy."

"Makes sense to me," said Thelma.

Fen asked, "Did Destiny tell you why she couldn't come until this evening?"

"She said she was going to Tyler with a friend. Lunch and shopping. She's excited about seeing our sketches."

Fen turned to Thelma. "I noticed the truck needed diesel. If you have time, fill it up today after you finish snooping on Talia Goldberg."

Pointing her spatula in his direction, Thelma said, "You worry about painting a mountain and solving a murder. I checked prices in both directions and found the cheapest diesel. I'll pick up some groceries while I'm gone."

Bailey retreated to her room after breakfast as Fen set up an easel and a canvas in the living room. He hadn't painted a mountain landscape in years, and the desire to do so rose within him. Even if Destiny chose a different sketch, he'd get started on this oil-on-canvas and sell it as a separate work.

Thelma received a text and went to her room without opening it. An hour later, she left to conduct a stakeout on Talia.

Fen put faint pencil marks on the canvas to delineate sky from mountains, and mountains from the foreground. He lost track of time, but the ringing of his phone brought him back to East Texas. With the phone pushed to his ear, he asked, "Did Talia leave?"

"She did," said Thelma with excitement. "You won't believe who's with her."

"Male or female?"

"Female."

"It's Destiny Roe," said Fen.

The disappointment in Thelma's voice caused him to smile. "How did you know it was her?"

"They're the same age, enjoy extreme sports, and live within five miles of each other. It wouldn't surprise me if they know each other from somewhere else."

"More likely it was a lucky guess," said Thelma.

Fen pretended he didn't hear her and moved on. "The only other woman you've met since we checked in is a lady named Florence at the RV campground. I can't see a young world traveler and fitness fanatic like Talia having much to do with Florence, so I eliminated her."

Thelma released a loud breath. "All right, I'll give you this one, but don't catch a case of pride. You have a long way to go before you solve the murder."

"I was right about something else," said Fen.

"I don't want to hear it."

"Yes, you do. You'll call me back if I don't tell you."

A few seconds passed before Thelma spoke. "I can wait, but I know you can't, so tell me before you bust a gut."

"Sheriff Blankenship called to tell me he released Derrick McDonald this morning."

"Did you call lawyer Chuck and rub it in?"

"Not yet, but I will."

Thelma attempted to sound serious. "Don't let Mr. Pride sit too long on your shoulder. He's a mean little fellow who'll push you into a muddy river. Some folks call him karma, but I think he's a demon."

"That's good advice, no matter what his name is."

The call ended as Bailey appeared at his side. "Did I hear you talking about Destiny?"

Fen turned to meet her gaze. "It seems Destiny and Talia Goldberg are good enough friends to go to Tyler together for the day."

"I wonder how they know each other."

"That's a question begging for someone to answer it. Lou will have a new research assignment to work on this afternoon."

A look of excitement filled Bailey's eyes. "Let me do it. Lou will be tired and grumpy from fishing all morning."

Fen scratched a mosquito bite on the back of his neck. "You're probably right. I've already given Lou too much background work to verify."

"Uh-huh, and I'm almost finished with my sketches to show Destiny."

He thought for a few seconds. "You're committed to caricatures and a portrait. Spring break won't last long, then you'll be busy with college. That leaves it to me to do the background research on Destiny."

The excitement left Bailey like air from a poorly tied balloon. "I wish now that I hadn't committed to do the caricatures. I'm letting you down."

"Nonsense. Don't be surprised if I need you to drive me somewhere. Be prepared to drop what you're doing at a moment's notice."

Thelma returned before noon carrying multiple bags of groceries and got to work in the kitchen. This wasn't unusual, but her silence about her exploits was.

Bailey came from her room with an offer to help Thelma put away some of the bounty, which earned her a quick rebuff. She changed direction and went to the living room to inspect Fen's work.

A notification sounded from Thelma's phone. She cleared her throat as she slowly approached from the kitchen. Bailey and Fen turned their attention to her as she wiped her hands on an apron and kept wiping.

Bailey broke the silence. "What's wrong?"

"Ain't nothing wrong."

"Then why did you snap at me when I offered to help, and why do you keep drying your hands when you weren't washing dishes?"

Thelma straightened her posture. "I've got something to say that's meant for Mr. Fen's ears only."

Fen sensed a quirk of a smile coming on, so he turned to put his pencil down. "When is Sam picking you up?"

Thelma stomped a foot. "I should have kept you knocked out with pain pills. A person has no private life."

Bailey covered her mouth with her hand, which did little to cover the gasp. She lowered it and grinned. "Someone has a steamy hot date, and it's sure not me or Fen."

Thelma glared. "You hush that kind of talk. It's not proper for a young lady."

Her gaze shifted to Fen. "I'd better not hear a word out of you either. There's plenty of food, but you're on your own to fix it."

Thelma took off her apron, folded it, and placed it in a drawer. She then went to her room, came back out carrying a seldom-used suitcase, and left the condo.

Bailey stood slack-jawed for several seconds. "I know she's a very private person, but I didn't think she'd blow up like that."

"She has deep hurts from her past. My wife helped her

cope with many of them when Thelma was in jail, and later when she became our cook and housekeeper. But things linger."

Bailey tilted her head. "How did you know Sam was coming to pick her up?"

"A series of little things. She wanted Sam to rest before driving home after he found the wallet and pistol. He turned down her offer to spend the night with her in a hotel. That hurt her enough to make her cry."

Bailey's eyes softened as she remembered that night. "I know. Thelma doesn't cry. Ever."

Fen let the comment pass. "Knowing Sam was coming to pick her up started this morning. She received a text notification but went to her room to respond to it. All her regular informants are back in Newman County and they know she's several counties away, taking care of us. I knew it probably wasn't one of them."

"It could have been her new informant from the RV park."

"True, but if it was Florence, she would have responded to her out here."

"Anything else?"

Fen pointed to the kitchen. "I watched her put away groceries. She bought things she normally won't buy. Quick-to-eat things that require little or no preparation. You picked up on her wiping dry hands with her apron. Did you notice she didn't answer the last text she received? There was no need. It was Sam's signal for her to meet him in the parking lot. When I put all the little clues together, everything pointed to her and Sam going away for some private time."

"Wow," said Bailey as her head made a slow, tick-tock movement. "Now I see why you solve so many crimes. You notice every little thing."

"There are plenty of things I miss, but you're right about not ignoring the little things."

Bailey asked, "How long will Thelma and Sam be gone?"

Fen raised his shoulders and let them fall. "Predicting the future is much harder than discovering the past."

A knock on the door ended the conversation. Bailey opened it and stood aside as Lou burst in. "Is there any liquor in this condo? I need something that will peel paint off a car after being with that jerk all morning."

Chapter Nineteen

L ou stepped into the kitchen and yanked open the door to the refrigerator. Bailey followed her as Fen moved to the dining area and said, "You've come to the wrong place for a stiff drink. There's tea, coffee, or water."

Lou reached for the coffeepot and let out a huff. "There's only half a cup."

"I'll make a full pot," said Bailey. "Why don't you sit down?"

"I'll take a cup, too," said Fen. He pulled out a chair and sat with his back to a wall waiting for Lou to join him.

"Catch anything?" he asked.

"Only two, and it's a good thing. A game warden checked us, and I received a ticket."

"What for?"

"Two illegal fish. They were both too small because that idiot guide didn't measure them." She wasn't finished. "The game warden also cited me for fishing without a license."

"Didn't Shane Wesley make sure you were fishing legally?"

Lou leaned forward and issued a hard stare. "He conveniently waited until we were at the far end of the lake before he asked. He told me not to worry, that the game wardens worked Lake Palestine yesterday and wouldn't be back for at least another day."

She leaned back. "Did I mention the guide is an idiot?"

Fen nodded. "Did the tickets come early or late?"

"Late. I had to put up with that Neanderthal's blather all morning. All he could talk about was his new bass boat. He wouldn't shut up about it."

Bailey entered the conversation while the coffee pot made gurgling sounds in the background. "Tran's boat isn't anything special. He told me it was a high school graduation present he gave himself."

"New or used?" asked Fen.

"Well used. He had to do a lot of work to it."

Lou folded her hands together. "Shane's boat is showroom new." She looked at Fen. "Do you want the details?"

"Please."

"It's a nineteen-foot Ranger Bass Boat with a 225 Mercury outboard motor. Came decked out with the trailer, trolling motor, depth finder, and two stick-like contraptions that poke down in the mud to keep the boat from moving. It has other gadgets on it, but I don't remember what they are."

Fen searched his memory. "That sounds like a boat Ranger calls their Cup Series. It comes fully equipped for professional anglers to compete in big fishing tournaments."

"That's his plan," said Lou before she shifted her gaze to the coffeemaker. "He also told me how much it cost. I could buy two or three new cars for what he paid, or six used Camrys like I drive."

"Paid or is paying?" asked Bailey.

"Is paying. He said he had to put thirty grand down."

Fen asked, "Did he brag about winning tournaments?"

"All he did was brag. He went on and on about last year's spring tournament on Lake Palestine."

"No others?"

"He mainly talked about the tournaments he'll win this year."

The coffee pot sputtered, then hissed. Bailey spoke as she opened the cabinet and took down identical white cups. "Did you ask him about Tran Wilks?"

"Yeah, but he didn't say much. Only that Tran attracted the ladies."

"What does he look like?" asked Bailey as she delivered coffee to Fen and Lou.

"Mid-forties, longish greasy hair the color of muddy water, inked arms sticking out of a plaid shirt with one too many buttons undone on the top and the bottom. Dirty blue jeans and tennis shoes held together with duct tape. If that's not enough, he met me on the dock with a cheek puffed out with chewing tobacco. He replaced it every hour and a half with a fresh wad. I spent all morning listening to him spit in the water. It didn't take long before a brown tobacco slick drifted past."

"Yuk. That's gross," said Bailey.

"Did he fish?" asked Fen.

Lou made a face that telegraphed to Fen that he'd asked a silly question. "Fished like he was trying to win a tournament. Sat up front operating the trolling motor while I stayed in the seat on the back deck. He'd catch a bass, weigh it, release it, and write some numbers. Then he'd get right back to catching the next one. If things slowed down, he'd pull up the trolling motor and tell me to reel my line in. I'd better have it in when he cranked the engine. He'd take off like a rocket, barely skimming the top of the water. That boat went about thirty miles per hour faster than I was comfortable going."

Bailey asked, "How could you hear him talking if he was going that fast?"

"I couldn't, and that seemed to please him. I know it made me happy to take a break from asking him questions he didn't want to answer. It was like pulling nose hairs to get him to answer my questions."

This was Fen's chance to ask his most important question. "Did you ask him if he took Dale White fishing?"

"Of course I asked," snapped Lou. "He told me I'd signed up for a guided fishing trip, not a guided gossip party. By that time, I'd had all I could stand of him."

Bailey leaned forward with her chin in hand. "What did you say to him?"

"That I didn't appreciate his attitude, how he spoke to me, or his nasty chewing tobacco." Lou lifted a proud chin. "It didn't faze him one bit."

Fen followed up. "How did he respond?"

"He told me if I didn't like the way he ran his business, I could get out and walk. I would have, but we were in fourteen feet of water when he said it."

Fen didn't react to the put-down, but he'd heard something that needed clarification. "It's obvious he overreacted when you asked him if he'd taken Dale White fishing. Do you believe he's capable of murder?"

Lou bought time by taking a series of sips from her cup. "If Dale White was as unlikable a man as the one I spent the morning with, I can see the two of them leaving in a boat and only one of them coming back."

Fen followed Lou's lead and bought time by sipping his coffee. He settled his mug on the table and brought his gaze to rest on the reporter. "I know you have a lot to do, but I need a background report on Shane Wesley. I'll take care of getting police and FBI reports. You and I both know those are a good place to start, but they're only as good as the reporting agencies inputting data."

Lou came alive. "It won't bother me one bit to lose sleep if it helps put him in jail." She pushed up from the table. "I'll be in my condo drinking coffee and using every trick I know to deliver a thorough report."

"Don't you want a sandwich to take with you?"

Fen responded before Lou could. "Bailey, get an empty bag and fill it with brain food. Lou's in for a long night."

Lou followed Bailey to the kitchen. "I prefer things with carbs, sugar, and caffeine."

"That's my version of brain food," said Bailey.

Lou informed them a hot shower was in her immediate future, followed by a nap and a marathon date with her computer.

With Thelma and Lou gone, Bailey announced she wanted to try the Activity Center's nine-inch meat lover's pizza.

The closing of the door behind Bailey meant Fen was alone for the first time since their arrival. It was as if the quiet room gave him a warm hug. He thought about his mental to-do list. It was empty until that evening when he and Bailey would meet with Destiny Roe.

Chapter Twenty

It was awkward with only one hand, but Fen built himself a ham and cheese sandwich with lettuce. He tried cutting a tomato, but the sharpest knife in the drawer wasn't up to cutting through the skin. The garbage disposal made quick work of the mangled, bruised mess. He settled for potato chips as a side dish and three cookies for dessert.

He returned to his sketch and spent two uninterrupted hours completing the pencil work. He took a break, put ice in a tall glass, and filled it with tea. The chair in the living room was his next stop. It was far enough away from the canvas to give him a different perspective. He saw room for improvement in a couple of places, but overall, it pleased him. Even if the deal with Destiny fell through, he believed the finished product would sell quickly.

The mechanical tune from his phone identified Bailey as the caller. "Things must be slow if you have time to call," he said.

"You won't believe what happened. A college fraternity is

staying at the resort, and they want individual caricatures plus one of the entire group."

"How many guys are you talking about?"

"Forty-six. Can you help me?"

Fen's initial inclination was to drop everything and come to her aid, but reason came calling. "I can give you advice on how to handle the order, but I won't be able to help."

"Why not?" snapped Bailey.

"Three reasons: First, I'm here to solve a murder. Second, I don't want to hear what Thelma would say. Third, I don't want Thelma to get in your eye like an onion."

An audible gulp came from Bailey. "You're right. She might make good on that threat to cut a limb from the peach tree and use it on me." She sighed. "Let's hear your advice."

"Schedule the individuals far enough apart so you won't rush. Don't sacrifice quality. Next, take photos of each finished caricature and the individual. Give them their sketch to take home with them. Find out who their leader is and tell him you need a group photo. Also say you'll mail the group drawing to him once you finish it. Give yourself time to do a good job."

"It will take me the rest of the day and half of tomorrow to do that many."

"One more thing," said Fen. "The agreement you made with the resort is for one caricature per person. Make sure you clarify that the group sketch is extra and you require half payment up front. Come up with a fair price. If they try to negotiate the price or when payment is due, hold firm."

"I'll do it. Anything else?"

"Don't worry about Destiny. I'll tell her to come here tonight to approve our sketches and sign a contract."

Background noise in the activity center intensified. "Do you have her phone number?"

"I haven't forgotten how to find things like that. I looked it up this morning after Thelma told me Destiny went to Tyler with Talia."

Bailey huffed a breath of regret. "When we work the next case, remind me not to take on another job."

"You're young and multi-talented. You can handle more than you think."

"I can't be in two places at once. You lost your driver for the rest of the day and a good portion of tomorrow."

He considered his options. "I expect Thelma to return tomorrow morning. If she doesn't, I know how to drive."

Bailey let out a hoot. "Make sure I'm not around when Thelma finds out." She spoke through chuckles. "I'll be home when I get there."

Fen placed his phone on the coffee table and stared at his work in progress. It wasn't long before he moved to the couch, fluffed a bed pillow for his head, placed another under his cast, and lost touch with the world without the aid of a pain pill.

THE CHIME of an incoming text brought Fen out of a deep slumber. At first, he didn't reach for his phone, but the spell of the long afternoon nap disappeared like morning mist. Without thinking, he tried to reach for the phone with his left hand because it was closest to the coffee table. "You big dummy," he whispered to himself as he realized he'd slept with his right side against the back cushions.

He then sat upright and swung his feet to the floor. He sat for several seconds as he gained his bearings. He stretched out the arm that wasn't encumbered by a cast and read the cryptic text message.

Call if able...A.

It was little more than an unscientific hunch, but Fen had a theory that unexpected phone calls had a fifteen percent chance of being wonderful news, a ten percent chance of being horrible or unwanted news, and a seventy-five percent chance of falling somewhere in between. He'd never tracked the results but stuck to the theory as if it were true.

He didn't need the phone's directory to find the number, even though he seldom used it. A soft voice answered. "Is the coast clear?"

His first words came out sounding like he'd just roused himself from an afternoon nap, which he had. "Hello, Audrey. Is anything wrong?"

"Now that I hear your voice, that's my question back at you."

Fen spoke through a yawn. "Waking up from a nap."

He cleared his throat and heard her ask, "Is that all? How's your head and arm?"

"They're both itching. Other than that, I've been taking it easy."

Fen could see the City of Smithville's attorney in his imagination, and he liked what he saw. They'd started a slow-burning relationship the previous year when Fen and his troupe of women assistants solved a murder that occurred on the Colorado River. He thought he'd never get over the death of his wife, Sally, nor did he want to rush into a relationship. By mutual agreement, they'd decided to allow five years to pass before taking action other than the occasional phone call. Audrey had a son to get through law school, and Fen needed to make sure his grief wouldn't ruin what could be a second chance at being with a woman who would share the rest of his life. He also felt obligated to remain single until Bailey found her place in the world.

Audrey asked, "Are you going to give me a more complete

answer to my question, or did the knock on the head result in amnesia?"

"I've always been a quick healer. I'm off prescription pain meds, and we're making progress on the case. Do you want to hear about it?"

"Normally I would, but I have an appointment in five minutes. Lou's article in the Tyler paper made me wonder if you were all right. Which of the two detectives do you think has the right man?"

"I'm exploring other possibilities."

"Oh my. That sounds interesting. Could one of the new suspects be a beautiful, rich, single woman?"

"Of course not. There's two that fit that description."

"I wouldn't doubt it a bit." She paused. "By the way, you said you were taking a nap. You wouldn't be with one or both women now, would you?"

"Not yet, but the cliff climber is coming to our condo this evening."

"It's going to disappoint her to find Thelma, Bailey, and Lou there with you."

Fen enjoyed the mildly suggestive banter with Audrey. It was something he and Sally had done frequently. He teased the new woman in his life by saying, "I assure you she won't be disappointed. Lou has her own condo with days of background work to do. Bailey's in a separate building sketching caricatures of almost fifty college fraternity guys. She won't be in until after eleven. Finally, Thelma ran away with Sam for a romantic night in a hotel."

A riot of laughter came through the phone before Audrey composed herself and said, "There's nothing wrong with your head if you can produce lies like those."

The call ended.

The knock on the door sounded at six thirty. Fen opened it and Destiny flashed a smile as she entered. "We meet again, Sheriff Maguire."

"I sign my paintings Fen Maguire. If I was going to have you arrested, it would be Sheriff Maguire, even though I'm no longer a sheriff."

The smile remained as she strode toward the living room. "Do you still arrest people?"

"Only the ones who contract for a painting then change their minds."

This earned a wider smile, and he followed up the banter with an observation. "I like the new hairstyle. It fits the shape of your face."

Her hand reached for her hair. It was much shorter than what he'd remembered. "I had it done this afternoon in Tyler. I was unsure, but the beautician promised I'd love not having to mess with it."

"Did you spend all day in Tyler?"

"I go there with a friend three or four days a week. She's into distance running but enjoys the burn from cross-training. The staff and equipment at the gym in Tyler are excellent."

This answered Fen's first unasked question. He'd wanted to verify that the woman Thelma saw in Talia's car was Destiny.

Fen took the time to inspect the new hairstyle. "I'll need to take new photos of you. Bailey's pencil sketch of a close-up of you has your hair pulled back with a scrunchie. There's not enough left now to pull back. She'll do another sketch with short hair."

"Can I see the one with long hair? I may prefer that look for the portrait."

"Of course."

He'd set up two easels in the living room. She followed him to the one on the right. He turned over Bailey's drawing, and Destiny nodded her approval. She moved closer and examined the details. "I love the pose. She must study human anatomy night and day. How did she know I grit my teeth and narrow my eyes when I climb?"

She cast her gaze to look at him. "I wanted her to capture how intense rock climbing can be."

Fen kept looking at the sketch. "Her best works fall somewhere between realism and hyper-realism." He took a step back. "I do like the determination she captured. Are you always that way?"

"I used to be a shy, girly-girl, but life kicked me in the teeth enough times that I got over it." Her voice changed to something much less serious, even playful. "It's a shame you have that cast on. I could teach you a few things about climbing."

He recognized that Destiny had let her guard down, if only for a moment. He changed the businesslike tone of his voice to match hers. "I never saw much need to climb cliffs. It's hard enough for me to stay on the ground and not get hurt. I have an artificial knee to prove it."

"I bet it was a football injury."

Fen laughed. "You're not even close. I got between a woman carrying a pistol and her future ex-husband. He walked away, she went to jail, and I took a ride in an ambulance. You're not carrying a pistol, are you?"

She pulled up the bottom of a form-fitting top and revealed black leggings from waist to ankles. She then turned in a slow circle and asked, "Do you see any need for a pat-down?"

He cleared his throat. "Uh... nope. Let's move on to my sketch. It's a distant view, and a different style, so you'll need to use your imagination more to see what the final product will look like."

Destiny took several steps back and tilted her head. She moved forward, then to one side and the next. Her gaze kept shifting from his sketch to Bailey's and back again.

"Please don't take this wrong," said Destiny.

Fen had heard the same sentence more times than he wanted to admit. It marked the slow, painful march toward a rejection.

"I know nothing about art other than what catches my eye. You're a world-class artist and I'd be a fool not to purchase any painting with your signature."

Fen thought to himself, *Wait for it... BUT...*

"But," said Destiny, "distant images simply aren't my style. I live life literally on the edge and that's what I want surrounding me."

He didn't want her to feel guilty. "In a way, I'm glad you don't want it. My biggest desire for the works I produce is that customers truly appreciate them. There are so many styles of art and plenty of people who will fall in love with this painting when it's finished."

"You're going to paint it anyway?"

"Sure. People love paintings of cliffs and mountains." He then got back to business. "What about Bailey's close-up?"

"Absolutely, and this isn't about the price difference between what she quoted for your painting and hers. I'll pay her what she was charging for yours."

"She'll appreciate that. It will support her college pizza habit."

"Does that conclude our business?"

"Almost. I made up three contracts to take care of any contingency. I had a feeling you'd reject one of them. All I need is your signature and half the money down. Bailey's already signed it."

"Do you mind if I pay it all?"

"That would thrill Bailey."

Destiny cast her gaze toward the kitchen. "Would you have any bubbly we could use to toast my first art purchase with?"

"There's a few cans of Dr. Pepper. Will that in a fluted glass do?"

"We'll pretend we're drinking champagne."

The fizzy, dark soda may have been a lousy excuse for sparkling wine, but it served the purpose. Glasses clinked after Fen offered a toast to art. They both took sips.

Destiny lowered her glass and gave him a sideways glance. "Talia told me she hasn't met you yet."

Fen watched the bubbles rise in his glass. "Why would I want to talk to her?"

"Let's not pretend. You're here to help the cops find out who killed her husband."

"Are you sure?"

"We both are. You were in a serious accident that delayed your arrival. You're here with Bailey to help you. Your housekeeper came to take care of you. I bet she drove."

Fen nodded. "She did." It was his turn to ask a question. "What does Talia want to know?"

"Which one of the two men the police arrested killed her husband? We also want to know why both are running free."

Fen nodded, hoping he didn't show partial relief. "Will Talia be home tomorrow morning?"

"She can be if you call her tonight."

"No need," said Fen. "You'll call her as soon as you get to your condo. Tell her to expect me at eight."

Destiny shook her head. "Nine thirty at the earliest. She takes long runs on the days we don't go to cross training."

"I'll be knocking on the door of her motorhome at ten o'clock."

Chapter Twenty-One

The texts Fen sent to Bailey and Lou the previous night were the same.

Meeting at 9:00 a.m., this living room. Don't ask why.

He made a point not to send it to Thelma, as the last part would keep her awake all night.

When Bailey opened her door at eight she looked like a bear coming out of hibernation. Fen acknowledged her presence but refrained from verbal communication until she instigated it. He doubted that would happen for almost half an hour.

Lou arrived wearing sweats and house shoes that should have gone to a thrift store several seasons ago. The faux fur looked especially bedraggled because she'd walked through heavy morning dew. Both women appeared to be leading participants in a bad hair day contest.

The greenish-brown discoloration under Lou's eyes made the lake's dark water look crystal clear in comparison.

At least Bailey had youth and a great complexion going for her. She was the first to loosen her tongue. "If one more frat boy comes on to me, I'm going to rearrange his face to look like his caricature."

Fen wanted to tell her to leave her hair like it was and she wouldn't need to worry about untoward comments. Of course he didn't, but he smiled at the thought of how she'd react.

Lou mumbled, "I'm too old for all-nighters. You'd better have a good reason for not sending me a text or email instead of making me get up so early."

Fen ignored the comment. "Thelma left us a box of assorted donuts. Does anyone want scrambled eggs?"

"Coffee and a sinker for me," said Lou.

"Brain food only," said Bailey.

Fen waited for the sugar and caffeine to take effect before he said, "I met with Destiny Roe last night. She paid in full for Bailey's painting but didn't want mine."

Bailey's head came up. "Why didn't she want yours?"

"For the same reason some people buy my paintings and not yours. It boils down to personal taste. The good news is she agreed to pay full price as if she'd bought my painting."

Bailey looked bewildered. "But—"

Lou lifted her head. "Don't question good fortune. Take the money, complete the painting for the woman who enjoys dangling like Spider Man, and be thankful."

"Good advice," said Fen.

He took a breath. "I wanted to talk to you about what I now know about Destiny and Talia Goldberg. They're closer friends than I imagined, and they know we're here to help the police find Dale White's killer."

Lou took a turn. "I tracked the travels of Dale and Talia for the last five years. Their paths crossed with Destiny's over two years ago in Bali. It seems Destiny went her own way for six months and then they wound up at the same exotic locations. Sometimes they'd stay at the same resort, but not always."

"Interesting," said Fen. "We know Dale and Talia could go anywhere they wanted, but what about Destiny? Where does her money come from?"

"She's a trust fund woman who bounces around the world living large and doing what she pleases."

"Did Talia come into her marriage to Dale with big bucks?" asked Bailey.

"Upper middle-class family. She's still waiting for her inheritance. The will needs to go through probate but the court won't be in a hurry because someone murdered Dale."

Bailey looked at Lou. "Why not?"

Lou seemed more focused on her soggy donut than the question, so she shrugged to communicate that she didn't know.

Fen had two answers. "If Talia was involved in Dale's murder, that would disqualify her from an inheritance."

Lou looked up. "I knew that."

Fen continued, "I haven't heard one good word about Dale White except he was brilliant and made money hand over fist. The chances of him getting along with his own parents are slim. They might want to contest the will, which would cause further delays."

"What's Talia living on now?" asked Bailey.

Once again, Fen had the answer. Candy gave it to him after he placed a phone call to her, asking for bank records. "Dale set up a separate bank account for Talia. It carries a balance of a million dollars, give or take a hundred grand."

"Must be nice," said Lou. "Talia enjoys the benefits of marrying a rich man." She looked at flecks of donuts floating in her coffee as she said, "At least she got one with plenty of money. My mother didn't tell me it was just as easy to fall in love with a rich man until after husband number three."

Fen fixed his gaze on Lou then Bailey. "I'm meeting with Talia at ten."

Bailey asked, "My first sketch is at ten thirty. Will we be back by then?"

"I'll drive myself."

The two women looked at each other, both shaking their heads and talking over each other. They expressed the same concern. Thelma would throw a wild-eyed fit and all three would experience her wrath.

Fen set his jaw. "I'll take the blame."

Lou said, "I'll send flowers to your funeral."

He ignored the comment. "Lou, get some sleep, but not too much. There's still much to learn about all the suspects."

"It would help if we had up-to-date financial statements on everyone. I can try, but—"

Fen cut her off. "I'll call Candy back. With any luck, we'll have up-to-date information tomorrow."

He shifted his gaze to Bailey. "You need to do something with yourself, put on a big smile, finish the individual sketches, and take a group photo. It won't be long before you're back at college and you'll have a complicated sketch to finish and a difficult portrait to paint. That's beside all your regular studies and assignments."

Bailey lowered her gaze. "I thought you wanted me to help you solve the murder."

"I still do," said Fen without a trace of sympathy in his voice. "You're the one who overcommitted yourself. The next time you help me with a case, I expect you to be available."

Bailey lifted her head. "Don't put all the blame on me. I told you what I was doing; you could have told me no."

Fen smiled. "That's better. A good investigator knows how to stand his or her ground."

Bailey squared her shoulders. "I scheduled the last individual sketch for one forty this afternoon. The group photo will take place at two. Give me something to do after that."

Fen wondered if he'd painted himself into a corner. Bailey wanted an assignment, but he couldn't think of anything. Something came to mind as he sipped his coffee, but he didn't believe it would satisfy her. "I'm not supposed to drive before the doctor clears me. I'm making an exception to the rule and I know I'll get an earful from Thelma. After today, you're to take me wherever, whenever I need to go."

"Can I stay with you and actively take part in interviews?"

"Sometimes yes, sometimes no. Don't push it."

He knew it wasn't what she wanted to hear, but he didn't like open-ended commitments.

It occurred to him to check the time. "We all have things to do. I'll be back after my interview with Talia."

Lou walked out with him but said nothing until they reached his truck. She placed her hand on his shoulder. "You make a wonderful substitute father to that young lady."

"I'm making it up as I go."

TALIA'S MOTORHOME stood out as a diamond among lumps of coal when compared to all the travel trailers and motorhomes in the campground. Fen gripped the steering wheel and took his time lowering himself to the ground. The one thing he didn't want to do was fall and return to the condo with a fresh scrape. His chances of bluffing his way past Thelma were poor enough.

Talia had the door open for him when he arrived. She offered no word of greeting but stepped back as he wished her a good morning.

"I thought one of your assistants would drive you."

After the previous day's conversation with Destiny, there

was no reason to deny the existence of his team. "They're busy trying to find the person responsible for killing your husband."

It wasn't a total lie, but he'd danced a wide circle around the truth. Bailey was drawing silly sketches of young men while Lou was back in front of her computer, and Thelma and Sam were... he didn't want to think about what they might be doing. Time to refocus.

As he stepped into the motorhome, he said, "I've only seen YouTube videos of top-of-the-line motorhomes. This is spectacular."

Talia gave a quick look at her surroundings. "It will be for sale if you and that obnoxious detective do your jobs. No one has given me a satisfactory explanation of why they released Dale's killer."

Fen measured her words against her body language. Talia looked like a woman who was trying hard to sound offended. Perhaps he could push her to discover if he was correct. He ignored her last complaint and focused on the motorhome.

"How many miles per gallon does a rig like this get?"

"I have no idea and even less interest in finding out. All I know is my life is on hold until there's an official ruling on where my husband died."

"Didn't a district attorney or sheriff tell you that?"

"They sent a messenger boy, that incompetent detective who apparently didn't do his job and properly arrest Derrick McDonald."

"Did he tell you why they released Mr. McDonald?"

"I've heard nothing. Everyone's dodging my phone calls."

It seemed possible, but unlikely, that neither Talia nor Destiny had read the story Lou wrote. If one of them had, they both knew unless...

Fen tested her. "I may be mistaken, but I think I remember Destiny telling me she read a story in the Tyler newspaper about Mr. McDonald's arrest. A detective from the neighboring county claimed jurisdiction and arrested a different man for killing your husband a few hours before McDonald's arrest. This put both counties in an awkward position."

Talia's eyebrows came together. "I don't care if it's awkward or not. What will it take to get someone arrested and officially charged?"

Fen rubbed his chin. "Additional evidence would do it, if it was good enough."

"Isn't there enough already?"

"None of it's conclusive. The altercation between your husband and Mr. McDonald is significant, but all it proves is on that particular day they had a scuffle. There's no proof they were anywhere near each other on the day of the offense."

"What about the other man? What evidence is there that he killed my husband?"

"None, other than he discovered the body and brought it to shore. He also took Dale fishing the week before he went missing."

Fen shifted the conversation. "The consensus among your neighbors and a lot of other people is that Dale didn't get along with many people."

Talia spoke under her breath. "That much is certainly true." She raised her voice back to normal. "You mentioned needing the right evidence. What do you mean?"

"Physical evidence. Blood, fingerprints, DNA, the murder weapon, shoe prints, tire tracks that match a suspect's car, phone records, a laptop, bank records, and credit card receipts, to name a few." He took a breath. "An eyewitness would be nice, but they're not always reliable. Video and audio recordings are better. But the best of all is a confession. You'd be surprised how many people can't stand the guilt of what they did."

Fen allowed a few seconds of silence to let the possibilities sink in. "Many times, when more than one person commits the crime, one of them will betray their co-conspirator. They will even plant evidence to take suspicion off themselves."

He noted the lecture had changed Talia's demeanor from antagonism to curiosity. "Do you believe Derrick McDonald had a partner?"

"It's possible. It's also possible the other man they arrested didn't act alone."

"Could they have worked together?"

"That's something I'm considering. So far, there's nothing to suggest it, but all it takes is one big break and the jailbirds sing. They say there's no honor among thieves and that goes double for killers. The stakes couldn't be higher for them."

Fen stood. "I've enjoyed my visit with you and promise I'll do all I can to catch the person or persons who killed Dale."

"Thank you. I hope it won't take too long."

"What will you do when you leave here?"

"Go as far away as I can. I caught the travel bug, and staying in only one country for more than a few months bores me to death."

"Not me," said Fen. "Give me my ranch and a blank canvas."

"Surely you want more than that."

"I enjoy the occasional challenge of a homicide."

"What about female companionship?"

"I speak to my late wife every morning. A framed picture of her travels with me everywhere I go."

He wasn't expecting, nor did he receive a response, so he changed the subject. "Good luck with the cross training and the marathons."

"Ah. Destiny told you."

"We had a long, interesting conversation. She told me quite a bit."

"Oh? Did she tell you we're each other's alibi?"

Fen gave her a parting smile. "That's the one thing I failed to ask her."

"She went with me to California."

He took extra care climbing down the steps of the motorhome and getting into his truck. The trip back to the resort went without incident. He drove with extra caution and not like a former highway patrolman trying to catch up to a speeder.

The conversation with Talia replayed in his mind as he entered the condo.

Thelma's voice rang out. "I knew you'd do something foolish if I left you alone. You couldn't stand not driving that new truck. How far did you go?"

Fen spoke in an even tone. If Thelma wanted a verbal sparring match, he'd oblige her. If not, he didn't want to provoke her into one. "I drove to the campground and interviewed Talia Goldberg."

Thelma shook a finger at him. "I hope you got driving out of your system because you're a passenger until Doc tells you otherwise."

It shocked him that the expected tornado was only a small dust-devil. Thelma turned to face the kitchen sink and hummed a nameless tune. "Ya'll didn't eat much. Are you hungry?"

Fen knew when he heard Thelma's off-key tune that all was well. He also knew that despite her bluster, she needed to know he appreciated her. Nothing pleased her more than feeding people. This was not the time to turn down her hospitality. Besides, the single donut he ate was a poor substitute for a meal from Thelma.

"As a matter of fact, I'm starving. Lou worked all night, Bailey's finishing her work with the fraternity, and all any of us ate this morning were donuts."

"Good. I'll have something on the table in half an hour that will stick to your ribs." She reached for the refrigerator door but didn't open it. "Do you need me to drive you anywhere today?"

"Not unless something happens between now and when Bailey finishes with the fraternity tonight. I told her that starting tomorrow, she's my driver until she goes back to college."

"Make sure you two take her truck. That girl drives like her hair is on fire."

Thelma wouldn't be herself if she didn't get in the last word of a conversation.

Fen walked to his sketch of the mountain and made a mental list of paints he would mix for the base coats of sky, cliffs, and foreground. A quiet afternoon with nothing to do but paint and think suited him.

The incoming text altered his plans.

Chapter Twenty-Two

The afternoon sun, fresh air, and brisk walk were the pick-me-up Fen needed after a belt-stretching lunch and standing for hours in front of an easel. One major change he'd made was to rotate a clean canvas a quarter turn and start over. The original work was to be one half of a two-painting set, a distant view on the left and Bailey's close-up portrait of Destiny on the right. Since the cliff-climber nixed the idea and chose only Bailey's work, it left his elongated landscape out of balance.

While walking to Destiny's condo, he noticed that spring break and warm temperatures brought people to the tennis courts and putt-putt golf course in droves, not to mention the crowds at the outdoor swimming pools.

He strode past them on his way to the condo complex where Destiny was staying. The text he received included her condo's number.

His brisk pace slowed so he wouldn't arrive panting like a hound. It proved fortunate that her condo was on the ground floor, saving him from climbing two or three flights of stairs. He knocked and heard the words "I'm coming" through the door.

The condo was a smaller version of the one he shared with Thelma and Bailey. The layout and decor matched, except for a shorter living room with one less club chair.

"Come in and make yourself comfortable. You have your choice of water, tea, or white wine. Have a seat in the living area and I'll bring it to you."

"Water, no ice, please." He continued to examine the rooms. "Is this a two bedroom?"

"Uh-huh. Two bedrooms and two baths. The bathroom off the living room is tiny, but the master bedroom has a shower and a jetted tub. I love to indulge in a hydro-massage after a hard workout."

"That's not an option for me with this cast on."

"You're getting around well. Any complications?"

"If you're talking about physical setbacks, the answer is no." He pretended to pout. "I'm a little bummed that I lost a sale to a nineteen-year-old upstart. She may never let me live it down."

"Face it, Sheriff, she out-hustled you."

Fen searched for a snappier comeback but had to settle for, "Youth is wasted on the young."

Destiny delivered his water and settled a second glass on the coffee table before sitting on the couch. The shorts she wore put two muscular legs on full display. A knit sleeveless top did the same for her upper body. Could the choice of wardrobe be a strategy to distract, or simply how the athlete dressed all the time? Up to now, he'd only seen her wear leggings and a form-fitting top. Either way, he focused on her face.

After a few moments of silence, Destiny moved past social banter. "Talia called me about your meeting with her this morning. She said it was most enlightening."

"We had a productive discussion. She's an interesting woman."

"Interesting and angry."

Fen nodded in agreement. "She was at first, and I can't blame her. She wants to move on with her life but can't."

"Why not?"

"It's complicated. There are two primary suspects the police arrested and then released."

He was prepared to say more, but she cut him off. "She told me about them and what you said about there's not enough firm evidence to hold either of them."

Fen nodded. "Not yet, but I'm hopeful there will be."

Destiny draped one smooth leg over the other. "What will it take to get an arrest that will stick?"

He focused on her nose and noticed a slight flaw on its bridge. Perhaps she broke it climbing? The thought came and went in less than a second. "Didn't Talia tell you what I explained to her? I thought I spelled it out clearly."

She shook her head.

Fen spent the next several minutes explaining the various categories of evidence and what the police needed to bring charges that would stick.

Destiny took in every word of the tutorial and asked, "Are you and your team working to find more evidence?"

"Of course, and so are the police. Believe me, both detectives are using every trick in the book to add to their cases against the men they think are responsible."

"What if they don't find any additional evidence?"

Fen looked toward the back patio. "They're each convinced they have the right man."

Destiny crossed her arms over her chest. "What about you? How are you proceeding?"

Fen gave an opaque answer. "Have you ever been raccoon hunting?"

Her head jerked back. "I didn't see that question coming, and the answer is never. In fact, the only thing I've ever hunted was my car keys. What's your point?"

He pulled his lips apart in a wide smile. "You haven't lived until you hunt behind a pack of well-trained coon dogs. The best hunts take place at night. The dogs track by following a scent. You turn them loose in a river bottom and wait for them to catch the scent of a raccoon. When they do, their barks shift to howls and they follow the scent until they run the raccoon up a tree."

"Do they always catch the raccoon?"

"Sometimes they go the wrong direction and need to backtrack. They can also lose the scent entirely, or one raccoon will cross the trail of another." He paused. "Am I making any sense at all?"

Destiny's eyebrows came together. "Are you saying that the two detectives are on the wrong trail?"

"Right now, they're backtracking. They'll keep looking until the trail goes cold."

"What then?"

Fen bought time by taking a long drink from his glass. "Detectives are a lot like bloodhounds. They keep looking until they find something or there's nothing left to find. All either detective needs is one piece of solid evidence, then it's the beginning of the end." He paused, "However..."

The words hung in the air like a piñata, waiting for a sharp blow to spill its contents. Fen swung the invisible stick. "I'm thinking more along the lines that they may be chasing the wrong raccoon and need to expand their search."

"Where do you start?"

Fen smiled. "You have a good head on your shoulders. Where would you start?"

Destiny let out a cackle, which broke the tension. "I enjoy the occasional detective story. They always start with those closest to the victim: a relative, business associate, or a friend."

"Those are all good places to look. Sometimes cops zero in on suspects through a process of elimination."

She fluttered her eyelashes and spoke with a drawl that was as sweet as a Georgia peach. "Sheriff Maguire, please say you don't suspect little old me."

Fen played along and laughed. "Little old you isn't kin."

He stopped the act. "Do you know if Dale White named Talia the sole beneficiary in his will?"

"Uh... I'm not sure he had a will. Did you ask Talia?"

"We didn't talk about it. Do you know if there's a big life insurance policy on Dale?"

"He didn't need one. Multi-millionaires are self-insured."

Destiny uncrossed her legs. "It occurs to me you're overlooking something."

"What's that?"

"Talia has an alibi. She and I were out of town together. We have hotel and credit card receipts to show where we went, stayed, shopped, you name it."

"Have the police asked for those yet?"

"They asked Talia, but not me. Should I gather them and give them to you?"

"That will save them time and maybe keep you from a needless interview with one or more frustrated cops. They're under a lot of pressure."

Destiny's brow wrinkled. "I'm a little confused about why the police would want to speak to me."

Fen spoke in a matter-of-fact tone. "As you said, you're her alibi. And other than Talia, you probably knew Dale White better than anyone else."

She bristled. "Are you insinuating there was something going on between me and Dale?"

Fen shot back, "Was there?"

Destiny's hands clenched and her suntanned face took on a rosy hue.

Not wanting to hear the explosion, Fen burst out laughing. "Gotcha'." He slapped his knee. "That's what you can expect in a police interview. They'll set you up, then slap you with a question that sounds like an accusation."

He continued to chuckle as Destiny stilled her emotions. It took less than thirty seconds before she said, "You're a sneaky man. What would you have done if I'd said there was something going on between me and Dale White? That he wasn't always fishing all day?"

Fen picked up his glass of water. "I'd have said it didn't surprise me. I picture Dale White and Talia as a couple who practiced an open marriage. You've known them for about three years and you three have a habit of staying at many of the same exotic resorts."

Destiny issued a pinched smile. "There's nothing illegal about anything we've done." She lifted her chin. "We shared many common interests."

"But fishing in tournaments wasn't one of them."

"Heavens no. Dale changed when he went bass fishing in Florida." Her gaze became more intense, as if she were trying to explain a hard concept. "To Dale, life was nothing but one competition after another. He played the game of earning money until he had more than he would ever spend."

"That's a lot of money," said Fen.

"Yes and no," said Destiny. "He had the Midas touch. He could look into the future and see what the next big thing would be. He invested infrequently but hit it big every time." She reached for her glass of water. "Talia can tell you more about the things he invented and invested in while they were in college and following."

Fen knew he'd speak to Talia again but didn't say he would.

Destiny continued, "He dabbled in business during the years I knew him, but it no longer challenged him. That was during their travel and extreme sports phase. Injuries took their toll on his body but the desire for new thrills remained strong."

Fen thought he knew where she was taking the conversation and said, "Some people say fishing is as addictive as drugs."

"He couldn't get enough of it." She quirked a smile. "Most of the time he couldn't get enough of it. He'd come calling on cold, rainy days when the fish weren't biting."

Fen schooled his features not to show either surprise or triumph at her admission. "Do you think you and Talia were the only fish on his stringer?"

Destiny cackled. "What a delicious metaphor and a unique way to ask a delicate question. To tell you the truth, we both thought about it, and discussed it, but neither of us really cared."

"No jealousy from Talia?"

"We're both cut from the same cloth. It's woven without a thread of shame in it for lifestyle choices."

Fen sensed the interview wind down when Destiny asked, "Do you think you'll ever arrest Dale's killer?"

"It's possible the police arrested the killer yesterday morning. Arresting is easy. Proving guilt beyond a reasonable doubt is the hard part." He stood and said, "That leaves me and the detectives, like the hounds, searching in the dark, looking for the fresh trail."

Destiny also stood. She moved to the other side of the coffee table and blocked his path. A teasing yet serious look crossed her countenance. "You don't fool me, Sheriff Maguire. The two detectives are on cold trails. You're the lead hound of the pack and you're not sitting in the dark waiting for the raccoon to make a mistake and scurry past you."

"Looking for and finding aren't the same. Many crimes go unsolved. Some raccoons are too smart to catch."

An alluring gaze bore into him. "Now that you know the way to my door, don't be a stranger."

Fen pretended not to understand the subtext of her words. "I may have other questions for you regarding the case, so I may take you up on the invitation."

Chapter Twenty-Three

Shadows had lengthened by the time Fen left Destiny's condo and retraced the path he'd walked earlier. His pace was more of an amble, as it involved traveling uphill. He wanted to process the interview. It was then he remembered to turn off the record function on his phone. It would aid him in recalling the details of this most recent interview.

He arrived at the condo to find Bailey eating a sandwich and Thelma delivering a glass of milk to the teen.

Bailey spoke after swallowing an enormous bite. "What did you learn?"

"To take small bites and chew them well."

"Hilarious," said Bailey with a deadpan look as Thelma's midsection jiggled.

He settled in a chair. "I learned that Talia and Destiny shared more than cross-training."

Bailey paused for several seconds. Her eyes widened, and she asked, "Are you saying what I'm thinking?"

Thelma burst in. "You'd better not be thinking it." Her gaze shifted to Fen. "And you'd best not be saying it."

Fen kept his gaze on Bailey and nodded to answer her inquiring gaze.

"Holy smoke," said Bailey. "Do you think those two women worked together to kill him?"

Fen puffed out his cheeks and released a gust of uncertainty. "It's an interesting development, but I'm not sure it means much. They have conclusive proof that establishes solid alibis for each of them. They were nowhere near the Neches River when Dale White died."

Bailey's narrow gaze told him she needed more convincing. "You always say that people can fake alibis. Why not these two?"

"There's too much evidence, and it's too specific," said Fen. "Credit card receipts, eyewitnesses, store cameras."

"Rich people can pay to have all those things altered."

Fen scratched his itching scalp. "You're right. I'll have Lou dig deeper and try to find discrepancies."

He turned to Thelma and pointed to his head. "How long do I have to wait before I can shampoo this greasy mop?"

"I'll spray it down with some more of that waterless cleaner. I know it doesn't work like shampoo and water, but it's the best we can do until the stitches come out."

Fen growled. "I'll try it again. Maybe I need to use more this time."

Thelma was already walking. "You stay sitting there. I'm the cleaning expert and you'll end up spraying it in your eyes again."

He shifted his gaze back to Bailey. "Did you finish with the fraternity?"

"Uh-huh. Well, kind of finished."

A cocked head preceded his question. "Did you finish or didn't you?"

She lowered her voice to a whisper. "I don't want to talk about it in front of Thelma."

The whisper wasn't soft enough. "What don't you want to talk about in front of me?"

Bailey groaned. "No offense, Thelma, but it's something personal. In fact, I'd rather not talk to Fen about it, either."

Thelma put the spray can on the table. "If it's that bad, we'll both hear about it before long. You'd best unburden yourself of the load."

Bailey closed her eyes for a few seconds then opened them again. "It's nothing bad in the true sense of the word. I'm confused about something and don't know what to do."

Fen interrupted. "If you don't want to talk about it, you don't have to."

Thelma huffed and placed the towel over the collar of Fen's shirt. "The best way to get rid of a boil is to lance it and squeeze hard."

Bailey protested, "It's not a boil."

Fen remained silent as Thelma's hand covered his forehead, and aerosol spray hit his hair. She continued to spray for much longer than she had two days prior.

"The directions say nothing about working this into the scalp, but I'm going to, anyway."

Fen had to admit the gentle scalp massage felt wonderful, but was it enough for removing dirt and oil? The dry towel came next. Thelma stayed clear of the stitches but gave the rest of his head a rub that left his scalp tingling.

She remembered to bring a hairbrush and comb. After making a couple of funny faces as she parted his hair, she announced, "That's as good as it's going to get until the stitches come out."

Fen thanked her and admitted it felt better. Bailey cast a

critical eye. "Using more product helped. It looks like you only waited one day to shampoo and not seven."

"I'll take it," said Fen. "Thanks, Thelma."

Bailey rose and moved her easel to her room. "I'll get this out of everyone's way. I need to do what Fen does. Think and paint."

Fen held up a hand to Thelma. Without words, he told her to leave Bailey alone. She may not have liked it, but Thelma silently took everything used to clean his hair back to where it belonged.

Bailey stayed in her bedroom until Thelma banged and clanged pans, a common prelude to supper. Fen sent her a text.

Would you rather have supper elsewhere?

Yes.

I'll distract Thelma.

Thanks.

Fen went to his bedroom, pretended to use the facilities, and closed the door louder than usual. Bailey's bedroom door remained closed until he was in the kitchen with Thelma. He leaned against the cabinets, which forced Thelma to look at him and not in the direction of Bailey's escape route. Out of the corner of his eye, he saw Bailey slide past on tiptoes. She'd showered, fixed her hair and changed her clothes from a paint-speckled shirt and cut-offs to something spring-ish and new.

Less than a minute passed before Thelma asked, "Was that Bailey sneaking out?"

Fen nodded.

"I thought so. She's going to see a young man, isn't she?"

"That's my best guess."

"One of those fraternity boys?"

"Most likely."

"Good," said Thelma. "She was getting too thick with Cory. That girl's got a lot of growing up to do and places to see before she's tied down."

Fen's initial response sounded melancholy. "I don't think Cory's willing to wait that long. He's older and plans on staying in one place all his life. I wouldn't doubt it if he already has his eye on someone else."

"Most likely," said Thelma.

The evening passed with Fen standing in front of his easel, considering the day's events. Thelma put the kitchen to rights before retiring to her bedroom. The volume on her television stayed low enough so he couldn't make out the words, only muffled murmurs and the occasional outburst of fake television laughter.

Fen's brushes were clean by ten o'clock. A soak in a hot bath followed. At ten thirty, he slipped between white sheets. He longed for the day when the cast came off and he didn't have to contort his body into strange shapes to put on his sleepwear.

The full day left him mentally and physically spent. With Sally's photo tilted so it was the last thing he saw, he turned off the light and fell into a motionless sleep.

THE KNOCK on his door intensified. "Wake up, Fen." Urgency seasoned the words hollered by Thelma.

He came out from under the covers with a firm grip on his pistol. "What's wrong?"

"I heard a scream coming from the parking lot."

Fen was up and out of the bedroom door. "Did you look to see who it was?"

"All I saw was a truck heading out of the parking lot like someone stole it."

Fen ran to the door and looked down at the rows of vehicles. He strained to hear. Tires screeched somewhere in the distance.

"This ain't good," said Thelma. "Bailey didn't come home."

Fen held up a hand. "Quiet." He didn't breathe in order to catch more of the distant sound. "It's too far. They could have gone either left or right on the main road."

"Help me get dressed."

It was awkward getting dressed with a broken arm, but Thelma did all she could to button, zip, tug, pull, and maneuver clothing and boots so he could appear in public.

Thelma left before he slipped his pistol in its belt holster. She met him at the door with his flashlight in her outstretched hand.

He took the stairs as fast as he dared with the flashlight tucked into his sling and his good hand sliding along the rail. He planned to start his search at Bailey's truck but never got that far. Her phone lay at the base of the stairway. Dime-sized splotches of fresh blood stained the white concrete. Jerking the flashlight from the sling, he followed a bright beam of light to the parking lot, where black asphalt made it harder to see the drops of blood. A thick white zip tie lay in one of the last tiny puddles.

An official-looking resort security SUV came quickly toward him.

The man's window rolled down. "We received reports of a disturbance."

Fen was in no mood to trade notes. "I'm Sheriff Fen

Maguire. I believe there's been an assault and abduction of a nineteen-year-old female. Her name is Bailey Madison."

"Are you sure?" asked the man.

Fen put on his sternest face and used a voice he saved for special occasions. "I'm sure, and you will not waste time asking me any more stupid questions. Get out of the vehicle and don't get in my way. I'm calling the Smith County Sheriff's Office and you're sealing off the crime scene." He pointed with his flashlight. "Follow the blood from here to the bottom of the stairway. Don't step in it, and don't touch the cell phone at the base of the stairs."

"Yes, sir. Anything else?"

"Are you working alone?"

"There's two more. One's an off-duty Tyler cop."

"Get him here."

"She's a her."

Fen didn't respond to the clumsy use of pronouns. Instead, he entered the patrol vehicle, shut the door, and placed the radio call.

The dispatcher needed no further convincing that the call was legitimate after Fen identified himself as a former sheriff and a ten-year veteran with the highway patrol. Out of habit, he used the Texas 10-Code to identify the crimes. He also gave his exact location. As an afterthought, he told the dispatcher to call Detective Bobby Sealy and have him respond.

Fen stepped out of the vehicle and found guests lined up on the railing. His phone rang. Thelma's pinched voice sounded. "Is it Bailey?"

"Yeah."

"Is she hurt?"

"Yeah, but I don't think she's hurt bad."

"What else?"

"She's gone."

"Lord, have mercy." A whimper followed.

If it had been anyone else, Fen would have ended the call. What Thelma needed was more information and something to do. He drew a full breath. "I found Bailey's phone at the base of the stairs. There's a trail of blood from the stairs to the parking lot. The size of the drops and their distance apart tell me she's hurt, but not badly. You heard a scream, so that's a good sign, too. In the parking lot I found a large white zip tie and a wide area of smeared blood."

"Oh, Lord," said Thelma. "They tied her up and took her."

"Thelma," shouted Fen. "I need you to pull yourself together and do something for me." He paused. "Are you listening?"

She sucked in a breath. "Tell me what to do."

"Call Lou. Tell her everything I told you and for her to get here and start interviewing the people standing along the railing. We need a description of the vehicle they put Bailey in."

Thelma repeated the short version of her instructions. "Call Lou and tell her to get a description of the vehicle."

"And the assailant, and anything else they can remember."

A second resort patrol vehicle arrived and a female officer bailed out. She asked, "Sheriff Maguire?"

Fen didn't remember if he cut off the call to Thelma before he stuffed his phone into his shirt pocket.

Chapter Twenty-Four

The female resort security officer proved to be a City of Tyler veteran cop by the name of Lisa. Fen showed her the evidence of Bailey's abduction and told her he was involved in investigating the murder of Dale White. A single eyebrow rose to signify she understood this might not be a simple abduction.

"Isn't Bailey the cute college girl doing caricatures in the Activity Center?"

"Correct. I have reason to believe she was meeting a fraternity guy staying here. I don't know his name."

"Do you think he could have abducted her?"

"Not likely, but it needs to be checked."

"I'll handle it. The management prefers that we keep police interaction with the guests to a minimum. It won't take me long to find the person or persons you need. Do you want to talk to him?"

"Absolutely."

"I'll bring him to you."

It was a good place to start, but Fen knew this would be only the beginning of the search for Bailey.

A black and white Highway Patrol SUV arrived with lights activated but no siren. A wave of familiarity swept over Fen and he found a small measure of comfort in seeing the ubiquitous khaki uniform, gun belt, and cowboy hat worn by the broad-shouldered state trooper.

The conversation was all business and brief. The number of people on the balconies increased as a parade of emergency vehicles wailed their impending arrival. Fen noticed Lou on the lowest balcony. Fen pointed to her. "Do you see that woman coming from the far end of the building?"

"Yeah."

"She's with me. A professional reporter who will get good information out of people faster than any three cops in uniform."

The state trooper tore his gaze from Lou and fixed it on Fen. "I'll have her back and make sure she's allowed to work. We need a vehicle description, and fast."

He hustled away as the first sheriff's department officer arrived. His girth spoke of too many late-night stops at convenience stores. Fen gave instructions for him to go to the top floor and start on the far end to interview guests. He may have stereotyped the deputy, but all Fen could think about was gathering solid information as quickly as possible.

Two more Smith County Sheriff's Department vehicles came to an abrupt halt. A man sporting sergeant's chevrons on his sleeve and collar arrived. Fen once again explained the cause for raising the alarm and the status of the response. The latter took much less time. In fact, he spoke only a sentence when a police radio came to life with numbers identifying the broadcaster as a highway patrolman.

Fen cast his gaze to where Lou and the state trooper stood

holding the microphone of his radio. The description of a white Ford pickup truck followed, along with the approximate age of the truck and that it had damage to the tailgate.

Lou stood on the walkway and gave the thumbs-up sign for Fen to see. He returned the signal. Another clue, and this one substantially reduced the size of the haystack the police would look in.

The night dragged on and interviews continued but gleaned nothing additional. An unmarked car arrived, and Detective Sealy stepped out and surveyed the scene. He acknowledged Fen with a brief nod but directed his inquiries to the sergeant.

While they were talking, Lisa arrived with someone in the front seat. She took stock of the scene and backed up. Fen went to her car where only the driver's side window was down.

Fen asked, "Is this the guy?"

"Yeah. I'll get out and let you talk to him."

After trading places, Fen inspected the young man with great care. He wore a long-sleeve sweatshirt with a fraternity crest and Greek letters boldly displayed. Loose-fitting shorts covered muscular legs, while sandals were the footwear for the evening. The young man's chin was square; worry filled his eyes. Pinched lips produced a deep dimple in his left cheek.

Fen tried to balance the need for answers and putting the young man at ease. "You're not in trouble, but I need to know what you did tonight."

"You must be Fen Maguire."

A single nod confirmed the young man's guess.

"Bailey talked about you. Is she all right?"

"That's why all these cops are here. We're trying to find her, and you're going to help us."

"I'll do anything to help. I offered to walk her home, but she wanted to go by herself. I guess you know how independent she is."

Fen knew better than to get trapped into allowing a witness to direct an interview. "Let's start at the beginning. What's your name?"

"Jeremy. Uh... Jeremy Watters, sir."

"I see you're in a fraternity."

"Yes, sir. I'm the chapter's treasurer. They usually choose a finance or business major."

"Which is your major?"

"Both. I'll graduate next year but stay on for an MBA."

With the ice broken, Fen moved on. "Tell me about your night with Bailey."

Jeremy didn't hesitate. "It really started a couple of days ago. I was waiting to get my caricature done when two brothers got out of line with Bailey. I told them to knock it off."

"Did they?"

The words tumbled out. "Yeah, but not right away. I had to threaten them with fines." He looked down then back up. "They had a few shots of tequila before they came to pose. That nasty stuff changes people's personalities."

Jeremy's speech returned to a normal pace. "Anyway, Bailey thanked me and we talked while she sketched me. We sort of hit it off and I hung out in the Activity Center. She talked a lot about you and Thelma. She also mentioned a woman named Lou."

"Did she mention anyone else?"

He tilted his head. "Sam, Cory, and her roommate Wren."

"What did she say about Cory?"

"That he's a county cop and they've been dating for a while, but she's unsure about their future."

Fen detected no evasion or exaggeration from Jeremy, so he moved on. "Tell me about tonight. Be very specific."

"We agreed to meet at the activities center and share a pizza." He chuckled. "For such a small frame, that girl can pack away the meat lover's. She called it brain food."

"Keep going. Did you stay at the activities center?"

"Kind of. We went outside to the couches by the fire pits. She wanted to know about my business classes, and I was interested in her sketches and portraits."

"How long were you there?"

"I sort of lost track of time until she left me to walk home."

"Uh-huh," said Fen. "Tell me about that, and don't omit any details. I'll know if you do."

A nervous chuckle came from Jeremy. "She told me how you could read people and the one thing people should never do is try to slip a lie past you."

"That's good advice," said Fen in a somber tone.

He held up his hands. "I confess, Sheriff. I kissed her, and she kissed me back."

"And?"

"She said she needed to finish one thing before she started another. She wiped her mouth like something had soiled it and told me she had to get back to your condo. I tried to talk her into letting me walk with her or drive her, but she was already ten yards ahead of me, almost running."

"What time did you go your separate ways?"

He looked down at his watch. "I have a thing about numbers. I track steps, am never late for class, and I can tell you my bank balance two minutes after I wake up. The last time I saw Bailey was 11:23 p.m."

"Did you see anyone following her or waiting ahead?"

"I turned and went to my condo. There were a few people out, but everyone was walking either by twos or in larger groups."

"Thanks, Jeremy. I'll pass on what you told me. Don't be surprised if a detective follows up with you."

"I sure hope Bailey's all right. She's special."

"That she is," said Fen. "Sit tight."

Fen stepped out of the patrol car and walked to Lisa. "I don't think he's a suspect, but he was with Bailey until 11:23 p.m. She walked at a quick pace to the condo, most likely on a straight path."

"Did she come from the activities center?"

"Yeah. From the couches in front of the fire pits."

"We call them the kissing couches. There's no telling how many teens and tweens had their first kiss on those couches." She got back to the business at hand. "I'll time a quick walk from the couches to the stairway. The exercise will do me good, and it will verify the time of the abduction."

Fen threw a thumb over his shoulder. "And eliminate that young man as a suspect."

He glanced toward the car. "Why did you park away from the action?"

"There's someone here with a detective's badge who prefers interviewing in a closed room at the sheriff's office in Tyler. I see no need in ruining a college boy's spring break." She cast her gaze to the condos where Lou stood opposite Detective Sealy, looking like someone had glued her feet to the concrete walkway. Her posture was straight as a flagpole and both their voices seemed harsh, even from a distance.

"I see what you mean," said Fen. "Can you help Jeremy disappear while I save my team member from an unpleasant and unnecessary trip to Tyler?"

"It will be a pleasure, Sheriff."

Voices were reaching a crescendo when Fen arrived at the spot of the escalating disturbance. He pulled Lou by the arm and spun her to face him. Once again, he used his best Highway Patrolman's voice. "Go to my condo, Lou."

Her face shone like a ripe tomato. "This clown wants to arrest me without cause."

"I know he does, and he will if you don't go upstairs and let me handle this."

He spun to face Sealy. "As for you, back off. She's working under my supervision and found information that could be critical to finding the abducted young woman. If you have a beef, it's with me, not her."

Fen spun around again. "Lou. I need your help to find Bailey. Go upstairs and calm Thelma down. None of the officers here have time to listen to a lecture on freedom of the press."

If possible, Lou's face turned a deeper shade of red. She spun on her heel and took angry steps away.

Fen turned to face Sealy, who poked him in the chest with an index finger. "Now it's my turn."

That's all he said before Fen grabbed his finger and bent it back. "Do you know the definition of assault?" He didn't wait for an answer. "It's any malicious touching. If need be, I have a dozen witnesses who will testify that you poked me before I defended myself."

He bent the finger back a little more, which caused Sealy's knees to buckle.

"Stop. You'll break it."

"Not until you and I come to an understanding. Someone abducted a young woman tonight. The presence of blood tells me they've already harmed her. I made sure you received a phone call because you should lead the search for her. Instead, you're hassling a reporter who discovered critical information about the truck used to carry out the abduction. That reporter is a member of my team, as is the victim, Bailey Madison."

Fen released the finger. "Do your job and find Bailey. After you do, come find me."

"Wait," said Sealy. "What else do you know about the abduction?"

Fen leaned into Sealy and whispered, "There's a connection between Bailey's abduction and Dale White's murder."

"How are they connected?"

"Find Bailey and I might tell you."

Sealy proved to have more gumption than Fen gave him credit for.

"You need to tell me now," said Sealy while rubbing the feeling back into his finger.

Fen took a step toward the detective, who stepped back. "Listen, Sealy. The only other thing I can do tonight is save you from yourself."

"What's that supposed to mean?"

Fen pointed upward. "There's an award-winning reporter in my condo who's banging out a story about an arrogant detective who prematurely arrested a Marine Corps veteran for murder and is now botching the search for a nineteen-year-old college girl abducted from an upscale resort on Lake Palestine. I'm having a hard time deciding if I'm going to stop her from publishing the story or help her write it."

Sealy's Adam's apple bobbed up and down as Fen gave a parting shot. "Finding Bailey alive before dawn would go a long way in helping me decide what I'm going to do about that story."

Fen went upstairs to check on Thelma and Lou. He wasn't expecting to see game warden Tim Gladly waiting for him.

Chapter Twenty-Five

Tim waited for Fen to speak. Lou didn't wait. "Don't you ever do that to me again."

Fen ignored her and turned to Thelma. "This will be a long night for many people. The cops downstairs like coffee and snacks. Warm cookies would be wonderful. The same goes for the crime scene technicians who will be here soon."

"What about Bailey? Was that her scream I heard?"

"Didn't Lou tell you?"

Thelma responded with a shake of her head and said, "All she talked about was how mad she is at you and Detective Sealy." She pointed to Tim. "He tried to tell me, but Lou wouldn't shut up."

Fen hooked his right thumb in the front pocket of his jeans. "I'm making a rule that will stay in effect until we find Bailey. No raised voices or cussing." He paused. "Agreed?"

Thelma gave her head a firm nod. "I'll agree to anything if you tell me what's being done to get Bailey back."

Fen turned to Lou. She pouted but plopped into a chair at the dining table. "I'll agree for now."

"Good. Lou, you go first. Tell us what you learned from interviewing people on the balcony."

"Three people heard a scream."

"Four," said Thelma. "I heard it, too."

Lou took out a notebook. "Four people heard a scream, one gave a description of the truck, and one six-year-old boy told me he saw a man pushing a short person into an old truck. There was a sack over the person's head."

"A sack?"

"It was white, so it could have been a pillowcase."

Tim asked, "Two or four-door truck?"

"The boy said four. Another witness didn't come out of her condo until the truck was driving away. The lady wasn't sure if it had a back seat or not. All she remembered for sure was the dented tailgate."

Fen asked, "Was she sure it was a Ford truck?"

"Her husband only drives Fords. She could tell by the taillights."

Lou's desire to gather details outweighed her anger. "Fen, did you discover Bailey's movements tonight?"

"There's a Tyler city cop who moonlights as one of this resort's security guards. I recruited her to find the young man Bailey spent the evening with. His name is Jeremy Watters."

Fen gave details as Lou scribbled notes and Thelma wiped her hands on a full-length robe. Silence reigned until he spoke of the kiss. Thelma moaned and whispered, "That gal."

The story continued with Jeremy and Bailey parting company and her hot-footing it home. Well, almost home. He then described the blood and her phone.

Lou asked, "Was that Jeremy in the resort's patrol car?"

"Lisa brought him to me. We talked long enough for me to know he's not a suspect."

"Where is he now?" asked Thelma. "I'd like to speak to that young man about walking a young lady all the way to the door."

"He feels bad enough about what's happened to Bailey without you piling on," said Fen.

He moved on. "Before Lou asks, Lisa took Jeremy somewhere on the resort where Detective Sealy can't find him for several hours."

Lou's head jerked upward. "That's almost enough for me to forgive you."

"There's more that I'll tell you about later. I came close to breaking Sealy's finger. I don't take kindly to people poking me in the chest and wasting time."

Tim hid most of a smile behind his hand. He cleared his throat and turned his gaze to Fen. "I thought you might like to ride with me."

Thelma moved to the coffeepot and spoke over her shoulder. "I know what that means. You two will drive down every rutted road and pig trail until you find her. I'll fill a thermos and pack some munchies. I'm glad I bought a sleeve of disposable cups with lids."

Lou spoke next. "Can I come along?"

Tim looked at Fen, who said, "It's your call, but I owe her a favor."

Tim looked at Lou and nodded. "I'll have to move some things around in the back seat, and Thelma's right. Expect a bumpy ride."

Thelma ran from the kitchen to Fen's bedroom and came back with a pillow from his bed. "Take this with you. That arm won't heal if you don't start taking better care of it."

It wasn't long before the unlikely trio of a game warden, a retired sheriff with a broken arm, and a newspaper reporter were bouncing down dirt roads, checking out derelict cabins, abandoned trailer houses, houseboats, and boathouses. They also stopped on dirt roads and checked for fresh tire prints.

They happened upon an older model Ford pickup, backed between pine trees off a rutted road. Only the front bumper shone. Tim kept going until they crested a hill and he coasted to a stop. Fen spoke over his shoulder. "You wait here, Lou."

He didn't think she would, but it was the right thing to say.

After slipping through the woods, they came upon a white Ford four-door pickup. The mismatched tailgate looked dark while the rest of the truck shone clearly in the broken moonlight.

Tim approached the driver's side while Fen crept from the opposite side. No heads were visible, but audible low moans told a tale of at least one person inside the vehicle.

They waited until they were sure what was going on inside the truck. Tim tapped on the window with his flashlight.

Two heads appeared from inside the truck. Fen holstered his pistol after Tim hollered through the gap in a partially rolled-down window. "Texas Game Warden. You two get dressed."

Lou's voice came from several yards behind Fen. "That was disappointing."

"We're not finished," said Fen. "Stand on the other side of the truck and listen. Stay back at least three paces."

Lou did as directed. It wasn't long before the driver, a young man in desperate need of a comb or hairbrush, exited the truck and produced a driver's license.

Tim asked, "How old is the girl?"

"Nineteen, same as me."

"How long have you been here?"

"About two hours."

"Someone abducted a young woman the same age. You can

see the dirt road from here. How many vehicles have passed by?"

"Only two that I saw. I heard another about ten minutes ago."

"Describe the first two."

"I wasn't paying much attention."

The girl shouted from inside the cab of the truck. "There were three. The first was an older white Ford half-ton. It passed but didn't come back. The road dead ends about two miles from here. The second was a one-ton dually. It came from the opposite direction, headed back to the blacktop. The truck wasn't brand new but looked newer than the one that passed earlier. A jeep came next." She pointed. "You should find one or two empty beer cans where they stopped, turned around, and left."

Tim thrust the license into the driver's hand. "You two go home."

Fen was already walking fast toward the road. Tim kept up the pace, but Lou got off to a slow start.

They were all breathing heavily by the time they reached Tim's truck.

"What's the rush?" asked Lou.

"They changed trucks," said Fen. "Look for tracks leading into the woods."

High-beam headlights cut through the dark woods. Fen's eyes strained and shifted to look for tire tracks leading from the dirt road. He occasionally checked the woods for a glint from a bumper or windshield. The road rose and fell twice, but the only tracks were on the dirt road.

"There!" shouted Lou. "Back up."

Fen spun to see Lou pointing to the woods. He grabbed Tim's flashlight and clicked it on. What looked like an army surplus tarp covered the rear end of a pickup.

They exited the vehicle and ran toward the shape that didn't match the surroundings. Fen issued words of caution to Lou. "Touch nothing." For the third time in less than four hours, he drew his pistol. He went to the rear of the truck and used the barrel of his weapon to lift the tarp. Tim's flashlight illuminated a dented tailgate.

It was a victory, but a hollow one. They'd found the truck, but not the prize. Bloodstains on the back seat showed Bailey had been there, but where was she now?

Tim returned to his truck to use his computer to run the license plates to ascertain ownership. It came as no surprise when the computer reported the vehicle stolen. He then notified dispatch of the find and gave their exact location.

Fen called Detective Sealy, who answered with a curt, "I caught the radio traffic."

"Good. We'll wait here until you arrive."

Lou gave him a look that reminded him of a confused puppy. "Why'd you call that jerk?"

"Protocol. The abduction took place in Smith County. He's the Smith County detective in charge of the case. We're still in Smith County. He's responsible for this crime scene unless the sheriff says otherwise."

"What else? I've known you long enough to watch you do plenty of things that bent the rules."

Fen looked at the trees as a stray breeze moved the tops of the pines. He brought his gaze back down to her. "The phone call was a peace offering. I almost broke his finger. The call told him I'm sorry for doing that."

When Sealy arrived, Tim, Fen, and Lou left to look for a white, six-wheeled pickup truck. That narrowed the search to multiple thousands in the state.

At five twenty-five in the morning, nature called loud enough that Lou asked if they could stop at a convenience store. Tim pointed his game warden's pickup truck toward the nearest blacktop road.

Lou completed her mission with fresh coffee as a bonus. She settled into her seat as first light changed the eastern sky from indigo to blushing rose. The dispatcher called Tim's badge number. He replied with the same numbers. "Are you 10-8?"

"I am now."

A coded message came over the truck's radio. Fen opened his door and dumped a fresh cup of coffee.

"What's going on?" asked Lou.

Tim had the truck in gear and slung gravel. He turned on the emergency lights and activated the siren.

Fen buckled his seat belt and spoke over the sound. "A fisherman found Bailey. She's at the boat launch next to the campground where Talia Goldberg is staying."

Tim added, "And where Derrick McDonald has his boat and travel trailer."

Fen took his turn and spoke as if he were thinking out loud. "And all within sight of where the Neches flows into Lake Palestine."

Lou spoke about the obvious. "That's the location where Tran Wilks brought Dale White's body to shore?"

Fen and Tim glanced at each other but said nothing. Both knew there were too many coincidences.

<h1 style="text-align: center;">Chapter Twenty-Six</h1>

Fen pulled out his phone after Tim turned off the main road. Thelma answered before the phone completed its first ring. "This better be good news."

"We're almost to her. Come to the boat launch where you spied on Talia."

The call clicked off. Fen expected no less from Thelma. She'd demand to know the smallest details of the ordeal, but that would come later. For now, she'd think only about returning the chick to the nest.

Tim brought the truck to a sudden, controlled stop as he reached for the radio's microphone. Fen had his door open and seat belt off before the tires stopped rolling. Two faces turned his way. The one nearest him belonged to Derrick McDonald. The second face he'd know anywhere, even caked in dried blood as it was now.

Fen hollered toward Tim's truck. "Tell the ambulance to step it up."

Bailey ran limping toward him. They hugged each other with an intensity that he felt throughout his body. Then, in typical Bailey fashion, she pushed him away. "What took you so long?"

He ignored the complaint. "How bad are you hurt?"

"Not bad. A bloody nose, and I lost one of my favorite tennis shoes."

Fen moved in for a closer look. "It's more than a simple bloody nose."

Before he could give a layman's diagnosis, Derrick spoke. "I told her it's broken. Saw plenty of them in the corps. Those knuckleheads were always testing to see who the top dog was."

Bailey didn't like the diagnosis. "If it's broken, that guy's going to get double for his trouble." She stomped her remaining tennis shoe and looked to the heavens. "Weren't the burn scars on my hand enough? Now I have to go through life with a crooked nose. I'll probably snore like a pig when I sleep."

Lou arrived with her phone out, taking pictures as she came. She spoke as she switched a setting to film the event for use on television. "How did you get away?"

"He pulled me out and drove off in a hurry."

"Did your assailant keep you tied and wearing that pillowcase over your head?" She pointed to a bloody cloth on the ground.

"Yeah. I was on the ground until that nice man cut me loose."

"Do you know the man who attacked you?"

"No. He put the pillowcase over my head. I didn't see him."

"Did you struggle?"

"I tried, but he had me on the ground before I could react. He was trying to roll me over on my back. I screamed like crazy and brought a knee up as hard and fast as I could. I think it hit home, if you know what I mean. I heard a loud 'OOF'. The next thing I know, I'm being dragged, with my hands behind my back, seeing white spots. We stopped, and he bound my ankles. That's when the pain hit me. Blood gushed from my nose, soaking the pillowcase." She pointed.

Fen put a hand on Lou's shoulder and whispered in her ear. "That's enough for now."

Lou turned to face him with a look of challenge in her eyes. He returned a look that didn't invite discussion.

Tim arrived with a silver emergency blanket and placed it around Bailey's shoulders. She gave him a nod of thanks.

Fen was so fixed on Bailey that he didn't see Talia Goldberg until she came to a stop. She pulled the headlamp off and asked, "What's going on?"

Fen and Tim took steps toward the woman decked out in running gear. Fen asked, "Out for your morning run?"

"Every day," she replied as she pointed to Derrick McDonald. "It looks like you caught him before he killed someone else. Did he beat this poor girl?"

Tim took over. "Ma'am, this is a crime scene. I need you to move to the other side of my truck and wait for other officers to arrive."

She gave him a wicked stare. "I'll move farther than the other side of your truck. Tell the detective I'll be in my motorhome until nine thirty. After that, I'm leaving for Tyler."

"With Destiny?" asked Fen.

"Not today. She said there was a big commotion at the resort last night and she didn't sleep well."

Talia's long legs put an amazing amount of distance between the boat launch and the tin hut with the dangling clipboard in a short amount of time.

Fen walked Derrick to the other side of Tim's truck. "I don't have time to explain, but you have to face Detective Sealy alone today. Call your attorney and follow his instructions."

"He'll tell me to say nothing, which is what I'd do anyway."

He looked at the lake and calmed himself. "Am I going back to jail?"

"I don't know, but I expect he'll take you in for questioning. Everything will turn out all right if you do what your lawyer tells you to do."

The scream of distant sirens announced the impending arrival of other first responders. Fen needed to act fast. He motioned for Lou and Tim to rejoin him around Bailey.

Fen cast his gaze to Bailey first. "The ambulance and cops will be here soon. I want you on the ground when they get here. Pretend you're still fuzzy-headed from getting knocked out. Don't act normal until you're well on the way to the hospital."

"Why?" asked Bailey.

"Do you want to answer questions from a detective for hours or go get cleaned up, get your nose straightened, and spend the day in a clean hospital bed?"

Lou added, "Your face and hair are a real mess. It sounds to me like you received a concussion, the same as Fen."

Bailey responded by placing her hand to her head. "I have a pounding headache and my nose hurts like crazy. Something for the pain sounds good."

"Good girl," said Fen. "Thelma's on her way. She and Lou will follow the ambulance to the hospital. They'll take you to Tyler and run all kinds of tests on you. Expect it to hurt when they straighten your nose. Lou will get more details from you about everything that happened last night. Thelma will demand you go home to our ranch with her when you're released. That will be your choice."

"There's no way I'm leaving you here when all I have is a broken nose. You're in worse shape than I am. I'll be back in the condo tomorrow night."

Fen looked at Tim. "Can I bum a ride back to the resort with you?"

"Sure. You can catch some sleep. I'll go home and come back in four hours."

"Make it six hours. I'm not used to staying out all night. The life of a retired sheriff and artist has made me soft."

"Six hours it is. I'm interested in how this ends."

"I'm making everything up as I go."

"He's lying," said Bailey. "This is when he really starts thinking." She moved to a grassy spot, spread out the emergency blanket, and rolled herself into it until she looked like a burrito covered with aluminum foil.

Detective Sealy's car came into view, followed by an ambulance and Fen's truck.

Sealy surveyed the scene after climbing out of his unmarked car. As expected, he approached the game warden's truck and directed his questions to Tim. "Why is Derrick McDonald here?"

Tim pointed to Bailey. "He was here when we arrived. Claims he found the victim of last night's abduction when he came to put his boat in."

The response caused Sealy to quirk a smile and respond with sarcasm. "That's interesting. Why was he out so early?"

Tim cast his gaze to Derrick's boat that was still on its trailer. "He said he wanted to fish at first light."

"I can think of a few other things he might be up to."

Fen let the innuendo pass.

Sealy then asked, "Anyone else see anything?"

Fen answered this one. "Talia Goldberg was out taking her morning run and stopped by."

Sealy scanned the area. "Why isn't she here?"

Tim answered, "I told her where to stand and to wait for other officers to arrive. She said she was going home and ran off. I had to secure the area."

Fen lifted his cast, but only an inch or two. "There's no way

I could catch her. She looked like a deer running toward her motorhome. She told us she'll be there until nine thirty. After that, she's going to Tyler. You can probably find her at the cross-training gym."

"Is that all?"

"She wanted Derrick arrested. She still thinks he killed her husband."

Sealy ground his teeth. "What about the girl? What did she tell you?"

By this time, ambulance attendants and Thelma hovered over Bailey while Lou had maneuvered to a spot where she could film Sealy's interaction with Fen and Tim.

Sealy asked, "Did you talk to the girl?"

"Not much," said Fen, but he didn't continue.

"Well? What did she say?"

Fen gave the detective a stare that could freeze water. "We've been talking for several minutes and you haven't asked either of us about Bailey's injuries." He stared harder. "By the way, her name is Bailey Madison, not 'the girl.' If you haven't figured it out yet, she's very much like a daughter to me."

The mini lecture hit home and Sealy's head dipped. "Sorry. I hope her injuries aren't bad."

Fen kept a stiff posture. "They're bad enough. My guess is she has a broken nose and suffered a concussion, but I'm no doctor."

Fen let out a huff of disgust. "Before you ask, she's fully clothed, except for a missing shoe. Bailey didn't give a description of her assailant." He pointed with a finger sticking out of his cast. "There's a blood-stained pillowcase in the parking lot. You'll want that. I also noticed a couple of zip ties."

"Did you cut them off?"

"No."

"Did McDonald?"

"Why don't you ask him?"

"I intend to ask him all kinds of questions."

"Good. The way I'm feeling now, I want the guy who did this to Bailey to grow old in prison."

A fire truck and additional police vehicles arrived.

Sealy took a quick glance at where Bailey lay then turned to go to where Derrick McDonald stood talking to a deputy.

Fen drew close to Tim. "Turn the truck around and get ready to leave. I won't be long." He turned and walked toward the first responders attending to Bailey. A quick movement of his head was all it took for Lou to understand that he wanted her to follow. Out of earshot, he filled her in then said, "I'd like you to take Thelma to the hospital and stay with her."

Lou nodded and said, "Of course."

Fen said, "Thanks." He looked toward Bailey lying on the ground. Thelma was on her knees beside Bailey, holding her hand and whispering something meant for her ears only.

An ambulance attendant looked up with pleading eyes. "Can you help us? This woman won't move, and we need to get the patient on the gurney and into the ambulance."

"Thelma," said Fen. He had to repeat her name three times and tug on her arm with his good hand before the words got through. "Move away from her. These people will take Bailey to the hospital. You and Lou will follow the ambulance."

"Huh?"

"I said, Lou will drive my truck and you're going with her to the hospital. I want you to take care of Bailey but not get in the way of doctors or nurses."

"Aren't you going?"

"Bailey needs you, and I need to find out who did this to our girl."

Lou put an arm around Thelma. "I won't let the ambulance get out of sight."

Thelma issued a nod of surrender. Fen took this to mean that the break-in period for his truck's engine was over. On second thought, he was sure Thelma had already taken care of exceeding fifty-five with her trip from the condo to the boat launch.

Fen waited until firefighters and the ambulance attendants placed Bailey on the mechanical gurney before he approached her. "If you can hear me, I'll go to the hospital if you want me to."

She responded with a mischievous wink of one eye.

He let go of her hand and watched as they loaded her into the ambulance.

Lou walked up to him and handed him her keys. "You might need my car. There's no telling where Bailey's truck keys are."

He nodded his thanks then walked toward Tim Gladly's truck. Detective Sealy was placing Derrick McDonald in the back seat of his car as they drove past.

Tim shot Fen a quick glance. "Do you know what you're going to do next?"

"Yeah," said Fen as the need for sleep hit him. "I'm going to bed for six hours, get up, drink strong coffee, paint, and hope divine revelation of what to do next comes calling."

"In other words, you'll make things up as you go."

"I call it waiting for creative inspiration."

Chapter Twenty-Seven

Fen grumbled a complaint as he swung his legs off the bed. He checked the clock on the nightstand and did the math; he'd slept a little over four hours. His gaze shifted to the west-facing window of his bedroom and discovered the thief who'd stolen two hours of sleep. It was the curtains he'd failed to close before he collapsed onto the fluffy duvet, fully dressed except for his boots.

He ran his tongue over his teeth and realized taking off his clothes wasn't the only thing he'd omitted in his pre-slumber routine. Last night's coffee and Thelma's peanut-butter cookies formed a film that would require extensive brushing to remove, followed by mouthwash.

He remembered to cover his cast but failed to take care not to shampoo his hair until the feel of stitches on his fingertips reminded him. He threw caution to the wind and completed the task, making sure not to scrub the sensitive line on his scalp. The absence of blood on a white towel told him the wound had all but healed.

His dirty clothes joined a growing pile in the closet, and he dressed for a new day, even though it was mid-afternoon. Entering the living room, he stopped to admire his two sketches depicting Destiny Roe scaling a distant cliff. The first rectangle was tall, and the second was wide.

He stood back to view from a different perspective and thought about eliminating both from consideration for a finished work. Both sketches showed the climber as little more than an unrecognizable smudge. Destiny was right to choose only Bailey's. Or were the drawings trying to tell him something?

After a quick trip into Bailey's room, he returned with the close-up sketch of Destiny and another easel. He lined up the third drawing with the other two. He took one halting step at a time to view the sketches from various angles. His focus increased until he lost track of time. The sketches were trying to tell him something, but it was like trying to read a book through a sheet of wax paper.

The trilling of his phone broke the spell. He slipped it from his shirt pocket, viewed the screen, and asked, "How's Bailey?"

Lou answered his question with one of her own. "Did I wake you?"

"You missed me snoring by almost an hour."

"That's what Bailey and Thelma are doing. All the tests on Bailey came back normal. Thelma threw a fit when a resident said he'd reset Bailey's nose. She insisted on a specialist."

"Good for her. Are they keeping her overnight?"

"Yeah. We'll try to be back by noon tomorrow, but you know how long discharging takes."

"You'll be back by noon."

"How can you be so sure?"

"Thelma."

"Don't say another word. You're right."

Fen moved on. "Did you talk to Bailey alone?"

"I had to wait until Thelma made a trip to the hospital kitchen and demanded a special tray for Bailey. The floor nurse made the mistake of telling Thelma that lunch was over and Bailey could have a protein drink or wait for the evening meal."

A snicker escaped from Fen, but he covered it by asking. "What did Bailey say about the assault?"

"Not much. The pillowcase stayed on her head the whole time. The zip ties cut into her wrists and ankles a little. I'm sure she'll have some bruising. Other than punching her hard enough to break her nose, there were no other acts of violence. The guy never said a word, made a phone call, or spoke to anyone else."

"A one-man job?" asked Fen.

"Yeah. No smells other than fish."

"No cologne, oil, gasoline, or diesel?"

"Just fish. Not overpowering, but distinct."

Fen was on the verge of concluding that Bailey wouldn't provide anything else when Lou continued, "Bailey got a peek at the shoes the man was wearing. She described them as, and I quote, 'Old, nasty, Converse high tops. No visible socks.'"

"That's not much to go on," said Fen with disappointment seasoning his words.

"You've solved crimes with less," countered Lou. "All you have to do is find a man who smells of fish and stinky feet."

Fen didn't laugh. "Has Detective Sealy shown up yet?"

"Not yet. How do you want us to handle him?"

"He'll want full access to Bailey without an audience. Do whatever is necessary to get Thelma out of the room. Sealy will be tired, frustrated, and in no mood to put up with an overprotective guard dog."

"One more thing," said Lou. "I sold the story of Bailey's abduction and release."

"Does that include the video of Sealy?"

"Everything. It's still a local story and won't show on television until this evening."

"That may help the investigation, but not you. Be careful. I don't want to post bail for you or Thelma."

"Speak of the devil," said Lou. "He's coming down the hall, and he isn't smiling."

The call ended.

Game Warden Tim Gladly arrived wearing a fresh uniform, but the dark crescents under his eyes told a story of not enough sleep. He started off with an apology. "Sorry I'm late."

Fen asked, "Coffee?"

"Yuk."

"Me, too. I thought about using a pressure washer on my teeth when I woke up from my nap."

"At least you got a nap."

"What happened?"

"The usual. It started with a guy running from another game warden on Lake Palestine. He had a new bass boat and a motor that could outrun anything on this lake. I got the call after I left here and went to a marina on the south end of the lake, hoping he'd pass by or put in there. No luck. They called off the search in the early afternoon, just in time for the usual."

"And what's the usual around here?"

"Spring break, alcohol, girls in skimpy bathing suits, and guys with more testosterone than brains. A fight broke out at the marina when one character thought it would be a good idea to pull the string on a girl's string bikini. For a girl who wasn't hiding much, she sure got upset about showing a little more."

Tim rubbed his eyes. "I went home, showered, changed into a fresh uniform, kissed the wife goodbye, and here I am."

Fen pointed at the shadow of whiskers on Tim's face. "You missed a spot shaving."

"I missed 'em all. The world's going to take me as I am tonight."

"You'd better sit down before you fall down," said Fen as he pointed to the couch.

"I'll take a chair. That couch looks too inviting. What do you have planned for the evening's entertainment?"

"An interview with Tran Wilks. He should be here any minute."

Tim settled into the chair. "I thought you cleared Tran as a suspect."

Fen gave his head a nod. "He and Derrick McDonald are alike in one respect. Detectives in both Henderson and Smith counties want them in jail, but for different reasons. One's an overprotective father and the other doesn't understand how complicated this case is. For now, I don't want Tran to think he's all the way off the hook and swimming free."

"It shouldn't surprise anyone that Tran and April got together when she worked as a dispatcher. Some people just look like they belong together."

Fen's thoughts turned to his former wife. "That's what everyone said about me and Sally."

Instead of reacting with words of sympathy, Tim yawned, which was best for Fen. This wasn't the right time to take a sentimental trip down the tunnel of lost love.

Tim followed his yawn with, "I don't know what you're up to with Tran, but you'll have to do most of the talking. All I can think about is clean sheets and a soft pillow."

"He won't be here for another hour. Why don't you stretch out on the couch so you can dream of your nice, warm bed?"

"I don't mind if I do."

Fen spent the next hour listening to Tim snore while he stared at the trio of sketches on easels. He hoped to recapture the message that the muse had tried to give him earlier. He concluded muses were flighty things. They came and left on their own schedule.

Chapter Twenty-Eight

Fen gave Tim a five-minute warning that Tran should arrive at any time. This was enough for the game warden to retreat to the bathroom, splash his face with cold water, and return wearing his gun belt.

"Do you feel any better?"

"Good enough for a couple more hours. It's amazing what an hour's rest can do."

A triplet of knocks on the door sounded. Fen pulled the door open as Tran jerked a baseball cap from a mound of thick hair. "Are you Sheriff Maguire?"

"Come in, Tran. Bailey told me about your fishing trip."

He spoke as he walked. "Wasn't much of a fishing trip. Is she here?"

"We'll talk about that in a few minutes. First, say hello to Tim Gladly."

"We go back a long time," said Tim. "Tran never gave me a moment's trouble. He always makes sure his customers have a valid fishing license and I've never issued him a citation."

Tran followed Fen's hand motion and sat on the couch,

running nervous fingers along the bill of his hat. He waited without speaking.

Fen took mercy and said, "You asked about Bailey. She's in the hospital."

"Hospital? What happened to her?"

"Someone abducted her last night."

Fen and Tim didn't have to wait long for a response. "Is she all right?"

It was the right question to ask, so Fen gave him the answer. "They broke her nose and there are some deep scratches."

Tran swallowed hard. "I hope you don't think I had anything to do with it."

Tim played along. "We're eliminating suspects. Where were you last night?"

His eyes shifted the way people sometimes do when trying to formulate answers. Sometimes the answers are true, sometimes not. His gaze moved to the hat in his hands and his voice dipped. "I wasn't where I was supposed to be." His head came up. "That's not exactly true. I misspoke. I was where I should have been, but—"

Fen finished the sentence for him. "But you weren't alone?"

He continued to examine his hat. "No, sir, I wasn't alone."

Fen and Tim exchanged glances before Fen continued. "Where did April tell her father she was going?"

Tran's head jerked up. "Please don't tell him. He'll shoot me, cut me up, and use the parts to bait a trotline."

Fen kept a straight face, even though Tim had to get up and get a glass of water. The plea from the young man might have been hyperbolic, but the fear was real.

"Sometimes," said Fen. "we do the wrong thing, and it still works out to our benefit. Can you get April on the phone?"

"Uh-huh. I got a burner phone I use for text messages. Sometimes her dad gets close enough to hear the voice of whoever she's talking to. If it isn't a female, he demands to talk to them."

Fen could only imagine what Bailey would say if he did that to her. He refocused. "Send her a text. Tell her to go somewhere private and call you."

"We have a code for that."

Tim returned while Tran punched in a message and sent the text. Fen held out his hand, gave Tran a no-nonsense stare, and received the phone. He then gave it to Tim. "You know her."

It took a long silent minute, but the phone rang, and Tim leaned back in his chair. "April, this is Tim Gladly. That's right, the game warden. A sheriff friend and I are here with Tran... No. He's not in trouble, but there's something we need to clear up so he stays out of trouble. Someone assaulted a young lady last night at the resort on Lake Palestine... No, not that kind of assault, even though they broke her nose... No. We don't have a suspect in custody yet. Earlier this week, Tran was the fishing guide for the girl who's in the hospital... No, we don't think he did it, but we need to rule him out. Did you stay home last night?"

Fen hoped she'd say no.

"What time was that?"

The back-and-forth conversation went on for another minute or two before Tim thanked her, cut the call off, and handed the phone back to Tran. "Where were you and April last night?"

Fen knew Tim had received the answer to that question from April.

"A bunch of the people from April's class are home from college. They had a party at a lake cabin. It broke up about two in the morning. I went home and April stayed with her best friend."

Tim turned to Fen. "That's the same thing April said."

Fen slapped his good hand on his knee. "That's one problem out of the way. Let's see if we can be more productive than we've been up to now."

It was as if the muse returned and whispered in Fen's ear that he should focus on the big picture first. He didn't know what it meant, but he felt the need to rearrange the sketches on the easels. "Don't pay any attention to me or what I'm doing. I'll ask you more questions in a minute."

After moving the views to the left and Bailey's close-up to the right, he focused on his two sketches. Something still didn't seem right. He took the wide scene and moved it to the left of the tall one. A shock, something like placing a small battery on your tongue, shot through him.

"I've been looking at the crimes all wrong," said Fen.

Tim and Tran looked at each other, waiting in silence for him to make sense.

"Tim, let's switch up the order of the crimes you've worked," said Fen. "What's the most recent?"

Tim chuckled. "I'd like to get my hands on the guy who outran the game wardens and went somewhere we couldn't find him."

"That's easy," said Tran. "It was Shane Wesley in that new Ranger with the 225 Mercury. He's only taken it out a few times."

Tim sat erect but said nothing. Fen knew that didn't mean he hadn't firmly implanted the mental note in his brain.

Fen asked, "It sounds like you don't much care for Mr. Wesley. Why not?"

Tran studied his hat again. "It's nothing I can prove." He looked up with a flash of anger coming from the otherwise docile young man. "He's the reason I get checked so often by game wardens while I'm on the water and by cops when I'm on the road. Everyone thinks I'm a poacher, a menace to wildlife management, and the Redneck Romeo. It's all because of Shane Wesley. He blames his illegal activity on me."

"How?" asked Tim.

"The most recent thing he did was place my name on his trot lines. He baited some hooks with fingerling bass. I took binoculars with me that day and watched him do it."

Tim and Tran kept talking about other instances when Shane Wesley played fast and loose with fish and wildlife laws and other people's reputations. Tran wasn't his only target, but he was the best guide on the lake, which made him the biggest target.

When the trading of notes ended, Fen stood. "Tran, is there any way you can get out of your morning session tomorrow?"

He grimaced. "Not really, but my late afternoon session is only for three hours. The days are getting longer, so I have early afternoon open."

Fen turned to Tim. "Can you join us?"

"Will we be trying to catch men or fish?"

"Something better than either of those. We'll be fishing for evidence."

"Count me in."

Chapter Twenty-Nine

Fen was hoping to sleep long enough that he wouldn't see the sun rise. The trilling of his phone and a look at the clock on his nightstand dashed that hope. He croaked out his name and waited for a response.

"It's Talia. I need you to come to my motorhome right away."

"Why? What is it?"

"Someone's trying to frame me for what happened to your daughter."

Fen did not correct the misunderstanding about the relationship. "Did you find something?"

"Yes. Come as soon as you can." The call cut off.

He blinked as the light went on and he saw Sally's photo. He picked it up and said, "I was waiting for something like this to happen."

He placed the framed photo back on the nightstand and dressed as fast as the cast on his arm allowed. Out the door he went, swishing mouthwash until he reached Lou's car in the parking lot, where he left a puddle of minty-scented liquid.

He couldn't remember the last time he drove something as small as a Toyota Camry, but it felt as if he were sitting only inches above the pavement. The pre-dawn traffic was non-existent, so he pushed the car up to eighty after turning onto the main road. In less than ten minutes, he pulled into Talia's driveway.

She greeted him outside wearing her running gear, including her headlamp. She reached for a switch and a white LED light came alive, shining with unexpected brightness.

"It's inside Dale's boat," she said as she walked to a cobalt-blue bass boat. It looked like a twin to the one Lou had described after her miserable fishing trip with Shane Wesley.

The headlamp's beam bounced and swayed until Talia stopped by the rear of the boat and fixed it on the back deck. "There it is. I haven't touched it."

Fen sucked in a full breath. "It's Bailey's, all right." He moved in for a closer look. "Bloodstains, just like the other shoe."

He reached into his pocket, took out his phone, and placed a call. A groggy voice answered with a single word, "Yeah."

"It's Fen Maguire. Let me know when you're awake enough to pay attention. It's important."

"It had better be."

"I'm at Talia Goldberg's motorhome. I'm looking at Bailey's missing cross-training shoe. There are bloodstains on it, just like the other one."

"Why am I not hearing about this from Talia or dispatch?"

"You can ask her when you get here."

"I'm on my way."

Fen returned his phone to his pocket and turned to Talia. "It will take Detective Sealy a while to get here. I wouldn't turn down a cup of coffee while we wait."

"Was it necessary to call that incompetent man?"

Fen let loose an uncovered yawn. "I take my coffee black, hot, and strong. You can tell me all about finding the shoe when you get back. I can't leave the evidence unguarded."

He snapped his windbreaker together as a shiver gave evidence that he was entering the coolest time of day, the moments before and after first light.

Thoughts shifted from the chill and dampness of the air to the unexpected discovery of Bailey's shoe. Who could have placed such a vital piece of evidence in such an obvious place? Why not throw it away? Any fool would have wrapped it in something and thrown it in the trash. Since landfills rarely reveal their secrets, this seemed like a deliberate plant. Was someone trying to frame Talia? If so, they'd done a lousy job of it.

The stars shone brightly on this cloudless early morning. Fen stared at the heavens. His thoughts shifted to the afternoon's appointment with the game warden and the love-struck fishing guide. How different that would be. This morning, evidence of one crime found him. This afternoon, he'd be searching for evidence of a different crime. He stood there thinking, waiting for first light to bring clarity to Bailey's abduction. This afternoon, he'd have bright sunlight, but would it be enough to solve a murder? Two very different crimes. Were they linked? His gut shouted, yes!

One thing was for sure: He felt fully alive, even without the aid of caffeine. Still, a nice hot cup of morning mud wouldn't hurt a thing.

Talia delivered a steaming mug of excellent coffee. She seemed to read his mind. "I don't drink the stuff, but Dale was a coffee snob. He tasted coffees from all over the world until he settled on a special blend that mixed beans from three different islands. He hired a man with an ancient roasting machine to prepare the beans to his exact specifications."

She turned toward the motorhome. "If you want the beans, there are boxes of them in the storage compartment underneath."

"I'll take you up on that," said Fen as he inhaled the heady aroma. He took a small sip, then asked, "Who was the first person that came to mind when you found the shoe this morning?"

"Derrick McDonald," said Talia without hesitation.

"Any others?"

Talia shook her head. "It all fits together like a puzzle. Derrick hated Dale for taking what he thought was his campsite."

Fen countered with, "You have to admit, Dale did sort of pull a fast one on Derrick."

"Dale said that's how things work in the world of business. The owner didn't have to agree to Dale's offer."

"True," said Fen.

Talia had more to say. "It's also true that Derrick McDonald is a grief-stricken former Marine. A violent man more than capable of killing."

Fen remained silent, waiting for more. None came, so he asked, "How does that explain Bailey's shoe in your boat?"

She corrected him. "That's my late husband's boat. I've never been in it." She took a full breath. "As for the girl's shoe in the boat, he put it there to point guilt at someone other than himself. He could have easily thrown it away, but he needed something to distract you and that clown of a detective." She paused. "I'm sure you've noticed, but Detective Sealy's not the sharpest knife in the drawer."

Fen nodded, not to agree with her, but to relay that he understood her point. He drained the last of the coffee and looked sadly at the bottom of his cup. Detective Sealy drove up as Talia climbed the steps into her motorhome. He spoke loud enough for her to hear. "Did you make enough for two?"

"There's plenty. Do you know how he takes his?"

"Same as me. Black, hot, and strong."

Sealy spoke with an accusatory tone as he approached Fen. "Did you send her inside?"

"Yeah," said Fen. "She's bringing us coffee. You didn't sound very chipper this morning. Any objections?"

"No," came the response wrapped in a meeker voice. "Thanks. Where's the evidence you called me about?"

"Over here, in the boat. You'll need a flashlight."

Talia's voice came from the doorway. "I have my headlamp. Detective Sealy, come get your coffee." She handed over his mug before stepping down.

She led the way to where Fen stood. He took his coffee and backed away. After reenacting the scene of finding the shoe, Talia repeated her accusation of Derrick McDonald while Fen savored his second cup of coffee. If anything, she sounded more certain with Sealy than she had the first time.

The detective nodded at all the right times, encouraging her to continue. He then asked a few questions related to the possibility of her hearing or seeing anyone around her campsite between midnight and the present time. The answer was a simple no.

Sealy then patted the pockets of his jacket. Fen handed him a pair of ultra-thin gloves and said, "Sorry, I didn't bring an evidence bag with me."

"I'll get one out of my car."

Talia leaned into Fen and whispered after the detective opened the car's trunk. "What happens now?"

"He'll take pictures then bag and tag the shoe. After that, there's two things he may do. The first option is he'll go inside with you and get a formal statement. The second is he'll tell you to go inside while he and I go talk to Derrick McDonald."

"Will you arrest him?"

"I won't, but he'll either arrest Derrick or detain him for further questioning." A thought came to Fen. "One of us will ask Derrick to agree to a search of his property."

"What if he doesn't agree?"

"He'll apply for a search warrant. Your statement along with Derrick finding Bailey and cutting off the zip ties, there's plenty for a search warrant."

"What do you expect to find?"

Fen wiggled his eyebrows. "That's what's fun about this line of work. You never know what you'll find."

Sealy returned, did everything Fen predicted he would, and told Talia he'd be back later that day to take a statement from her. She asked if she could stop by his office after her cross-training workout. "It will save you time," she added.

"That's even better," said Sealy.

Fen followed Sealy to Derrick McDonald's travel trailer. First light had come and gone by this time and sunlight shone through the pines to the east.

Derrick was sitting in a lawn chair, balancing a coffee mug on his leg, when they arrived. Sealy took the lead. "I guess you know why we're here."

"It probably has something to do with me finding that girl in the parking lot yesterday."

"When did you get there?"

"Early-thirty."

"Can you be more specific?"

"Zero-five-twenty-two hours."

"Uh-huh. Someone abducted her the night before."

"The bloody pillowcase and zip ties gave me a clue that's

what happened, which is why I called the sheriff's department."

"Had you ever seen her before?"

"I'm not sure."

"Either you did, or you didn't."

"Like I said, I'm not sure. She looked a lot different with blood all over her face and hair. If it's the same girl, I saw her fishing with Tran Wilks several days ago."

Sealy looked at Fen for confirmation. He gave his head a nod. "I paid for Bailey to go on a guided fishing trip with Tran."

Sealy moved on. "Where's the knife you used to cut off the zip ties?"

Derrick pointed to a leather case on his belt. "Right here."

Sealy's gaze shifted to the home on wheels and back to Derrick. "We can do this the easy way or the hard way. You can either give me permission to search your truck, boat, and trailer, or I'll detain you until I get a warrant."

"You already searched and found nothing."

"That was before I suspected you of being involved in the girl's abduction. You admitted to recognizing her and you were alone when you claim you found her. There's also additional evidence found this morning that could implicate you."

Derrick looked at Fen with pleading eyes. "Can he do this to me again?"

Fen nodded.

Derrick stood, unlatched his belt, slid off the leather case, and tossed it to the ground at Sealy's feet. "I do not give you permission to search my home, truck, or property." He walked to Sealy's car and placed his hands on the hood. "If you don't mind, read me my rights so I can tell you I refuse to say anything more without having my attorney present."

Fen watched as Sealy searched Derrick, handcuffed him, and placed him in his car. He gave 50-50 odds that the eventual search of Derrick's truck, boat, or trailer would yield something useful. Perhaps Talia Goldberg wasn't the only person to receive something of Bailey's.

Sealy rounded the hood of his car. Fen blocked his path. "Did you search the truck used to abduct Bailey?"

"Yeah."

"Did you find anything that belonged to her in it?"

"No. The truck was unusually clean. All the paperwork was in the glove compartment, and it belonged to the truck's owner."

Fen thanked him and went to Lou's car. Between the two cups of strong coffee and the flood of new information, his brain was firing on all cylinders.

Chapter Thirty

Fen made his way to the main highway and pointed Lou's car toward Tyler, a city affectionately known as the Rose Capital of Texas. Before going to her room, he took the time to make a stop in the hospital's gift shop to get something for Bailey to bring her a little cheer. A delicate chain with a sterling silver rose seemed an appropriate gift. He bought a single long-stem red rose to accompany it.

He navigated the maze of rooms and arrived to find Thelma pushing Bailey's over-the-bed table away from her. It contained the remnants of the hospital's version of a healthy breakfast. White tape covered the bridge of her nose and she was well on her way to looking like a raccoon with dark bruises spread out underneath both eyes. The corners of her mouth pulled up when she saw him.

Thelma took one look at him and said, "You shouldn't be driving."

"It beats walking," said Fen. He took Bailey's hand. "How are you feeling today?"

"Sore, tired, and ready to leave." She wasted no time. "What's the latest on the case? What did you do yesterday?"

Before he could answer, Lou walked through the door. "Well, look who showed up. I hope you didn't wreck my car."

"It's all in one piece and I didn't drive it over eighty."

Lou gave him a sideways look, unsure if he was joking or not. "If you drove eighty, it was for a good reason. Let's have it."

"Not until I hear if they're releasing Bailey today."

Nurse Thelma had the answer. "They said it would be later this morning."

Fen turned back to Bailey. "Do you feel well enough to go back to the condo?"

"I was well enough yesterday after the doctor straightened my snoz. He said it will look normal after it heals."

"Do you want to help me this afternoon?"

Thelma gave him a look and a wag of her head. "The only thing Bailey's doing for the next few days is rest and eat food that's good for her. There's no way the eggs they served her this morning came out of a real hen."

Bailey ignored her. "What are we doing?"

"We're looking for the boat used in the murder."

Lou perked up. "Do you know where to look?"

"I know someone who does." He paused. "At least I think he can help us."

"Who?" asked Bailey and Lou at the same time.

"Tran Wilks. Tim Gladly and I made arrangements last night to meet him after lunch."

Fen reached into his pocket, pulled out his phone, and opened it. "Here's a recording of what I was doing this morning. I think you'll both be able to hear it if I put it on speaker."

Thelma moved out of the way and plopped into a recliner. "Don't let me get in the way of you three playing cops and robbers."

After listening to the recording of the time spent with Talia, Detective Sealy, and Derrick McDonald, Lou asked, "How much of this can I use, and when can I make it ready for sale?"

"Not everything, and not today. We'll discuss it on the way back to the resort."

"We? Like in you and me?"

"Uh-huh."

Bailey spoke up. "Are you both leaving without me? Why can't I go with you?"

Fen countered with, "Any complaints and you'll stay in the condo with Thelma this afternoon."

It was a hollow threat, but it served its purpose. Bailey stilled her tongue.

"Next," said Fen as he looked at Bailey. "You've already figured out that someone is trying to frame Talia Goldberg for abducting you last night. Right?"

"Correct," said Bailey. "I kicked off a shoe to prove I'd been in the truck."

"Anything else?"

"I'm missing the bracelet the fraternity gave me for doing their caricatures. It had those funny-looking markings on the beads. I managed to wiggle it off my wrist and left it in the truck, too."

"Is that all?"

She shook her head. "I don't know where I lost it, but I had my hair in a scrunchie on the walk home. Did they find them in the truck?"

"No, they're still missing."

Fen made the presentation of the flower and the gift to Bailey. "A little something to help you remember this adventure."

"You don't have to worry about me forgetting. Every time I sneeze or blow my nose, I'll remember this trip." She lifted the lid and removed the necklace. "This is now my favorite piece of jewelry. Thank you." She held out her arms to signify she wanted to hug him. He bent closer and received a kiss on the cheek.

Fen pulled back, cleared his throat and looked at Lou. "Have you had breakfast yet?"

"No, and it's the one thing I need more than a shower."

Thelma spoke from the chair. "We may beat you back to the condo. Between you and Bailey, I've had my fill of hospitals." She stood. "I'm going to see what's taking them so long."

Fen had no doubt Bailey would be home in plenty of time to join him in the search for more evidence.

<hr>

THELMA AND BAILEY didn't beat Fen back to their condo, but they all sat down to lunch together.

As she opened a plastic container of salad from the resort's cafe, Thelma let him know what she thought of his choices. "You should have waited for me to fix a proper meal."

Fen opined, "Face it, Thelma. Even you can't rush hospitals. I really wasn't sure when you two would arrive."

She grumbled something under her breath he probably didn't want to hear.

Bailey took over. "This is the perfect get-well meal. After this morning's runny eggs and plastic bacon, I could eat both pizzas plus salad."

Thelma placed her fork on her plate. "I won't fight you for it." She stood. "I need a bath and a bed more than I need to eat."

Her plate went into the sink. "I'll do the dishes later. You two can ruin your health if you want to."

Two lone slices of pizza remained when Bailey pushed back from the table. In the meantime, they'd heard water running in the small bathroom and Thelma snoring in her bedroom.

Bailey asked, "Should I do the dishes for her?"

"Leave them in the sink or she'll accuse us of wanting to steal her job."

A knock on the door brought Fen to his feet. "Are you expecting company?"

"Nope."

"Me neither." He went to the door and opened it. A young man with keen eyes stood with a bouquet in his hand. He spoke with polite confidence. "One of the brothers said they saw Bailey come back. Can I talk to her?"

Fen stood aside. "Why don't you ask her yourself?"

Bailey met him in the entryway. "Jeremy. What's with the flowers?"

"We were all worried sick."

"We?" she asked.

He raised his square chin. "Me and the rest of the fraternity brothers. Rumors have been flying. I came to make sure you're all right."

Bailey pointed to her face. "Other than this, I'm fine. No permanent damage."

Fen interrupted. "You two will be more comfortable sitting. Hand me the flowers and I'll put them in water."

Jeremy thanked him, handed him the flowers while keeping his gaze focused on Bailey, and followed her to the living room.

After stuffing the flowers into a half-full pitcher of water, Fen retreated to his bedroom. He may have a broken arm, but his eyes worked fine. Mutual attraction had a look of its own and he had no trouble recognizing it.

He left them to talk as long as he could, then made enough noise to let them know he was coming out. They didn't stop holding hands when they stood.

Bailey spoke with pride. "They want me to include my caricature in the group drawing. They even named me their Chapter Sweetheart. Can you believe it?"

"That's quite an honor," said Fen.

Jeremy gave his head a quick nod. "It really is, and it helps several of the brothers out of a tight spot. Their girlfriends were each hoping to get the title and things were getting ugly. The vote for Bailey was unanimous."

He turned to Bailey. "I'll come by and get you this evening."

Jeremy looked Fen in the eyes. "Sir, you don't need to worry about Bailey. I'll make sure she's safely inside from now on."

Fen rested his forearm on the pistol in its holster. "That's an excellent idea."

The door closed, and Fen turned to Bailey. "What are you going to do about Cory?"

Bailey flipped away the question with her hand. "I took care of that last night while Thelma went to supper. I called Cory from Lou's phone to break up with him. He said he tried to call me the night before to break up with me. We agreed it was for the best and there were no hurt feelings. He said I sounded like I had a cold. We talked about the murder case, but he knows nothing about what that creep did to me."

Fen slipped his sunglasses on. "Are you ready to catch some bad guys?"

"More than ready. I'm glad he didn't take my license, cash, or debit card. All I'm missing is my phone."

"Yeah, the police took it. I'll get it back for you. Let's go."

"Where are we going?"

"To a marina on the south side of the lake. Tim Gladly and Tran Wilks will meet us there."

Chapter Thirty-One

Tim's game warden truck was nowhere in sight when Fen and Bailey arrived at a waterside cafe in the small town of Coffee City. The business was more diverse than it looked from the parking lot. Once inside, it proved to be a combination tackle shop, convenience store, bar, and entertainment center for an enclave of cabins and places to park travel trailers. There was even a small area for live entertainers to plug in on the inside and a much bigger stage and seating area outside, directly on the waterfront.

Tim and Tran sat on stools at the bar, overlooking the lake. The game warden was drinking a bottle of root beer, while Tran pushed away the remnants of a hamburger and fries.

"No uniform today?" asked Fen as he came up on Tim's blind side.

"Less conspicuous. We're taking Tran's boat today."

Tran spun around and looked at Bailey. "Holy smoke. I'm so sorry."

"No need for you to apologize," said Bailey. "You didn't do it."

Tim challenged her. "How do you know it wasn't him?"

"The shoes," said Bailey. "I'm looking for someone with extra wide high-top Converse."

"You saw them?"

"Only a quick glance before he took me to the ground. After he bound my hands and feet, he put a bungee cord around my neck. It didn't choke me, but was tight enough around the pillowcase so I couldn't see."

"You didn't tell me that," said Fen.

Bailey shrugged. "It just came back to me."

Fen threw several bills on the counter. "I'll get your lunch. Do we need anything else before we go?"

Tran had the answer. "I always carry water and some snacks for my customers. I had a diabetic once that passed out. Scared me enough to where I don't go on the lake without something with sugar in it."

They exited through the back door and followed a walkway to a pier with uncovered stalls for boats. Tran explained, "This place is hopping on holidays and summers. The bands bring people in from all over. Many come in boats."

Fen and Bailey followed behind Tran and Tim as they made their way down a long line of boats in individual slots on a pier. Bailey spoke to Fen as she nodded at an older bass boat. "That's Tran's in the next stall."

It wasn't new, but Tran kept his boat clean. He spoke over his shoulder. "The motor is only two years old. It's not the fastest boat on the lake, but she gets me to where I'm going."

Fen asked, "Where does Shane pick up his customers?"

"Various places, but mainly at a marina on the east side of the lake. We're going to check out the west side first."

"Why?" asked Bailey.

"That's where Shane keeps his boat. He has a boathouse with a lift. He even has a garage door on it."

"On the lakeside?"

"Yeah. He has a remote that operates the door. It raises, he goes in and shuts it. When his boat is on the lift, you can't tell if it's there or not."

Fen took in the information and put it into a mental file. He then asked, "Do you know if he's on the lake today?"

"He was earlier, but when I passed by before lunch, he was pulling in."

In no time they were skimming across Lake Palestine, headed toward the west bank. Tim sat in the front, left-hand seat, while Tran operated the boat. Fen hollered above the sound of the Mercury 150 motor. "It's a good thing the lake is calm. It might jar something loose in Bailey's nose."

Tran turned to look at her, eyes wide. "Are you all right?"

"Fine. I enjoy going fast."

Boat houses, docks, and piers dotted the banks of this section of the lake. Tran throttled down, and the boat settled into the water. Fen and Tim lifted binoculars to their eyes. Tim spoke first. "The door's down, and I can't make out a boat."

Tran turned to look at Fen. "He's probably gone to lunch and lifted that new boat out of the water."

"We need to make sure," said Fen. He pointed to the bank next to the boathouse. "How close can we get to the shore?"

Tran had the answer. "There's a spot on the left side where I can pull up all the way and still be able to back out."

"Let's do it," said Fen. He turned to Bailey. "You're the lightest. Go to the bow when we get closer. Hop off and look for his truck. You know what to do if it isn't there."

Bailey grinned.

Tran pulled to a knoll on the bank, Bailey stepped off, and the boat backed up. Tim said, "I don't want to know what she's doing, do I?"

"No, you don't," said Fen. "We're just three guys enjoying a sunny day at the lake."

Fen kept track of the time, and nine minutes later, Bailey returned to the knoll. She stepped from the ground to the front deck of the boat with no slips, trips, or falls.

No one spoke until they were in the middle of the lake. Tim placed his hand on Tran's arm. "Cut the engine."

Silence prevailed, and Bailey gave her report. "It's just like Tran said. A red and white Ranger bass boat with a big, honkin' motor is hanging from the rafters."

Fen nodded his approval but asked, "What took you so long?"

"I checked to see how much gas he has. There were two tanks. One was all the way empty. The second was down to an eighth remaining."

Fen took out his phone and punched in a number. It rang twice before he heard, "I was wondering when you'd call."

"Lou, I have a job for you. Call Shane Wesley and ask if he could take you out again on his new boat. It needs to be this afternoon."

"I'd rather have major surgery without anesthesia." She paused. "Now that you've had your fun, what do you really want?"

"I need to know if Mr. Wesley booked a fishing trip this afternoon. I also need to find out where he bought his new boat." He took a breath. "Hold on, I need to ask Bailey something." He didn't cover the phone's microphone. "Did you see another boat and trailer in the driveway?"

"Nothing but empty beer cans and grass that needs mowing."

Fen lifted the phone back to his ear. "Did you hear?"

"Yeah," said Lou. "Where are you?"

"We're boating with Tran and Tim. I need that information. Call him now."

Fen ended the call before Lou could object. He looked up to find the fishing guide watching him.

Tran glanced at his watch. "Anything else?"

"I'll know when Lou returns my call."

"Who's Lou?"

"A woman looking for a good story, and she's going to get it."

It was a response that wouldn't make sense for another day or two, but it was all Fen wanted to give until he settled one more thing.

Bailey spoke to Tran. "Don't try to make sense of what he says. Fen gets secretive before he solves a case. Take us back to the cafe. He's going to pull into his shell now and think."

Lou called back as Tran secured lines fore and aft to the dock.

"I'm listening," said Fen.

"Item one," said Lou. "I'm not fishing with Shane this evening, and neither is anyone else. He's taking the afternoon off to fill out fishing tournament applications."

"And the place he bought his boat?"

She gave him the name and said, "It's off of 155, on the way to Tyler."

"Thanks, Lou. Come over tonight and I'll tell you everything."

"You never tell me everything."

"You're right. I'll tell you almost everything."

Fen shifted his gaze to Tim and Bailey. "Let's sit down and make a plan."

Tran looked at his watch again. "I need to head north and pick up my next client. He's at the marina where you're staying."

Handshakes and nods of appreciation ended Tran's time with them. They found an empty table inside the cafe and treated themselves to iced tea. Fen was the first to speak. "Something occurred to me this morning on the way back from Tyler. I failed to focus on an important piece of this puzzle."

"What's that?" asked Tim.

"The fishing boat Dale White was in when someone murdered him."

Tim leaned back and rolled his eyes. "Of course."

It took Bailey a few additional seconds before she realized what Fen was saying. "Holy smoke. We need to find Shane Wesley's old boat."

Fen nodded. "Let's see what the folks at the boat dealership have to say." He turned his gaze to Tim, eyebrows raised, in a half question, half suggestion. "A spray bottle of luminol and a UV light would be nice to have if we find it."

Tim reached for his phone. "I'll have someone come to the dealership if we get lucky." His eyebrows came together. "Should we pick him up today if we find the boat and blood?"

"Let's hold off on that decision until we're sure."

Bailey asked, "What if he cleaned it real good?"

"Everything hinges on the answer to that question."

Fen and Bailey left the boat dealership late in the afternoon. They rode home in silence until they turned off the main road. Fen asked, "Are you all right?"

"I guess. I know I should be happy, but I'm sort of bummed."

Fen shifted in his seat. "The reality of someone killing their fellow man hits hard, even for a crusty old cop like me."

"I won't be able to sleep tonight."

"Me either," said Fen. "Let's paint."

"That's a good idea. I need to start on Destiny's portrait."

Bailey brought Fen's truck to a stop. His thoughts shifted to

Destiny and Talia. Then he remembered Derrick McDonald and wondered if Detective Sealy's search had turned up anything interesting. It was then he remembered he'd received a call while looking at the blue glow of luminol reacting to blood at the dealership.

He punched in the voicemail and listened. "This is Detective Sealy. I thought you might like to know that we found a scrunchie in McDonald's truck. We also found long, blond hairs in it. They're the same color as Bailey's. I'll send someone out after you call me back to do a DNA swab on Bailey. I need to make sure they match what we found. Looks like I'll get credit for solving a homicide and a kidnapping. Until we get results, McDonald stays in jail."

Bailey looked at him as he ended the call. "Did things just get more complicated?"

"It only seems that way."

That night, Fen received one more phone call.

Chapter Thirty-Two

The sun dipped into the pines on the west side of Lake Palestine. Fen, Bailey and Lou climbed out of his truck, but he was the only one who took time to notice the sky's orange streaks waving goodbye to another day. He caught up with them as Lou knocked on the door to Talia Goldberg's motorhome.

Standing in the elevated doorway, the hostess looked over the tops of the two ladies' heads and addressed him. "Come in. You're the first to arrive. I can't wait to hear what you have to say. You said it was astounding news."

Fen answered with a pinched smile. "I know it's asking a lot, but I have to ask you to wait until everyone arrives before we discuss things."

Tim Gladly parked his game warden's truck with one wheel on asphalt and the other on grass. Destiny Roe pulled in behind him. Bailey and Lou went in while Fen waited outside. Fen asked Tim, "Is everything going to plan?"

"The bird is still singing, loud and clear."

Destiny gave Fen a sideways glance. "Is that some sort of code?"

"Let's get inside," said Fen. "I believe Talia has drinks for everyone."

He was the last to step inside and stopped after closing the door. "I'm responsible for arranging this meeting, but each one of you played a part in making it possible. Get something to drink and settle in." He looked at Bailey. "No bubbly for you."

"No problem. I'm going back to college in a couple of days. There's plenty there if I want it."

Fen moved to the far side of the living room and stood in front of a fireplace with fake logs. Tim stood in front of the door. Couches and chairs covered in supple leather were soon occupied by the hostess and guests. The extended slides on both sides of the motorhome made for plenty of space.

Tim spoke, which caused everyone to shift in their seats to see him. "I bring good news. This morning, Texas Game Wardens arrested the man we believe killed Dale White. He's currently in the Smith County Jail."

"Wait," said Talia. "I thought the police arrested Derrick McDonald yesterday. Isn't he in jail?"

Fen delivered an overly simple answer. "He's there, too."

Talia said, "Would you mind explaining? I thought him planting a shoe in my husband's boat showed a link between the two crimes."

Tim asked, "Why would you think that?"

"Because Derrick McDonald hated my husband, and he tried to frame me for kidnapping Bailey. Detective Sealy said as much when he took the shoe."

Everyone shifted again when Fen spoke. "That was a clumsy attempt to shift blame." He waved a hand to show it meant nothing. "Let's leave Bailey's abduction for now and focus on the murder of your husband."

"Good idea," said Bailey as she gave a shudder. "I doubt I'll ever get a full night's sleep again."

Fen kept talking. "It might have been chance, or a brilliant person who planned the murder of Dale White. The first obstacle the police faced was determining where someone killed him. Two counties claimed jurisdiction."

Bailey interrupted. "Tim Gladly found the pistol in Smith County while Dale's wallet ended up in Henderson County."

Lou asked, "Did the police ever determine the location?"

"Not really," said Fen, "but the evidence showed it was more likely he died in Smith County."

"Why?"

Fen cast his gaze to Talia. "Where did Dale carry his wallet when he went fishing?"

"When he was fishing, he kept it in a zipper pocket in his all-weather cargo pants."

"That's interesting," said Fen. "That leads me to believe that the killer had to unzip a pocket, take out the wallet, and throw it, or plant it, on the other side of the river."

Tim stepped in. "That's the working theory now that we have solid evidence."

Destiny spoke up. "I don't understand that."

Fen explained. "It turned out that both arrests were based on flimsy circumstantial evidence. The one from Henderson County proved the flimsiest." He stopped. "Is flimsiest even a word?"

"Yes," said Lou. "Keep going."

Fen obliged her. "The next thing to happen had to be one of those rare coincidences. A fishing guide found Dale's body in the lake directly over the line dividing the two counties, which is the underwater riverbed. The young man took it to the boat dock past the entrance of this park."

Bailey spoke next. "There's more to that story, too."

Fen quickly added, "But we won't go into that now since the killer is in custody."

Destiny raised her hand and spoke at the same time. "Who killed Dale, and how do you know this person did it?"

Fen nodded toward Tim. "I'll give you his name, but Fen will give you the details of how he, Bailey, and Lou worked everything out."

"You left out someone," said Bailey. "You did a lot."

"That's right," said Fen. "Tim deserves most of the credit."

Tim took over. "The man who killed Dale White is a part-time fishing guide named Shane Wesley."

Fen looked for a reaction but noticed nothing, so he took over. "The cops had virtually nothing to go on when the fishing guide found Dale's body floating in the lake. They soon discovered who he was and that he lived nearby. With nothing to go on, one detective began by questioning Talia, who had an alibi."

"Thank you," she said. "That awful Detective Sealy wanted to take me to Tyler for questioning until he found out that Derrick McDonald had assaulted Dale."

Fen picked up again. "Further investigation revealed Dale had a desire, some might say an obsession, to become a professional fisherman. He bought the bass boat parked outside and set out to learn and practice until he was a professional angler. He solicited the advice of area fishing guides."

Fen held up a hand to pause. "We're getting a little out of order. Let's pick up after the arrests of the young man who found the body in the lake and Derrick McDonald. The detectives from both counties all but stopped investigating. This is about the time we came to lend a hand in the investigation."

Tim added, "They came with no preconceived notions of who might have killed Dale White and expanded the search beyond what had been done."

Fen took a sip of water and continued, "This arm was in no shape for me to spend half a day on a bass boat listening to professional guides tell me if, when, and where they went fishing with Dale. Bailey went with one guide, the young man who found the body, and Lou went fishing with Shane Wesley."

Lou lifted her head. "Mr. Wesley picked me up in a brand-new boat with a motor so big I thought it would sink us. It has everything a tobacco-chewing redneck could want. I looked up the price of the boat and all the goodies it came with. When did catching fish become so expensive?"

Fen looked at Tim, and the game warden continued the narrative. "One thing led to another and, like I said, we arrested Mr. Wesley this morning at a marina while he was filling up with gas. We talked to the manager of the boat dealership where he bought the boat and discovered Mr. Wesley paid one-third of the sale price as a down payment. That included his old boat and motor. Thankfully, the boat was still waiting to be detailed, so there were still traces of blood in the boat he traded for the new one."

Lou summarized. "They have the killer, a boat he'll never use, and the old boat he used to commit the crime in."

"Right," said Fen. "There's one question that remains."

"What's that?" asked Destiny.

"Why did he assault and kidnap Bailey?"

The room went quiet.

Bailey said, "You forgot the second question."

"Oh yeah," said Fen. "The second question is, who paid Shane Wesley to kill Dale White?"

Chapter Thirty-Three

Fen's question brought new meaning to the term *stunned silence*. Bailey, Lou, and Tim knew the answer to why Bailey was abducted, but they'd agreed to allow everyone to have their moment in the spotlight.

Fen took the lead. "It's unnecessary to dwell on the mistakes I made in the early days of the investigation other than to say I had to take a step back and rethink the case."

Bailey posed a question. "Don't you think any mistakes you made had something to do with a severe concussion and a broken arm?"

"Perhaps," said Fen. "Clarity in my thinking only came after Destiny and Bailey met. Destiny expressed an interest in Bailey painting her portrait."

Bailey jumped in. "When I discovered she's a mountain climber, we agreed it would be super cool if the portrait showed her straining to hold on. Fen tried to help me make the sale by suggesting he could do a distant view of the mountain she was climbing. Some people buy his landscapes for investments."

Fen added, "It was a lousy idea to mix a landscape with a

portrait. Destiny had sense enough to reject it." He took a breath. "Anyway, I did two sketches of the distant view and stared at them for hours. It came to me that I needed to back away from the sketches—and the investigation. It's important for both that you look at them from different angles. One theory stood out to me, which I'll get to in a few minutes."

Lou spoke up. "He has trouble keeping a story in chronological order. Listen closely, so you don't miss anything."

A sour glance came from Fen, which put a grin on Lou's face.

"Back to the investigation," said Fen. "It surprised me that Destiny had such a close relationship with Talia, *and* an intimate relationship with Dale at the same time."

Talia and Destiny opened their mouths, but Fen held up a palm to stop them from commenting. "No judgment, only the facts."

Talia ignored the hand. "Destiny and I are not bound by your narrow-minded conventions. We're both women of the world who proudly lead non-conforming lives."

"I realize that," said Fen. "Still, if you were a true nonconformist, you'd never have married."

Lou added, "I interviewed several people who attended your wedding. They described you and Dale as strictly monogamous. You were even regular attenders and members of a mainstream church."

Talia started to say something, but Fen spoke over her. "No need to defend yourself. People and times change. Let's get back to why Shane Wesley kidnapped Bailey."

Destiny held up both palms. "Stop the bus. Are you telling us that this guy named Shane Wesley not only killed Dale, but he also kidnapped Bailey?"

"And broke my nose," said Bailey.

"Are you sure it was him?" asked Talia.

"I got a look at the old-school tennis shoes he was wearing. They were black and white high tops with duct tape."

Lou added, "That's what he wore when I went fishing with him."

Tim added, "And it describes what he had on this morning."

Destiny took her turn. "Is that enough to prove he abducted her?"

"Not by itself," said Fen. "But there's more to talk about than shoes."

"Tell them about there being too many clues," said Bailey.

"Good idea." Fen cast his gaze around the room. "It occurred to me last night that someone was trying hard to shift the blame for Bailey's abduction to others." He paused. "Think about it. Someone put Bailey's shoe in Talia's boat. Of course, she blamed Derrick McDonald."

Talia crossed her arms. "If I was wrong, it's because Detective Sealy suggested it."

Bailey said, "He was wrong about something else, too."

Talia looked at Fen. "What's she talking about?"

"A search of Derrick's truck produced a hair scrunchie with strands of long, blond hair."

Bailey pointed to her head. "My hair."

Fen mumbled a single word, "Redundancy."

"What did you say?" asked Talia.

"Too much redundancy."

"Explain what you mean," said Lou.

A professorial tone came into Fen's words. "These were two well-conceived crimes. Most murders are relatively simple to solve. This one is in a class by itself. It was carefully planned out, well financed, meant to confuse, and it almost worked. Even the weather cooperated by sending a flood. Someone went to great lengths to build in redundancy by planting evidence to blame others. Talia received Bailey's shoe to implicate her. A scrunchie with Bailey's hair showed up in Derrick's truck. It won't surprise me if something else were to show up that Bailey was wearing in the abductor's stolen truck."

He paused. "Bailey's abduction was the first step in another elaborate plan to make Derrick McDonald spend the rest of his life in prison for a murder he didn't commit."

Fen scanned the room. "There's no doubt in my mind Shane Wesley shot and killed Dale White." His gaze rested on Talia. "He did it to chase the same dream your husband had. To become a top bass professional. Dale was a man in need of the next thrill, the next conquest, another trophy on the mantle. Shane was looking for his first trophy and would do anything to get it."

Silence once again fell on the room until Fen added, "Lou. What was your impression of Shane Wesley when you went fishing with him? Was he smart enough to plan a complex murder plot?"

"The fish had higher IQs."

"Did he have any money?"

"Not until after the murder, then he sank all he had into his dream. That included his old boat, motor, and trailer."

"Was there any money left over after he bought the new boat?"

"A few hundred."

Tim said, "That's not enough to pay for gas and food to go to a fishing tournament."

Fen slowed his words. "That's the reason he went back to the person or persons who paid him to kill Dale. Shane may have been a dim bulb, but he was crafty. Stand back from the murder and consider what Shane needed. Money. He knew he had leverage over the person or persons who hired him, and he went back to them, asking for more."

"That's a dangerous game to play," said Tim.

Fen agreed but added a twist. "It may have been dangerous, but he got what he wanted... sort of. All he had to do to get more money was steal a truck, kidnap Bailey, rough her up, take personal items, and plant the evidence. The police would do the rest."

Bailey interrupted. "So, he kidnapped me, broke my nose, and threw suspicion on Mr. McDonald."

Fen jumped in. "Cops aren't necessarily bad, but they are under pressure to produce results. Detective Sealy wanted someone in jail, and to his credit, he had reason enough to question McDonald, perhaps even enough to arrest him, especially after the police found Bailey's hairband in his truck."

He heaved a sigh. "Unfortunately for Detective Sealy, we now know that McDonald played no part in either crime."

Lou then showed her caustic sense of humor. "I can see the headline: *Detective Catch and Release Strikes Again.*"

Fen moved on. "All this led me to wonder who else had the brains, motive, and resources to have Dale White killed and Bailey kidnapped and assaulted?"

Tim added, "We recovered the stolen truck he used. He soaked the back seat in gasoline but forgot to bring matches."

"How do you know that?" asked Destiny.

Fen took over. "Two Texas Rangers and I spent the morning talking with Shane. We began by discussing Bailey's abduction. We might have made him believe that's all we wanted to talk to him about. It took a while, but those Rangers know every trick in the book to get a man like Shane to talk. He waived his right to an attorney. They won't stop until they get a full confession."

Talia shifted in her seat.

Tim took his turn again. "Forensics has the stolen truck.

They'll find plenty of fibers, hair, fingerprints, and other things to convict Shane of abducting Bailey."

Fen added, "He's already confessed to killing Dale. If anyone helped him, they'll find that out, too."

Talia sat still and said nothing. Destiny, however, pulled something small enough to fit in her hand from her purse. "Talia, I found this in my car when we returned from Tyler today. It must be yours."

Bailey shot to her feet. "That's mine. Jeremy gave it to me. I had it on in the back seat of the truck."

"It's not mine," said Destiny.

Talia sat rigidly upright, her countenance as cold and unmoving as a statue.

Tim took possession of the bracelet and placed it in a plastic bag.

Fen shook his head. "Talia, you overplayed your hand."

Destiny came out of her chair and gave Talia a look that spoke of betrayal. "Were you trying to blame me for killing Dale and hurting Bailey?"

Talia's countenance took on a venomous hatred as she matched Destiny's raised volume. "You tramp. Dale wouldn't end our marriage. You couldn't win him, so you killed him."

Fen shouted, "Sit. Both of you."

When the two women stood glaring at each other, Tim took a step forward. "I insist you do as Sheriff Maguire says."

They reluctantly complied. Fen remained standing and lowered his voice. "It's redundancy, Destiny. If it's any consolation, you were the fourth in line that Talia was willing to frame for your involvement in Dale's murder and Bailey's abduction." He paused. "I guess we shouldn't count the man who discovered Dale's body in the lake."

It seemed like everyone in the room was holding their breath. Not a sound could be heard as he stared at Destiny for a long moment. "There's still a question in my mind that deals with how much you knew about Talia's plans. After all, you two shared a lot."

Destiny narrowed her gaze at Fen, her mouth set in a hard line.

Fen paused and regrouped. "Destiny, let me ask you about the night of Bailey's abduction. Someone had to help Shane stage his truck down a dark dirt road then take him to the truck he needed to steal. My guess is a check of your car and Talia's will reveal some trace of Shane Wesley in one or both of them."

He cast his gaze to Talia then turned back to Destiny and spoke in an accusatory voice. "Where were you the night Bailey was kidnapped?"

"In my condo."

"A likely story," hissed Talia.

"What's your alibi?"

"I was, uh..."

Destiny raised a haughty nose. "I was at home and I can prove it. He's a very handsome graduate student. A sports medicine man with plenty of stamina. He stayed all night."

Fen turned back to Talia. "Too much redundancy. You outsmarted yourself when you left Bailey's shoe in your boat, hoping the cops would believe McDonald was shifting blame to you."

"It worked, didn't it? They arrested him."

Tim answered the question. "It might have if you hadn't planted evidence in two other places."

"I'm not saying anything else," said Talia.

"You don't have to," said Fen. "I'll talk to Destiny." He looked at her and asked, "What do you think about your friend now that you know she tried to send you to prison?"

"I don't have words strong enough to describe what I think of her."

"Tim will help you find some."

"Am I being arrested, too?" she asked incredulously.

"Do you need to confess to something?"

"Absolutely not."

"Then all you'll need to do is answer questions from Tim and two nice Texas Rangers. I promised you'd tell them everything you know about Talia, Dale, and your relationship with them."

"But I know nothing about the murder or the kidnapping."

"Then it will be a quick interview."

Two men wearing white long-sleeve dress shirts, western cut slacks, boots, and cowboy hats entered the motor coach. On each of their shirts, they wore the small silver badge of a Texas Ranger.

Fen received thanks and handshakes from both men, who then left with Talia in handcuffs.

Tim performed the same ritual with Fen, giving a nod to Lou and Bailey. He turned to Destiny and motioned for her to stand. "Come with me. There's a lot to discuss."

Lou and Bailey rose to their feet and Lou said, "I have a story to put together."

Bailey issued a sigh of contentment. "This is one spring break I'll never forget."

Fen snapped his fingers and huffed. "Darn. I forgot something important."

"What's that?" asked Bailey.

"I didn't get the coffee Talia said I could have before the Rangers arrested her."

Bailey grinned and suggested facetiously, "I could come back and get it late tonight."

Fen shook his head. "One thing I don't need is to bail you out of jail. A Smith County detective will be here soon to process the motorhome. I missed my chance to get the best coffee I ever tasted."

"Will Detective Sealy conduct the search?" asked Lou.

Fen shook his head. "The sheriff thought it best for Sealy to take some time off."

Chapter Thirty-Four

Bailey jabbered all the way back to the resort. Instead of going to their condos, Fen drove to the activities center.

"Why are we here?" asked Bailey.

"I thought you might like a pizza to celebrate."

"Thelma will kill us if we don't eat her cooking."

Fen let the warning pass. "Let's live on the edge; I'll take the heat. After all, it's my idea."

The dome light came on after Fen parked and opened his door. Bailey sat with her seatbelt fastened, not making a move to get out.

"Aren't you coming in?" asked Fen.

"Are you kidding? There's a strip of white tape holding my nose in place and both eyes are black, blue, green, and yellow. I'm a walking billboard for abused women."

Lou tried to help. "It's not that bad. Come in with us."

Bailey set her jaw. "No way. I hate it when people stare at me."

Fen gave Lou a wink that Bailey couldn't see. "If she

doesn't want to go in, I guess we should let her sit out here alone."

Lou climbed out of the back seat and waited until they walked far enough from Bailey before she asked, "What's your plan?"

"I have two plans. The first is to use fresh bait to lure her inside."

Lou nodded her approval but added, "What if that doesn't work?"

"If she won't go to the party, the party will need to come to her."

The door swung open, and Jeremy stepped out. "Where's Bailey?"

"In my truck. She's embarrassed to come in with her face looking like she went ten rounds with a professional boxer. Do you think you can change her mind?"

"I believe I can, with a little help."

Jeremy opened the door to the Activity Center and let out an ear-splitting whistle. He motioned for his tribe to follow him outside. Once there, he explained the situation. He turned to Fen. "Where's your truck?"

Fen pointed, and Jeremy led the way. Forty-six young men approached the truck. Bailey slumped down in the passenger's seat. Undeterred by her feeble attempt to hide, Jeremy motioned for Bailey to roll down her window. She did, but only a few inches.

"Bailey," said Jeremy. "The sketches you drew of each of us made this the best spring break ever. We can't stop talking about them. Since we're leaving tomorrow, we're having a party tonight and it won't be complete without our sweetheart. Please come inside and join us."

He turned to the men standing near the truck. "What do you say, brothers? Do you want Bailey to join us?"

Hoots, hollers, whistles, and applause erupted.

Jeremy turned back to Bailey and said something meant for her ears only. Whatever it was, it worked. Bailey opened her door and Jeremy helped her down. They walked hand in hand as the crowd swallowed them.

Thelma's familiar voice sounded from behind Fen. "You did good by planning the party for her."

Lou added, "Real good."

Without turning to look at either of them, Fen pulled a bandanna from his back pocket, dabbed his eyes, and blew his nose. He cleared his throat and turned his head toward the fire pit. "I'm starving. Let's get some pizza before it's all gone."

If you enjoyed this book, please consider leaving a review at your favorite retailer, Bookbub or Goodreads. *Your* review could be the one that helps another reader discover their next great mystery!

To get in on the fun in my reader community, scan below or go to brucehammack.com/the-fen-maguire-mysteries-reader-gift/ to join my mailing list and receive a free eBook copy of *Murder On Caddo Lake,* a Fen Maguire short mystery.

Happy Reading!
Bruce

About the Author

Drawing from his extensive background in criminal justice, Bruce Hammack writes contemporary, clean read detective and crime mysteries. An avid Hercule Poirot and Sherlock Holmes fan, he believes the world can never have too many whodunits!

He is the author of the Smiley and McBlythe Mysteries, the Fen Maguire Mysteries, the Star of Justice series and the Detective Steve Smiley Mysteries. Having lived in eighteen cities around the world, he now shares his home in the Texas hill country with his wife of thirty-plus years.

Follow Bruce on Bookbub or Goodreads for the latest new release info and recommendations. Learn more at brucehammack.com.